PRAISE FOR EMILY CAVANAGH

"Emily Cavanagh's *The Bloom Girls* unfolds as smoothly as petals on summer flowers. This novel will be nectar to anyone who has a deep secret, a troubled love, or a wonderful, irritating, comforting family."

—Nancy Thayer, author of *Secrets in Summer*

"Cavanagh hits all the right notes with her characters. They are complicated and messy, one and all, which makes this an emotional and satisfying read."

—*Library Journal*

This
Bright
Beauty

To Cat,
Wishing you a world of
bright & beautiful things!
xo

ALSO BY EMILY CAVANAGH

The Bloom Girls

This
Bright
Beauty

Emily Cavanagh

LAKE UNION
PUBLISHING

Text copyright © 2018 by Emily Cavanagh

Published by Lake Union Publishing, Seattle
www.apub.com

Amazon, the Amazon logo, and Lake Union Publishing are trademarks of Amazon.com, Inc., or its affiliates.

ISBN-13: 9781542047791
ISBN-10: 154204779X

Cover design by Kimberly Glyder

Printed in the United States of America

To my parents, for allowing me to take risks by always leaving the door to home open

Lottie

I once heard that memory doesn't develop in a child until age three. But I remember this: sleeping in the crib with Franci, our faces nearly touching, inhaling the milky scent of each other's breath. The sun refracted through the slats of the crib, washing Franci's pink skin in gold. Her thumb was tucked tightly between my lips, and I was vaguely aware of the warm, wet feeling of my own thumb in Franci's mouth. A light wind ruffled the curtains. We slept, we breathed, our arms woven to share thumbs.

Whenever someone asks me what it's like to be a twin, this is the image that comes back to me. I wish I could pluck it from my mind and hold it up to the light like a slide.

"*This* is what it's like," I would say.

We were born twelve weeks early, our tiny bodies already tired of sharing such a small space. I'm sure I started it, always eager, needing to be first, not even born and already sick of sharing. I picture myself flexing my scrawny limbs, all two pounds and four ounces, arching my back in the warm, cramped space of our mother's womb, and deciding, *Enough.* I began the long descent into the world, like an animal burrowing through a tunnel, trying to find the hole on the other end.

And then I picture Franci. Two pounds and one ounce, and perfectly content to spend another three months curled up beside me.

Someone should have told me there was no hurry. Things would be no different outside that safe warm space. We'd share tight spaces all our lives.

We weren't ready. Oh, our bodies had formed. We had fingers and toes and hearts and lungs and kidneys. We had brains. But Franci wasn't ready. And maybe I wasn't, either. For six months we'd lived as one being, our bodies nearly fused together. In the moments we prepared to part our solitary space, I wonder if my mind was doing its own splitting, fracturing into the Black and White that would eventually rule my life. Later I'd wonder if things would have been different had we been allowed those extra months that should have been ours.

I began the slow and awful descent, and Franci had no choice but to follow, out into the cold and gaping world, the bright light of life already blinding.

I was born six minutes before Franci, and I waited patiently for her to arrive. In our separate incubators we drank oxygen, and plastic tubes were secured to our translucent skin with tape. I must have been so pleased to have my own bed, inches of empty space surrounding me, no elbows crammed into my face, no feet squashing my belly. In those crucial minutes, I was surviving on my own, and I held on to that knowledge so many times later in life.

But Franci's heart was beating too fast, her breath coming in short and jagged gasps. *Put me back,* her body screamed. *I'm not ready.* Did I feel guilty then, for what I had started? I wonder if she ever forgave me for it.

It was one of the first stories I remember hearing from Mother. The rest of the story goes like this: Franci was dying. Or not dying yet, but not coming into life, either. Then a nurse suggested putting her in the same incubator as me. They placed her at my side and immediately she calmed down. Her heart rate slowed, and she began to breathe more regularly. And though I imagine I relished the unfamiliar feeling of all that space to myself, I also know that I was more comfortable once Franci was beside me again. In our new shared bed, I coiled my body around my sister, encircling her in a cocooning embrace. There's a picture of it in one of the musty yellow photo albums. Two tiny black-haired babies in only diapers, tubes stuck to splayed legs, and the one on the left curved around the one on the right, shielding the other baby from . . . what? From life? Not even a day old, and I'd saved her life.

It wasn't until I was older that I wondered: Why would you repeat such a tale to children, a tale of failure and inability that was present from the beginning? A tale so filled with powerlessness and dependency that it seemed innate. But Mother told the tale because she thought it explained our twinship, how close we were, even then.

How different the rest of our lives turned out to be. In the end, Franci would be the one to save my life over and over again. And then one day, she couldn't.

Franci

I was bathing the girls when the call came. I leaned over the tub to knead shampoo into Autumn's hair. She whined, pulling away from me.

"It hurts," Ana whimpered beside her.

"No it doesn't, Ana." I rubbed the shampoo into Autumn's hair, realizing too late that a drop of soap had found its way into her eyes. Autumn began shrieking, and Ana splashed bathwater at me.

"Ana, stop it!" I yelled.

"Mommy, there's soap in my eyes. You got soap in my eyes!" Autumn cried.

"Okay, hold on, sweetie." I wet a cold washcloth at the sink and brought it to her eyes, dabbing gently at the soapy rim. Ana splashed me one more time. "Ana!" I snapped. Ana looked back innocently, even though my sweater was completely soaked through.

It had taken nearly thirty minutes to get the girls into the tub. Getting them dressed and undressed took three times as long now as it had just a year earlier. They insisted on dressing themselves or sometimes each other. I often had to hold back my frustration when I watched Ana spend three minutes sticking both arms into the same hole of a shirtsleeve or Autumn misbutton her cardigan so that the collar stuck up at her chin. Sometimes it was all I could do not to throw the twins onto the bed, yank up their pants, pull down their shirts, snaps snapped, zippers zipped, everybody dressed.

But I couldn't do that anymore. Now that Autumn and Ana were in kindergarten, apparently it was no longer acceptable to be dressed by one's mother. I partly blamed their teacher for this, the bouncy, blond Miss Colletti, so chipper and bright that she put most kindergarten teachers to shame. With her red buckle shoes and cute checked skirts, she somehow managed to look like both a Polly Pocket doll and one of the designers on *Project Runway*. (Also, what young woman actually preferred *Miss* these days over *Ms.*? I knew of none besides Miss Colletti.) I was convinced she had planted the seed in the minds of her students that by the time they hit their fifth birthdays they should be dressing themselves. And now that Ana and Autumn were in charge of putting their clothes on, they wanted to be in charge of picking their clothes out, even if the red velvet Christmas dress wasn't exactly appropriate for an ordinary Tuesday in February, or if the "really, really soft blue corduroys with the pretty purple flower thingies" were in the wash.

Mark had been in New York for work for the past two nights and was scheduled to come home tomorrow evening. When Mark was away, I found it more difficult to keep to the regular routine. We'd all sleep in and stay up later, eating eggs or pancakes for dinner. By the time I'd wrestled the kids into the tub that night, it was nearly eight, already a half hour past their bedtime.

Recently my daughters had become self-conscious about their playtime. I wondered if this was a by-product of entering school and becoming more aware of the rest of the world outside the tiny bubble they shared. They'd taken to lowering their voices if Mark or I came into the room, looking anxiously at the doorway as they spoke softly to their dolls. Sometimes if I asked what they were playing, they would brush me off.

"Nothing," Autumn would say in her new bossy voice. "Just a game." Ana would nod soberly beside her sister. I saw a glimmer of what they would be like as teenagers, whispering into cell phones, closing the bedroom door against me, music turned up so that I was fully excluded.

But during bath time these new rules were suspended. Maybe it was the absence of clothes, maybe it was the bubbles or the steam or the soapy hair piled high on their heads. Whatever the reason, I was allowed into their secret world. I'd sit on the closed toilet seat and watch my babies pretend that they were at the beach in Florida, or that they were sea cows, or that they were helping lost animals onto a boat during a storm. Midway through, the story would change when a fairy entered the scene, splashing bubbly pixie dust over the rubber bath toys. The complexity of the games reminded me of the Louisa and Mirabella tales our own mother had told me and Lottie at night, stories that made sense only in the fractured way of dreams.

Some nights I drew the girls. Sitting on the edge of the closed toilet, my sketchbook open in my lap, I used a charcoal pencil to capture the fine edges of their wet hair, the curve of a mouth open in a giggle, or the serious concentration etched on their faces as they bowed their heads together over a plastic boat. The girls loved it when I drew them, and they'd often turn to me, faces frozen in mock poses, until they forgot and went back to their games. They were the only people who I ever showed my sketches to with any regularity. Even Mark had only seen a few of the better drawings of Ana and Autumn, and when he tried to get me to frame one for the girls' bedroom, I'd put the sketchbook away in embarrassment.

On the night that I received the call, I had finished washing their hair and had begun to draw their hands. Autumn held a rubber mermaid protectively while Ana brushed the doll's hair with a plastic comb. Though they only engaged in the activity for a minute or two, the image had stuck with me, and I was shading in their tiny fingernails when my phone rang. I picked it up from the sink and saw the Berkeley area code, though it was not Lottie's number. I held the phone for a moment while it rang another time. My sister and I hadn't spoken for ten months, since the previous April, the longest we'd gone without speaking. Every day her absence was a loud echo in my heart.

After one more ring, I answered.

"Is this Francine Weaver? Charlotte's sister?" An unfamiliar female voice was on the line.

"This is Franci. Is Lottie okay?" My chest tightened in nervousness. My sister was Charlotte to the rest of the world, but she'd always be Lottie to me.

"This is Sally, Charlotte's neighbor. I'm so sorry to have to tell you this. She's been in an accident." The woman sounded young and close to tears. "When I went to pick Mia up at daycare, they told me that Charlotte was hit by a car. She's at the hospital."

I watched, as if in slow motion, as the sketchbook slipped from my fingers and into the tub where it landed with a small splash. The girls looked up in surprise.

"Is she all right? What happened?" The black book bobbed in the water, the pages quickly becoming sodden, but I was unable to move forward to reach it. I tried to wrap my mind around what this woman was telling me.

"She was hit on College Avenue while riding her bike. She's at Highland Hospital."

"Oh my god," I breathed, imagining my sister's mangled body. "Is she going to be all right?" I asked again.

"I don't know her condition. I'm sorry. But I have Mia. Can you come to take care of her?" Sally asked.

"Who?" I became aware of the dull headache I'd had for the past few hours, the phantom pain that often indicated my twin's distress.

"Mia. Charlotte's baby. I watch her a few evenings a week. Can you come take her?"

"I don't understand. Charlotte and I haven't spoken in almost a year." I swallowed my shame as I admitted this. "But she doesn't have a baby." As soon as the words were out of my mouth, I knew they were wrong. In the background I heard the thin wail of an infant as if she were trying to prove her existence.

There was a shuffle on the line, and I imagined Sally trying to hold the phone and the baby at the same time. "Charlotte had Mia in September. She's five months old."

"But what about Whit? Where is he?" Whit and Lottie had been together for over ten years, since before I had left California for Boston.

"Whit?" Sally sounded confused. "Charlotte and Whit broke up. Sometime last year. And Whit's not Mia's father." There was another silence while I processed what she had told me. "Can you come?" Sally asked, the impatience starting to creep into her voice.

I turned slowly toward my own daughters, my head heavy and fogged. Ana had put the sketchbook on the edge of the tub, and the soaked pages dripped down the outside, charcoal-stained water trickling onto the bath mat. I watched Autumn bob her head into the tub, fill her cheeks, and blow a perfect waterspout in her twin sister's face, the water arcing gracefully in the air.

"Of course," I said, and Ana giggled, catching the stream in her own open mouth. "Tomorrow. I'll be there tomorrow."

I called Mark and explained in a hushed whisper what was going on. He said he'd book me a flight to California and switch his own flight to be home in time for me to leave the following morning.

The bathwater was cold when I finally got them out of the tub. Ana's lips were purplish, and Autumn's fingers were wrinkled and pruney. I was distracted, bundling them into giant terry-cloth towels, my mind conjuring images of my broken sister as I ushered the girls into the bedroom. Neither complained when I tugged the pajama tops over their heads; Autumn's eyes were heavy with fatigue, and Ana's head was beginning to loll like a rag doll's.

I ran the brush first through Ana's hair and then through Autumn's. Their hair hung halfway down their backs, wispy and honey-colored, flecked with streaks of red and gold and amber. I often wondered where this magical hair had come from, as my own was curly and dark, and Mark's was an indeterminate shade of light brown. Tonight I didn't have the energy to blow-dry it, which meant tomorrow it would stick up in awkward crimped curls.

"No story tonight, okay?" I said, peeling back the matching pink quilts. I was barely holding it together, and I worried I'd fall apart if they insisted on the regular bedtime routine—the endless books, songs, and cuddles. Each girl slid into her own bed without complaint, either too tired to argue or sensing my own fragile state. I leaned down to plant kisses on cheeks and foreheads, necks and lips, breathing in the fragrant scent of shampoo and bubble bath. "Good night, baby girls," I whispered into their hair.

"Good night, Mama," each said, eyes growing heavy. *Mama.* It was what they called me only in moments of great tenderness. Usually I was Mommy, or Mom. Never Mother, the formal name Lottie and I had for our own mother, more a title than a term of affection, though our mother had done the best she could. But I was Mama in the early hours of morning before they had fully roused from sleep, or when they woke from a nightmare and came racing down the hallway into the bedroom, climbing on top of me and Mark, crying, "Mama, Mama, I had a bad dream, Mama."

I slipped from the bedroom, flipping on the goldfish night-light and turning off the overhead light on my way, leaving the door slightly ajar. There were rituals that needed to be abided by, even tonight. I made sure the hall light was on before going into my own bedroom.

I sat on the bed, scrolling through the numbers on my phone till I found Lottie's. It had been months since I'd dialed it, though every day I thought about calling.

The sweet sound of my sister's voice filled my heart, tugging me closer toward her. "Hi, it's Charlotte. I can't get to the phone, but leave me a message and I'll call you back."

"It's me. Are you okay? Please call me if you get this. I'm on my way." My words came out quickly, and I thought about saying more but hung up instead.

I found the number for Highland Hospital. After being placed on hold several times, I was told that Lottie was in surgery, though they couldn't give me any more information. I got up from the bed, taking a shaky breath, trying to maintain control. California had never felt so far away.

Atop my dresser were several framed photos, including one of me and Lottie taken before the girls were born. We'd spent the afternoon hiking a trail on Mount Tam, and the deep blue of the Pacific churned in the background behind us. In the picture we were shiny with perspiration, our faces flushed and healthy looking.

I shivered and realized I was still wearing the soaked sweater. I pulled it off along with the long-sleeved shirt I wore underneath, leaving both in a sodden pile on the floor. I kicked off my sneakers and slid out of my jeans, fumbling in the drawer for pajamas. I found a long white flannel nightgown that I rarely wore. Long ago it had belonged to my mother, and I pulled it over my head, letting the heavy cotton billow around my legs, the closest I could get to her distant embrace.

I sat down cross-legged on the bed and tapped out a quick text to Lottie. Are you okay? Please call. What happened?

There was no response, so I sent another message. I'm so sorry. I'll be there soon.

I waited to see if Lottie would write back, which I knew was unlikely as I'd already been told she was in surgery. But even if she hadn't been, I wasn't certain that Lottie would respond right away. Her hurt likely equaled my own guilt. And when Lottie was wronged, she liked to turn the knife just until the sting was too much to bear.

There was only one other person I could call who would check on Lottie for me. Though I hadn't spoken to Whit in nearly a year, I still had his number saved on my phone. I pulled it up, wanting to postpone the call yet knowing I had to make it.

I'd known Whit since he and Lottie started dating ten years earlier. Caring for Lottie and making sure she was taking her medication was often a tag-team effort. I didn't apply to graduate programs in Boston until Lottie and Whit had been together for over a year—not until Whit had seen Lottie go off her medication, and I was certain he'd recognize the signs and know how to get her back on it. Not until I was confident that Whit wouldn't leave her.

Whit learned about Lottie's illness firsthand when we were twenty-six. It was just a few weeks shy of the anniversary of Mother's death, which was always a difficult time for us both, but the ten-year mark was particularly hard for Lottie. I could sense the encroaching depression that was settling in around the wooly edges of her spirit. I counted her pills in the plastic bottle in the medicine cabinet each day, making sure that the number decreased. But Lottie was too smart for me by then, and she later told me that every morning she removed a pill and wadded it up in a piece of toilet paper that she flushed down the toilet.

Both Lottie and I had gone to Berkeley for undergrad and then stuck around after graduation. Lottie was working on her PhD in literature, and I was working as a copyeditor for the alumni magazine. Most nights when I got home I was exhausted, my eyes tired and dry after hours scanning for missing commas and misplaced apostrophes. That evening when I opened the front door to the house, I wanted nothing more than to take a shower and order takeout, but I heard yelling coming from the back of the apartment. There was the sound of something heavy hitting the floor and then more yelling, and I hurried into Lottie's bedroom.

Lottie and Whit stood intertwined in the center of the room, and Lottie writhed to free herself from Whit's arms. She was thrashing about, kicking at his shins and twisting in his grip. Whit stood awkwardly behind her, his arms encircled her body, trying to stop her without using any force. Lottie's hair was damp and matted to her face, and she still wore pajamas though it was nearly five thirty. She was barefoot and her feet were bleeding from the hundreds of china and glass shards embedded in the tan carpet. I recognized the wreckage of six or seven of the vases that Lottie collected in fragments on the rug.

"Lottie! What are you doing?" She looked at me, and for a moment her body went still. Then she kicked at Whit again. "How long has she been like this?" I asked him.

"Five, maybe ten minutes."

I rushed toward Lottie. "Stop it," I ordered, taking her hands in mine. She locked eyes with me, my familiar grasp pulling her back from the edge once more. "Stop it," I repeated as if she were a child.

"What's wrong with her?" Whit asked.

"She's bipolar. I thought you knew." Lottie struggled with how to break this news to men. It was hardly first-date material. But Lottie had been dating Whit for over a year; it was the most successful relationship I'd ever seen her in. She had told me that Whit knew.

"She said she'd struggled with depression in the past, but that it was under control now. That's all she said." Lottie stood between us, swaying slightly on her feet, her head bent forward, all the fight drained from her now that I was here and we were talking about her as if she weren't in the room. Whit's grasp on her loosened.

"Help me get her over to the bed," I ordered. He lifted her up gently, cradling her in his arms like a groom carrying his broken bride over the threshold. He laid Lottie down on the bed, away from the glass, and then turned to me expectantly.

"Go into the bathroom and get some Band-Aids and rubbing alcohol. Get her prescriptions from the medicine cabinet and a glass of water and some paper towels," I directed. While Whit got the supplies, I took off my coat and turned back to Lottie.

"Why did you stop taking them?" I asked her quietly. Lottie turned her head imperceptibly, just enough for me to know she heard and understood the question.

Her face was red and teary, and her eyes were hooded as if lacking the energy to stay open. It was eerie to see her like this. Lottie was my mirror image, but I could not imagine ever looking like she did right now. I patted her cheek gently. "Why, sweetie? Why did you stop taking them?"

Lottie didn't answer immediately, but when she spoke her voice was hoarse and raspy. "I miss her so much. Franci, don't you miss her?" I nodded miserably. "I thought I would feel better. I wanted the White to make me feel better."

The White. It was what Lottie called her manic episodes. She described it as the White because when she was in the highs of mania, the whole world was bathed in an incandescent white light. Everything was glowing and white and beautiful. The thing that Lottie never seemed to remember was that when she went off her medication suddenly, she very rarely went into the White. Usually she was plunged headlong into the Black.

Whit came back into the bedroom. "Here," he said deferentially, handing me the supplies. I dampened the paper towels with rubbing alcohol and dabbed at Lottie's torn feet. A few of the cuts still had tiny shards of glass in them that I had to pick out with my fingernail. I tried to be gentle, but it must have hurt like hell. Lottie didn't even flinch. She lay on the bed, her eyes glassy and vacant, staring blankly at the ceiling. Whit peered over me, watching as I tended to Lottie, but after a moment he dropped to his knees and began to bandage the cuts that I had washed. When her feet were finally cleaned up, he looked at me.

"What now?" he asked.

"She needs her medication." I reached for the pills on the floor and uncapped the bottle, shaking a pale blue pill into my palm. I turned back to Lottie. "You need to take your medicine now, Lottie." She didn't answer but instead shook her head, just one small shake left and then right. I sighed, knowing she wasn't going to make it easy. "Lottie, you need this medicine. It will make you feel better."

"I don't care. I want to die," Lottie whispered. Even though I knew she wasn't in her right mind, the words still terrified me. This Lottie was so unlike my vibrant and energetic twin that I constantly had to remind myself that it wasn't her talking, it was the Black.

"We're going to have to force her to take it." I turned to Whit who was watching the exchange patiently. I wondered how long he would wait before breaking up with her.

"What do you mean?"

"I'm going to need you to hold her down, and I'll make her take the pill."

He looked horrified, as I'd known he would be. "Franci, I can't do that," he said, shaking his head. "If she doesn't want to take the medication, maybe she shouldn't take it. She's an adult. She should be able to make that decision for herself."

I stared at him evenly. "She's sick. Obviously you can see that. She's not in her right mind to make that decision."

Whit nodded slowly. "I get that. I just . . . I can't hold her down and force her to take drugs. It's not right."

I turned to him forcefully. I'd had this argument with Lottie many times, and my anger was suddenly directed at Whit. "These drugs have saved her life. It's not like I'm asking you to shoot heroin into her veins. A doctor prescribed these, and they will make her well." I paused, trying to make him understand. "Don't you get it? She can't function without them, not well anyway. She can't live a normal life without them." Whit didn't say anything, and I turned away. Lottie lay motionless on the bed during the conversation, but I knew she was about to muster up whatever energy she had left to fight me.

"Fine. I'll do it with or without your help. All I ask is that you don't let her hurt herself or me. Can you do that?" Whit nodded uncertainly, and I turned back to Lottie, the pill in my outstretched hand, the glass of water in the other. "Take the pill, Lottie." She shook her head like a petulant child. I held the glass and pill out to Lottie again, but this time she reached out an arm and swatted the pill out of my hand, knocking the glass of water to the floor in the process. The glass bounced off the bed, spilling water on the sheets and then landing unbroken on the floor. "Stop it!" I yelled at her. I got down on the floor and found the pill. "Fine. We'll do it the hard way." I went into the bathroom to refill the water. When I returned, I was steeled for a fight.

I put the glass down on the bedside table and held the pill in one hand. Both Whit and Lottie eyed me warily. I took a deep breath and then lunged toward my sister, holding her upper body down with one arm and the weight of my shoulder, hating myself, hating Lottie for making me do this. I brought my hand to her mouth, trying to force the tiny blue pill inside her pursed lips. Lottie turned her head away, using her free arm to swipe at my face.

"Just take the pill, Lottie. Just take it!" I yelled.

"Get away from me," Lottie shrieked. "Get *off* of me. Just leave me alone! You stupid bitch. You stupid fucking bitch. I hate you. I hate you!"

Maybe it was Lottie's words that made Whit spring into action. Perhaps her torrent of curses was enough to convince him that this really was a different woman than the one he'd fallen in love with. Whatever the reason, Whit was suddenly up from the foot of the bed and at my side. He grasped Lottie's wrists and held her arms away from her body in the shape of a cross. He threw a leg over Lottie's torso and straddled her, his weight bearing down to keep her legs from kicking. He moved quickly and efficiently with an athletic grace, and I couldn't help but be impressed.

"Go on," he said to me. Tears were streaming down Lottie's face by now, and she was moaning softly, still keeping her lips closed so that I couldn't slip the pill inside. I brought my face close to Lottie's, catching her chin between my thumb and forefinger. I pushed the pill against Lottie's closed lips with the fingers from the other hand. Tears stung at my own eyes, but I blinked them back, refusing to let them fall until this was done. I pressed harder and felt Lottie's lips part slightly. Suddenly the pill was on the other side, trapped in her mouth.

"Swallow," I instructed, but Lottie shook her head in stubborn defiance. I brought my hand back to Lottie's mouth, holding my fingers against her lips so she couldn't spit the pill out. "Sweetheart, please swallow," I pleaded. Whit was still holding Lottie down, but she had stopped fighting. She was motionless on the bed, the pill likely trapped under her tongue. This was for her own good, I told myself as I swallowed back the shame that rose in my throat like sour bile. I refused to cry as I reached up and pinched Lottie's nostrils shut, keeping my other hand over her mouth, cutting off the air. Lottie's eyes filled once again, but I refused to look at her this time.

Lottie held out for as long as she could. I could see her breaking. I saw the realization as it sank in, the acceptance of her fate. This was the worst part, worse than the cursing or the physical restraint. Watching my sister submit, watching her spirit as it drained right out of her, leaving her depleted and wasted. That was the worst part of all.

I had only done this a few times before, but it was the first time someone had helped me. Whit watched with a mixture of horror and shock, still holding Lottie down though she was now motionless.

And then it was over. I could see the contraction in Lottie's throat as she swallowed the pill; she nodded to indicate that it was gone. I removed both of my hands from my sister's face, and Lottie took in a gulp of air, closing her eyes. Following my cue, Whit removed his hands from Lottie's wrists. She didn't move, staying still on the bed with her arms splayed.

"Open up," I said, and Lottie obeyed, opening her mouth wide and lifting her tongue so that I could see that the pill was gone. "Good girl," I whispered. "Have some water." Lottie lifted her head slightly off the pillow and allowed me to bring the glass to her lips. She took several sips and then dropped her head back on the pillow. "You'll feel better soon. Get some sleep now. I'll come back in a few minutes to check on you." I stood up from the bed and motioned with my head for Whit to follow. He looked helplessly at Lottie as if he felt like some apology or at least a few words were in order. He opened his mouth several times to speak, but Lottie wasn't even looking at him, and after a moment he followed me out of the room.

I left Lottie's door open and went into the kitchen to find something to drink. I found an open bottle of red wine on the counter and poured two glasses. I handed one to Whit, and we each took several swallows before saying anything. It was Whit who spoke first.

"Fuck," he whispered, shaking his head.

"She'll be okay in a few days," I assured him. The sky was pink outside the kitchen window, and the terrace was dotted with the drooping shadows of trees. The clock on the stove read five till six. The whole episode had taken less than fifteen minutes.

"Why did she stop taking it? If it makes her better, why would she stop?"

I tried to explain. "She doesn't like the way the medication makes her feel. She says it dulls her senses and emotions. After a while she convinces herself she's cured and doesn't need the medication anymore." I poured more wine into our glasses. "But bipolar disorder isn't something that's cured; it's something that's managed."

"How long has she had it?"

"It started at the end of high school. The year after our mother died. We didn't realize what it was." I lowered my body onto a stool and rested my elbows on the counter. "It didn't get really bad until freshman year. That's when she was finally diagnosed. That's when she first went on medication."

Whit nodded. His expression was serious and attentive. He was a handsome man, nearly ten years older than us. He had a calming presence, and I suspected he was the type of person people ended up confiding in. I understood why Lottie had fallen in love with him.

"She must have someone she sees? A psychiatrist or something?"

"Sometimes. She's bounced around a lot. She hasn't had a lot of luck finding someone she really trusts and connects with. She still harbors this fantasy that maybe one day she'll be able to live without the medication, and most therapists won't even entertain that idea. Bipolar disorder is not something that's treated successfully with talk therapy alone." I took another gulp of wine. "She had someone whom she really liked for a while, but then she moved and the referral didn't work out." I gave Whit a weak smile. "And I'm here."

He raised his eyebrows. "That's not the same thing."

"Well, I know a little about it. When Lottie was first diagnosed I did a lot of research."

"That's a big responsibility. You can't feel good about what just happened in there." He gestured to the bedroom.

"Of course not," I said, the anger flaring up in me. "But if I had her committed, some orderly would do the same thing. Isn't it better that it comes from me?" Whit didn't say anything. "She's my sister. My *twin*. What choice do I have?" I asked, looking away. It was the question I had wondered since Lottie became ill. What choice was there other than trying to keep her well? We were both quiet for another minute, and I felt the warmth of the wine spread through me.

"So, are you going to break up with her now?" I asked, mostly just to change the subject, but also because I wanted to know. Breakups were hard for Lottie.

"Why would you think that?"

"Well, it wouldn't be the first time. This is pretty intense. It scares most guys off."

"I don't scare that easily," he said, and I was so surprised at the relief I felt that my eyes filled with tears all over again. I looked away so Whit wouldn't see them, but he already had. "Hey." He reached for my hand and gave it a light squeeze. "It's okay."

I nodded and stood up from the stool. "I'm going to go check on her. You want to order some takeout or something?"

"Sure," he said, opening the drawer where we kept the menus.

I walked unsteadily down the hall to Lottie's bedroom, wiping at my eyes. She was asleep on her back, her mouth open and her breath coming in heavy pants. I stood staring at her, my head resting on the frame of the door. It was the first time I'd had anyone to talk to about Lottie; I felt as if I had been given an unexpected gift.

"How does Indian sound to you?" Whit called from the kitchen.

"Sounds great," I called back. "Sounds good," I said, more quietly this time so only Lottie could hear.

In the quiet of my bedroom, gathering the strength to make the call, I thought back to that night all those years ago. When I stopped speaking to Lottie the previous year, Whit had called and texted several times, and I made it clear I didn't want to talk to him. If he wanted to continue to be Lottie's keeper, that was up to him, but I didn't want to hear about it anymore. It was a terrifying and wicked role we played in my sister's life, even if we thought there was no other choice.

I pressed his phone number and waited. After a few rings, he answered.

"Franci."

"Hi, Whit."

"What's wrong?" Of course, he knew. That was the way we operated. It was a careful dance, us passing Lottie's unbalanced frame back and forth—until we both dropped her at once.

Lottie

How to describe the descent? I have tried, to Franci, to lovers, to doctors.

It's like a black velvet cloak is wrapped around me.

No, that's not right.

It's like being locked in a room with black paper covering all the windows, taped so tightly that not a fragment of light can get in.

No.

It's like a black hand extending from the sky and holding me down, pressing me into the bed, into the ground, making my movements slow and heavy, each step a tremendous effort.

But that's not right, either.

Really, it is blackness that cannot be put into words, a blackness like nothing a person should live through to describe. Black, black, blacker, blackest. If I repeat the word enough times, I disappear into it and all that is left is the blackness. I *become* the Black.

Franci

The night before Mark flew to New York, we argued. It was the same argument we'd been having all year, about Mark working too much. I was tired of having it, yet I continued to start the fight, like a scab you pick off every time it starts to heal; I couldn't seem to help it.

The argument started over dinner. I was complaining to Mark that Miss Colletti was assigning homework to her kindergarteners.

"Thirty minutes of reading with an adult each night and twenty minutes of letter practice. Doesn't that seem a little excessive to you?" I asked, stabbing an asparagus spear with my fork.

"Yeah, I guess so," Mark said.

When we first moved in together, dinner was my favorite part of the day. We cooked elaborate meals and drank a nice bottle of wine almost every night. We stayed at the table long after we'd finished eating, talking about work or the future or our families. But over the past few years, dinners became hurried affairs. As a financial advisor at a large firm downtown, he frequently worked late or was expected at functions, which meant he often came home after the girls were asleep. If he was home early enough, I insisted on having Ana and Autumn join us at the table, but occasionally I'd cook something special for just the two of us, the closest we ever got to a date these days.

That night I'd fed the girls early and cooked Mark's favorite meal, but he didn't get home until after eight. By the time we sat down to dinner, the pork was dried out from sitting in the oven and I was irritable. Mark ate quickly, and I knew he was anxious to go watch the news in the living room.

"You guess so? Mark, they're five years old. Did you have homework when you were five?"

"I don't know. I don't remember." He placed his fork and knife on the half-empty plate and pushed it away from him, then folded the cloth napkin.

"You definitely did *not* have homework in kindergarten. No one had homework in kindergarten when we were growing up."

"Well, I guess they do now," he said mildly.

I let out a sigh of frustration. "This doesn't bother you at all?"

"Look, she's the teacher, right? You didn't like it when parents second-guessed your judgment while you were teaching. I'm sure she's up on what the other schools are doing. Maybe this is what they need to be prepared. Besides, what's the big deal? You read with them anyway. And twenty minutes of letter practice? That doesn't sound like the worst thing in the world," Mark said as he finished his glass of wine.

"I know, but you don't think it's just a little over the top?" I pressed. "I mean, I want them to do well in school, but I feel like we're supposed to be grooming them for the Ivy Leagues starting now. You know, Joseph Bensen's mother actually told me the other day that since Harvard is their first choice for him, they make sure to read with him for *two* hours a day. The child can barely tie his own shoes, and they're talking about Harvard."

"Franci, I don't know what to say," he said, throwing his hands up in the air.

"What does that mean?" I leaned back in my chair, crossing my arms.

"It means I'm tired. I had a long day. It's after nine, I have to be on an eight o'clock flight to New York, and all I really want to do is go watch a little television before I go to bed." He hadn't changed from his work clothes, and there was a small splatter of grease on his white dress shirt. The skin around his eyes was puffy, giving him the look of someone older.

"Fine. I'm sorry to bother you with conversation about our daughters' education." I despised the sarcasm in my voice, but I couldn't help it. "You're excused," I told him, as if I were talking to one of the girls.

"Oh, don't give me that," he said.

"What? What do you want? I make a nice dinner and just want to talk for a few minutes. Is that asking so much? You get home at eight o'clock and want to go watch TV. I should make you a Hungry-Man frozen dinner from now on, and you can eat in front of the television."

"Do you think I like staying 'til eight?" He was getting angry now, his voice rising. I'd been pushing all of his buttons, and as always happened when we got to this point, I wished I could rewind the conversation back five minutes, but it was too late. "You think I like getting home when the girls are already in bed? You think I like being too tired to have a decent meal and talk with you? Well, I don't. But that's what it takes. If we're going to continue living like this"—he gestured around at the dining room—"then this is what it takes."

Silver candlesticks gleamed on the long farm table. The walls were painted a cherry red, and the plates were heavy and of high quality, ordered from an Italian catalog. When I was teaching just a few years earlier, I shopped at Target and Marshalls and T.J.Maxx like all of my colleagues. But since I'd left to be a stay-at-home mom and Mark had accepted several promotions, I'd taken to shopping in places like Williams Sonoma, Crate and Barrel, and Pottery Barn.

"I never expected this. I would have been happy living in an apartment in Brighton." When we were first married, we lived in a cramped one-bedroom on the Allston-Brighton line, only steps from the T station. At night, we'd hear the distant rumbling of the train, the squeal of brakes, and the little bell indicating that the doors were closing.

"No, you wouldn't," Mark said, rolling his eyes.

"Yes, I would. You wanted this, not me. That's why you went into business. I never asked for all this," I insisted, though I knew the truth was more complicated.

"Well, you might not have asked for it, but you certainly manage to enjoy it. I see the bills, Franci. I see the charges on the credit card—the hundred-dollar haircut, the three-hundred thread-count sheets from God-knows-where. I see the clothes you buy for the girls. I'm not criticizing. I'm glad we can buy those things. But don't tell me that I'm the only one who's living this lifestyle." He held my gaze until I looked down at the table, shamed. He was right. I might not have asked for the big house or the Volvo and SUV in the driveway, but I'd certainly learned to enjoy them.

"Do you want me to go back to work?" I asked quietly. A part of me desperately wanted him to say yes. Since the girls had started preschool two years earlier, I was paralyzed with indecision about what to do next. If Mark said we needed the money, I would have been relieved to start looking for a job, but I didn't seem capable of making the decision myself.

"You know what I want, Franci? You know what I really want?" He leaned forward in his chair till he was just inches away from me. There was something seething in his expression—frustration, rage, or just bewilderment. "I want you to do what makes you happy. If working will make you happy, then work. If staying home will make you happy, then stay home. If taking up underwater basket weaving will make you happy, great, go for it. But it seems that no matter what you do or what I do, you're not happy. This isn't enough for you." He gestured again at the dining room. "You don't seem happy and I don't know why, and I don't know how to fix it."

"I'm grateful for everything that we have," I said softly, suddenly close to tears. "I am."

"I know you are. But you don't seem very happy." His voice was gentler now, the anger gone, replaced now with weariness. I wearied him.

"I'm happy." I looked down at the half-eaten food on my plate. Tears pricked at my eyes, but I refused to let them come. "You make me happy. The girls make me happy." It wasn't a lie. I loved them more than anything. But he wasn't incorrect, either. "I'm happy," I repeated, but this time I was only trying to convince myself. Mark didn't say anything. "Go watch TV. I'll clean up in here."

"Franci," Mark said, catching my eye. I looked up from my plate and flashed him a quick smile.

"Really, it's fine. You have an early flight tomorrow. Relax for a little bit. I'm sorry."

Mark stayed where he was for a moment, most likely weighing the benefits of continuing to talk against his own desire to escape. He rose slowly from the table and kissed me on the forehead. *When did we stop kissing, really kissing?* I wondered. "Thanks for dinner," he said. There was more to say, and we both knew it. The trouble was, neither of us ever had the energy to finish the conversation.

He crawled into the warm bed with me the morning after I got the phone call about Lottie. I'd spent the whole night tossing and turning, dozing off every now and then before startling myself awake, imagining my battered sister and the niece I hadn't known existed. A baby. How could Lottie have a baby? And how could I not have known? Mark lay down in his pressed suit and shiny black wing tips, and I loved him for it. He still smelled stale from the airplane and early morning flight, but I pressed myself into his body, eager to escape my own mind.

"Any more news?" he asked.

"I talked to Whit last night. He said he'd go by the hospital to check on her." The collar of Mark's jacket chafed at my neck, and I struggled to sit up. "She has a *baby*. How could she have a baby?" I shook my head, the familiar fury and frustration against Lottie rising up. In my mind I ticked off the months since I last saw Lottie. Last April's trip was over ten months ago. Lottie must have been in the early stages of pregnancy then. Mia, Sally had said. A baby girl named Mia.

Mark took my hand and squeezed it. "I booked your flight. You're on the one o'clock to Oakland. You have a room at the Marriott." I looked at him in confusion. There were half-moons under his eyes and a tiny nick under his nose where he must have cut himself shaving. He looked tired. Mark's eyes were gray, almost the same color as his suit. When we met ten years ago in grad school at Boston University, I would have sworn they were blue. A grayish blue, yes, but blue. Maybe it was the nondescript hues that he wore now that drained them of their previous color. I frowned at his lack of understanding.

"I can't stay in a hotel," I told him. "She has a baby. I'll have to stay in her apartment."

"There must be someone else—the father maybe?" Mark asked.

"I don't think so." I eyed him coldly, throwing the covers off, and I felt my heart going hard toward him. It wasn't his fault that he didn't understand that nothing was ever simple with Lottie, yet still I held it against him. As I got out of bed, Mark looked at my mother's long white nightgown with puzzlement.

"What are you wearing?"

I just shook my head as Ana and Autumn came running into the bedroom, their hair sticking up at odd angles from sleeping on it wet.

"Daddy!" they cried in unison, and Mark was on his knees, encircling them in his arms. And then I loved him again.

Lottie

The White is easier to describe. The White is power. It's like flying. It's like living the way I've always wanted to live. In the White, I can do anything, be anything or anyone. It is a glass prism, the rainbows reflecting off the walls in fractured diamonds of color. I am perfect. In the White, I'm a poet, an artist, a musician, a scholar. I'm a star in the sky, nestled into the soft atmosphere, watching the world around me.

From my perch in the sky, I understand it all. Everything is connected; everything makes sense. The man in the grocery store struggling to choose between two brands of bread is my soul mate. The woman with the surly grin at the post office—I understand the fear that really plagues her, the frustration that makes her bark at customers, and I smile magnanimously as I dash off my packages: presents for Franci's daughters. Expensive china dolls that I have purchased for them, identical black-haired girls that will have likely broken by the time they arrive, their porcelain skin cracking. But if they crack, then they crack, and that is meant to be. Everything happens for a reason; the universe is aligned in harmony, even if you cannot see it.

But I can see everything.

Franci

When I said goodbye to the girls, they cried and begged to come see their aunt. I gave them each a tight squeeze, and Mark must have sensed how close to falling apart I was because he grasped them firmly by their hands and led them to the door.

While Mark took the girls to school, I packed a small suitcase for California. Staring into my closet, I gazed mindlessly at the rows of muted button-down shirts, heavy wool sweaters, corduroys, jeans, and khakis. Not even on the plane, and I already felt the familiar anxiety and exclusion that California seemed to bring out in me. I selected several pairs of jeans and a few light sweaters and cotton shirts and stuffed them into a suitcase.

"You ready?" Mark asked. He was sitting at the dining room table with his laptop. I nodded, though I wasn't ready at all.

I put on my long winter coat, aware that the heavy down parka would be absurd as soon as I stepped off the plane in California. The temperature outside had dropped nearly twenty degrees overnight, and in just the few hours that Mark's car sat on the driveway, the windshield had crusted up again with frost. As he pulled out onto the quiet street, Mark sprayed the windshield and put on the wipers to clear the ice. But it was too cold for water, and I watched as crystals bloomed like flowers. He sprayed more water and the same thing happened, an intricate lat-ticework of flakes webbing across the glass, making it impossible to see the road. I rested my head against the seat, watching the frost flowers blossom. It would have been beautiful if it weren't so dangerous.

The drive to the airport felt longer than usual. Brookline was less than thirty minutes to Logan, but time dripped by slowly, each drop containing a memory: Lottie as Dorothy in *The Wizard of Oz* in the spring of seventh grade, her curly black hair in pigtails, bowing onstage in her sparkly red shoes; Lottie our freshman year at Berkeley during her first episode, before we realized it was an episode, at her computer at 4:00 a.m., a pencil holding back her hair, a cup of black coffee beside her while she tapped frantically at the keyboard, oblivious to my loud sighs of frustration in the twin bed across the room; Lottie in the delivery room in Boston on the morning that Autumn and Ana were born, a look of pride and awe and, yes, envy, on her face as she held her nieces for the first time.

At the airport, Mark pulled up to the taxi stand and let the car idle. He took the suitcase from the trunk and then pulled me into a tight embrace. I buried my face in the clean smoothness of his wool coat. I closed my eyes, the bustle of the airport terminal around us, the whoosh of cars driving past, and Mark's chin resting firmly on my head. Then a taxi honked, and a traffic guard was hurrying Mark along, and I had only a moment to kiss him goodbye and tell him to take care of the girls, the "I love you" getting lost in the sounds of departure all around us.

Lottie

It wasn't always like this. It wasn't supposed to be like this.

Every twin knows there is a sibling who is older, even if only by a few minutes. Once there was a time when *I* was the strong one. That was the way it was supposed to be, the way it was for many years. I was the one who took care of Franci.

I remember a birthday party at our old house in Palo Alto the year Franci and I turned eight. Mother invited all of the girls in our class, and Franci and I helped string pink crepe streamers from the doorways. They hung like the curling tentacles of squid, and every time we entered or left a room, we'd feel the papery softness against our cheeks.

It was the last year that we let Mother dress us identically, and we'd picked out matching white dresses that tied in the back with satin sashes. We wore lace ankle socks and shiny black patent leather shoes, and the only way to distinguish us was that my sash was green and Franci's was purple.

The guests were scheduled to arrive at two, and we sat by the dining room window, watching for the station wagons that would come bearing our classmates. Soon they began to arrive, pretty little girls in party dresses, holding brightly colored packages carefully in their arms.

Second grade was the year that I made different friends. Until then Franci and I had been inseparable, a private party of two. But in second grade, I pulled away from her and toward the other girls in the class. Though she tried to follow me, I found myself freezing her out for the first time in our lives, pushing her away and ignoring her when in the presence of my new friends. With no one else to turn to, Franci befriended Enid Brown, a shy redheaded girl who was lactose intolerant and whose mother carefully packed her a thermos of soymilk and a lactose-free cheese sandwich in the days before everyone ate soy.

As the girls arrived one by one, I went to play with my new friends while Franci and Enid sat in the corner of the living room by all of the packages, talking in hushed whispers.

Mother tried to engage us in several games as a group—she was aware of the drift between us, and while I'd heard her tell our father that it was healthy, I knew she was secretly disturbed by it too. She brought us out to the yard, and we played pin the tail on the donkey and then she gathered us on the patio for apple bobbing.

Each girl bent over the large silver pot, and some of us arose victorious with bright red and green Macintosh apples clenched precariously between our teeth. When it was Franci's turn, she kept diving headfirst into the pot, but each time she came up with a dripping wet face and no apple. The other girls began to giggle as Franci kept at it, doggedly aiming for the apples but only spilling water all over her pretty new dress. Mother watched helplessly, finally pulling Franci gently aside and handing her a dish towel while ushering another girl forward.

The piñata was meant to be the highlight of the party, just before cake and presents. It was in the shape of a giant pink-and-yellow horse, and as we were falling asleep at night over the past few weeks, Franci and I discussed the type of candy that might be inside. Lollipops? Chocolate bars? Miniature bags of M&M's? Those soft caramels with the sweet white centers? The possibilities were endless, and we were both dying to take a wooden bat to the horse, waiting for the crack that would shower us all with candy.

Franci went first. Mother knotted one of our father's old ties across her eyes and spun her in a circle three times. When she released her,

Franci was dizzy and disoriented, the yellow paisley tie still blocking her vision. She swayed on her feet, her back to the piñata, the wooden bat limp in her hands. She took several steps forward, swinging awkwardly at the air. A few girls giggled as Franci wandered several feet farther away from the hanging horse. She swung again, as if she were a farmer with a scythe, slicing fields of wheat.

I looked helplessly at Mother as the giggles grew louder.

"Hang on a minute, Franci," Mother said, stepping forward cautiously so that Franci wouldn't knock her with the bat. She placed her hands on Franci's shoulders again and turned her around so that she faced the piñata, walking her forward a few feet. "Okay, try again," she instructed. Franci tried. She did. But it was as if the bat were too heavy for her slim arms. Each swing that she took was at least a foot below the piñata. The snickering started again, soon erupting into howls of laughter. Only Enid, Mother, and I were silent.

Marissa Dawson was a pale, skinny girl with long brown hair, the ends of which she often sucked on, leaving her hair in wet points around her shoulders. In second grade this was not seen as the disgusting habit it would later become; it marked her as cool and self-assured, like gum chewing or eye rolling. Marissa was in my new group of friends, though I didn't particularly like her. Even then I recognized the streak of meanness that coiled through her personality.

Marissa was nearly bent over with laughter, her lank brown hair a skirt of sharp wet peaks. She covered her mouth with one hand, the other pointing at Franci, who swung uselessly several feet away from the piñata.

"Oh my god, look at her," Marissa shrieked to the other girls.

"Shut up, Marissa," I hissed. Mother looked at me in disapproval, but didn't say anything.

Marissa continued to howl with laughter. "What's wrong with her? Is she retarded?" she asked the group. The giggling of the other girls quieted. They looked at me, their eyes wide, and then they turned away from Marissa, quickly distancing themselves from her. They might not have been friends with Franci, but the others understood that there were some lines that shouldn't be crossed.

Franci stopped swinging, lowering the bat to the ground. She was now directly under the piñata. There was no chance that she'd ever be able to reach it. This seemed to dawn on her at the same time she heard Marissa. The bat hit the grass with a soft thud, though Franci didn't remove the tie. I knew that when she did, her eyes would be red and filled with tears, her birthday party ruined.

Eyes darted nervously between Marissa, me, and Mother, waiting to see who would intervene.

"What?" Marissa asked, her voice growing whiny and nasal. "She can't even hit the stupid piñata. I'm just saying, maybe she's retarded."

It was that word being used one more time that did it. I might have let it go. If she'd just shut up, I might have let Mother handle it. But she'd said it yet again, causing Franci's shoulders to hunch over even more, her head hanging on her neck like a broken doll's.

Before I even realized it, I lunged at Marissa. I felt the weight of her body against me as I knocked her to the ground. Marissa was small for her age and young too. She wouldn't turn eight till the following spring. It was easy to hurt her.

I scratched at her face and caught the bony curve of her shoulder in my fist. "Don't you call my sister that ever again! Do you hear me? Don't you ever call my sister that!" I screeched at her and tore tiny slivers of skin from Marissa's tender flesh. She didn't even try to fight back, only squealed and wailed like an injured kitten.

I couldn't have been on her for more than a few seconds, though it felt like minutes. Pretty soon Mother was behind me, shouting my name as she dragged me roughly off Marissa. Mother's strong, thin fingers dug into my arms, momentarily bringing me back from my feral daze. I allowed myself to be pulled away, though I was still yelling and kicking. Marissa lay on the ground, curled into the fetal position, her body convulsing in sobs. My new white dress was soiled with grass stains and a few dots of blood, but I didn't care.

I looked at Franci then. She had removed the paisley tie, and it hung around her shoulders. Her eyes were wide and frightened, though I was glad she wasn't crying. Her small mouth was pursed, and she looked at me like I was a stranger, some wild animal that had been allowed into her birthday party. But then I watched as her mouth softened, her face relaxing. I smiled at her across the patio, a tiny secret smile I hoped Mother didn't see. *For you,* it said. *I would do anything for you.*

The rest of the party went by in a blur. Daddy came down from his office to tend to Marissa's cuts. They weren't actually that bad, but she was covered in shiny antiseptic and several Band-Aids. She spent the rest of the party watching television in the den with my father, waiting for her mother to arrive. I would receive a severe lecture later that night, but I think my mother was secretly proud of me, and I was allowed to attend the rest of the party.

I no longer remember the presents or the cake, but I do remember that no one knocked the piñata open. It never rained candy down on us in a sweet autumnal storm. Instead, Mother sliced it open with a kitchen knife, a clean split right down its middle. When we peered into the cardboard belly, we were disappointed to find only an assortment of hard candies, jawbreakers, and plastic toys—not a single piece of chocolate in the whole horse.

Franci

When the plane landed at Oakland International Airport, I made my way down to baggage claim. Standing at the carousel, I scanned the crowd. Just as I spotted my black suitcase with the pink ribbon, I realized: I was looking for Lottie. The recognition caught me off guard, enough that I missed my suitcase the first time around and had to wait for it to make another long rotation on the conveyor belt.

I picked up my suitcase and made my way to the taxi stand outside. It was February, but it was close to seventy degrees in Oakland. I tipped back my head and let the sun warm my face. It hadn't been warm in Boston in a long time, and my skin hungrily drank in the heat.

A yellow cab pulled forward, and the driver stepped out to take my suitcase. The interior of the cab smelled faintly of cigarettes and cologne, and I leaned my head against the window and watched the gold cross medallion that hung over the mirror. It swung gently on its chain in a hypnotic rhythm, and I nearly drifted to sleep as I thought about what I needed to do.

I would go to Lottie's to pick up the baby, and then we would go to the hospital. I had called Lottie again while waiting at the airport that morning, and though she hadn't answered, she'd sent me a quick text. I'm okay. Banged up and on pain meds, but I'll live. Take care of Mia and I'll see you soon.

My relief that she was okay was quickly replaced by a swell of resentment. No matter how far I went, she'd always expect me to pick up the pieces for her.

I'd been to Highland Hospital once before, while in college. Freshman year had started off all right, but following winter break, which we had spent with our father, Lottie plunged into her first major depressive episode. She stayed in bed all day, skipping classes and ignoring the friends she'd made during the first semester. I became more isolated as well, going to Lottie's classes on top of my own to help keep her up to date with what she was missing. It was strange that it took me a full month to realize something was seriously wrong with Lottie. "I'm just tired" was all she said when I tried to get her out of bed. "I have a headache," or "I can't deal with that class right now." The excuses were vague and insubstantial, but I chose to believe them.

Until one afternoon when the resident advisor for our dorm came knocking on the door, asking to see Lottie. Sheera was a senior, and she'd seen enough in her three years as an RA to know when something was wrong. After being told four afternoons in a row that Lottie was resting or had a headache, Sheera barged into our room, took one look at Lottie buried in bed, and called Health Services.

The doctor Lottie was referred to diagnosed her with bipolar type 1 and sent her home with a bottle of pills.

"How can they diagnose you so quickly? This is the first time you've been depressed," I argued.

"It's not, Franci. Remember last year?" Lottie reminded me.

I thought back to the previous winter when we were still in high school. Lottie had gone through several weeks where I felt her disconnect from me. Her movements were slower, requiring great effort, and she barely talked to me, returning home from school to spend the rest of the afternoon in the fuggy air of her bedroom. She ate little more than sleeves of Ritz Crackers and vanilla yogurts, the area around her bed littered with empty containers and wrappers. It happened right before

Christmas and then again in March, around the one-year anniversary of Mother's death.

It didn't seem fair to call it depression. Our mother had *died*. Wasn't Lottie allowed to be sad, even if the severity of her mourning was belated? Our mother's absence was a tender bruise that ached every day, and just because I got out of bed every morning didn't mean it wasn't painful. Both times Lottie eventually stripped the sheets and climbed into the tub with no intervention from anyone. She emerged from the bathroom pale and thin, but she was herself again.

"It makes sense," Lottie said softly, and I thought about how, last year, she had returned to me slowly, her mood growing higher and brighter as she threw herself back into all of the things she loved: school and drama club and the flutter of friends that always surrounded her. That was just Lottie. It never occurred to me that something might be wrong.

When she first started taking the medication, I waited anxiously for it to take hold of my sister's fractured mind. After several weeks, I started to see Lottie through the gray haze of her depression, and I was able to let go of the breath I'd been holding for so long.

But Lottie hated the drugs. She said they dulled her senses and made it so she couldn't feel anything. It was like watching spring awaken but not being able to see color, the soft buds on the trees and flowers pushing through the ground all a hue-less gray. That was how she described the medication to me.

And it made her physically sick too. She was dizzy and nauseated, and she sometimes threw up. The depression had made Lottie lose weight, but now she was gaining it, her hips growing pillowy and soft, a slight roll hanging over the top of her waistband. The drugs affected her eyesight, and Lottie could no longer read for long periods of time, so I read aloud to her from her textbooks and class assignments. I didn't mind; Lottie was safe for the first time since the cycle started. The medicine might not be perfect, but it kept Lottie straight and even, and her moods more regular.

I hadn't realized just how much Lottie hated the drugs until the night it became clear she'd stopped taking them. She'd been on them for several months at that point. In recent weeks, though, I'd noticed that her mood seemed a little lower, but the medicine didn't prevent Lottie from having some highs and lows—it merely kept them in check. So it didn't occur to me that she might have gone off her meds, at least not this time. Later, when it would happen again and again, I knew what to look for, and I would immediately go to the medicine cabinet and search for the amber bottle of pills, checking the date of the last prescription and how many of the little blue tablets were in the bottle. I would even check the wastebasket underneath the layers of used tissue.

But I didn't yet know the signs or realize how sick Lottie had become until I opened the door to our dorm room that evening. It had been raining all day, a bleak and tearing rain, and as I fumbled with the lock, my fingers were slick with water. My coat was soaked from the walk across campus, and I was eager to get inside to make sure that none of my books or notebooks was ruined.

As soon as I opened the door, I knew something was wrong. The window beside Lottie's bed was wide open, the screen removed. Wind and rain blew fiercely into the room. Papers were scattered across both desks and the floor, and there was a puddle of rainwater by the window. Lottie's tee shirts and jeans lay piled on the floor, soaked through. Several candles burned on her dresser, fat glass jars with pictures of Our Lady of Guadalupe that you could buy at many shops in town. The blessed woman on the glass, her head bent in prayer and palms pressed together, cast an eerie glow throughout the room.

Lottie was in bed, a motionless heap beneath the blankets. Tiny whimpers came from under the sheets, and I approached her slowly, terrified of what I might find. Reaching out a hand, I pushed the lump that was my sister. I could feel her shape through the thick webbing of cotton and fleece.

"Lottie, what's wrong?" I asked.

Lottie didn't answer, but her whimpering continued. I couldn't see any part of her, not her fingers or her feet or even her hair. With a tentative hand, I reached out and peeled back the blanket, revealing my sister.

It took a moment to see the cuts. At first, all I saw was Lottie's naked body curled into a tight little ball. It was the same body that I had—the same slight shoulders and tiny breasts—though Lottie's was thicker now, her thighs meatier. Despite the extra ten pounds, I could still see the knobs of vertebrae in her bowed back, and the bones in her rib cage showed through the thin layer of skin like the legs of a spider.

Lottie's eyes were closed tightly, her arms clasped around her body in an empty embrace. There was a dark smear on the white skin of her stomach, another against the sheets, and another against her hip bones. I sat on the side of the bed, reaching out to unlock her arms. When I lifted one, I nearly dropped it in horror. It was flecked with little lines of red, each dash a tiny straight incision.

"Oh my god, Lottie—what have you done?" Lottie didn't answer, but she released her tightly clenched fist. From her palm fell the silver scissors from my nail kit. I snatched them from the bed as if they were a loaded gun or some other obvious weapon. I brought the sharp instrument close to my face, peering at the silver blades.

"Why did you do this?" I demanded. Lottie's other arm was clean. She hadn't gotten to it yet. I pressed my palms to my forehead, trying to understand what was happening. And then, abruptly, I knew. "Are you still taking your medication?"

Lottie didn't answer the question directly.

"I couldn't feel anything," she murmured, and my heart dropped a few inches in my chest, a quiet sigh that would become familiar as the years passed. "I had to make sure I could still feel something."

"And could you?" I asked.

"Sort of. But it didn't even really hurt." Lottie opened her eyes for a moment and looked incredulously down at her handiwork. "Why didn't it hurt?" She closed her eyes again.

"My god, Lottie." I was close to tears. I turned away from her, suddenly so revolted that the naked, bleeding heap on the bed was half of me. I walked to the doorway and flipped on the overhead light. The room was suddenly bathed in a blinding and incandescent yellow, and we both winced at the ugly brightness. I picked up the phone and dialed 911.

The rest of the evening was a blur I only half remember. I dragged Lottie from the bed and struggled to get her into a bathrobe. She stared vacantly into space, unwilling or unable to meet my gaze. I remember the small crowd that assembled in the hallway of the dormitory when the EMTs arrived. The medics were kind, young men only a few years older than us, and they were careful and respectful, letting Lottie shuffle down the hallway by herself while supporting her by the elbows like a frail old woman. I trailed helplessly behind and sat in the back of the ambulance with Lottie.

They didn't use the siren, and I choked on the silence. Perhaps it wasn't really an emergency after all. The only sounds were Lottie's occasional moans and the quiet assurances of an EMT. I didn't try to reassure my sister. I had already begun to hate her a tiny bit, a little black kernel the size of an apple seed that would slowly grow over the years. I wondered if maybe I'd been too rash by calling 911. Maybe I should have taken care of it myself, cleaned and bandaged Lottie's arm and gone to the pharmacy to refill the prescription. If I had taken charge, then the whole floor wouldn't have seen Lottie in her bathrobe and slippers being escorted to the elevator like a crazy person. A crazy person. If I had taken care of it myself, then maybe it wouldn't be true.

Lottie

Mia came to me in the white heat of mania, a blessing and a curse, my redemption, my demise. Like everything that happened to me during those flashes, it seemed a brilliant idea at the time.

The idea started as tangentially as anything else that happened during the White. I was walking down College Avenue on an October day so beautiful that it was excruciating. *Excruciatingly beautiful, excruciatingly beautiful, excruciatingly beautiful*—the phrase looped through my mind like a telecaster's news prompt as I made my way past the panhandlers, students, and professors.

I was on a mission. In a matter of minutes, I'd become obsessed with finding a bramble, the sweet jam-filled pastry that Mother used to buy on special occasions. She bought them at an Irish bakery in Palo Alto, but I was determined to find one in Berkeley, and I rushed into every coffee shop, bakery, and deli on the street, breathless, asking for brambles. Most of the workers shook their heads in confusion, either at my request or my frantic appearance. I began to formulate the plan in my head, how I could drive to the bakery in Palo Alto and go past our old house—not the condo our father bought after Mother died, but the house we lived in till high school. I would park my car outside, eat my bramble and sip a cup of sweet coffee and wonder who lived there now. After I finished eating, I'd knock on the door and the new owners would let me in, walk me through the bedroom that Franci and I once shared and the kitchen where our father made homemade pizzas every Sunday night, rolling the dough out on the long wooden table. Miraculously, each of the rooms would look exactly the same, untouched by time or strangers.

A little girl. My attention was diverted within a second, and then everything changed. As I barged out of the last bakery in town, I nearly ran into a woman and her daughter. The little girl, though she was dark skinned and dark haired, reminded me of Autumn and Ana, as little girls always do. She was with her mother, a beautiful black-haired woman in a fuchsia sari, her wrists and neck decorated with gold jewelry. I imagined they were from India, a place where I'd never been but had always wanted to visit. India seemed like a place full of enormous color, scents, and unfathomable poverty, and my addled brain quickly jumped from brambles to home to little girls to India.

The child held her mother's hand, and though I was barreling out of the tiny bakery with an aggressive force, the girl beamed at me sweetly.

"Hello," she said, looking up with a beatific smile. The mother nodded and tightened her rein on the girl's hand.

"Hello," I breathed back, transfixed by her deep brown eyes and liquid voice. A second later, they were inside the bakery and I was outside, standing on the sidewalk once again, people rushing past, the brambles forgotten and a new idea planted in my mind.

A child. My own child.

Franci

The cab dropped me off at Lottie's apartment. Like my own street back in Brookline, Lottie's was lined with trees. However, this street was narrow, the houses spaced only a few yards from each other so that it was possible to peer into someone else's kitchen while you were making dinner. Lottie's apartment was in an old, yellow Victorian that had been converted into a two-family home. I lived here with Lottie after college, and she'd lived here since, paying practically nothing in rent.

I fumbled with my key chain and found the house key I'd had since I left California. When I opened the door, I expected to be greeted by Sally and the baby, but the apartment was quiet. I rolled the suitcase over the threshold and closed the front door.

The smell hit me immediately. The acrid odor of garbage was ripe in the air, mixed with the faint scent of the Egyptian musk oil that Lottie had worn since she was a teenager. I slowly made my way down the hall toward the kitchen where the smell was strongest. Fruit flies circled lazily around a bowl of brown bananas, shriveled apples, and avocados. A mango lay open on a plate, its dull orange flesh dotted with flies. A compost bucket had been left open and several larger black flies buzzed around eggshells and coffee grounds. The anxiety in my chest tightened from the hovering insects and the realization that I would have to clean up the mess, but also out of fear of what I might find elsewhere.

The living room was not as bad, though candle wax had melted on nearly every surface. The dried splotches were glued to the coffee table and mantel, the purple and red stains like Rorschach inkblots. Several days' worth of newspapers lay in an uneven heap by the couch along with a stack of student papers, Lottie's messy red scrawl bleeding over the pages. Unwashed mugs were all over the room, a sticky circle of coffee in the bottom of each one.

I continued the disquieting tour, entering the bathroom slowly. The last time I was in this room, an EMT had been sitting with Ana. There had been blood and water on the floor, the scene of an accident. I hadn't been here since that awful night, since I packed my daughters up with me and flew home to Boston.

Today all I found in the bathroom was a yellowed toilet bowl and a garbage pail overflowing with tissues.

There were two more rooms left, Lottie's bedroom and the spare room. I stood on the threshold of Lottie's. From the doorway I saw the unmade bed, the sheets and quilt twisted in a rumpled pile. There were more unwashed dishes and stacks of books. Lottie's open closet door revealed piles of dirty clothes on the floor. I stepped back into the hall.

Last April I'd slept in the guest room with Ana and Autumn, the room that had once been my bedroom. It was white and had a futon that pulled out into a double bed, which I slept on with the girls cocooned around me. The room overlooked the garden Lottie shared with the neighboring apartment, and sun streamed through rice-paper venetian blinds. The room was peaceful and serene, the kind of room perfect for reading or writing or painting. It would be Mia's room now, and I was fearful of what I might find. I pushed the door open and peered inside.

The white futon was gone and a crib stood in its place, a black-and-white mobile hanging above it. The paper blinds had been replaced with heavy purple curtains that blocked out the light. There was a lavender shag rug on the polished hardwood floors. Lottie's desk was gone; there sat a changing table stocked with plastic baskets filled with diapers and wipes, powders and lotions. The room smelled like baby oil.

Everything was neat, everything in its place. For some reason, this was what brought me to tears. It was worse to see how hard Lottie had tried to keep it together. She'd worked to keep her illness from affecting her baby. Tears slid silently down my face.

Hanging on one of the walls was a collection of paintings. Stepping closer to examine the artwork, I was startled to recognize them as paintings I'd done in college. I hadn't seen them since the university's gallery opening more than fifteen years earlier, and it was jarring to see them arranged so carefully in Mia's room.

The pieces were from a series I'd done of my mother from photographs I found in old albums. Mother had been dead for almost four years when I did the paintings. In one she wore a form-fitting red suit in brushed silk and sat perched on the edge of a wooden chair, primly holding a cigarette. She stared off somewhere just to the left of the viewer, a small, private smile poised on her lips. In another picture she was on a beach in the evening hours of the day, the sun throwing shadows across her bare legs. She leaned back on her elbows, a striped blanket beneath her, wearing just a sheer white blouse and yellow bathing suit. She was laughing, her nose scrunched up, dark hair blowing around her face. I couldn't remember ever seeing her look so relaxed.

In my favorite picture, Mother held me and Lottie as newborns while she nursed. She sat on a couch, several pillows propped in her lap, and we were spread upon them, our dark heads nearly touching. I was amazed by the ease with which she nursed two infants at once, knowing firsthand how difficult it was. There were the telltale new-mother circles under her eyes, and her pale skin was drawn, but she looked down tenderly at us in her lap.

There were others: Mother in a snowstorm with my grandmother, a woman I'd never met; Mother beside a packed car, waving goodbye. I'd used a tiny paintbrush to capture each scene, and I did the whole series on canvases the size of the photographs—small, meticulous four-by-sixes or five-by-sevens, the details so fine that the viewer had to look closely at the paintings. I had called the series *Mother, can you hear me?* and I invited Lottie and our father to the opening of the group show, though I hadn't told them anything about my work.

The night was a disaster. I still felt the cringe of shame and sadness, remembering it now. When my father and Lottie arrived at the show, the gallery was already crowded with students, parents, and professors. I was on the other side of the room, away from my work, talking with another artist. Waving to them, I watched as they made their way to the wall that featured my paintings. I excused myself from the conversation, but I didn't go to them right away; instead, I observed their reaction to the show. My father took in each painting, peering closer to examine the details, at one point bringing his hand up to the canvas and reaching out to touch his wife's face with a thumb. I watched as he mumbled something to Lottie, his head bent low, and then made his way to the exit.

I hurried over to where Lottie stood by the paintings.

"Where's Dad going?" I asked.

"Oh, Franci," Lottie said as her eyes filled with tears.

"What? What's wrong? Where did he go?"

"Franci, these are beautiful. They're lovely. He was overwhelmed." Lottie shook her head, the tears spilling onto her cheeks. "He left. He went home."

"What?" I couldn't believe it. "He went home?"

"He couldn't handle it, Franci. It was too much for him. You should have warned him." Lottie turned back to the paintings, leaning in to examine the one of our mother in the red silk suit. "She looks so happy in these. But she wasn't. She wasn't happy." Lottie's blue eyes were bright.

"That's not true," I argued.

"Where did you come up with these?" Lottie asked, without agreeing or disagreeing.

"They're from photographs."

"Where did you get them? I've never seen them."

"In some albums in Dad's closet."

"In his closet?" I nodded, suddenly feeling guilty, though I wasn't yet sure why. "Did you ever think about why they were in his closet?" There was a note of accusation in Lottie's voice. "Did you ever think about why we've never seen them before?" I didn't answer her, instead focusing on the painting of us as babies in Mother's lap. "He doesn't want to see them. It's too hard for him to remember her," she said gently.

I felt a surge of anger then, at both my sister and father, and inexplicably, Mother too. "Just because he doesn't want to remember her doesn't mean that I don't. He doesn't get to decide that for me. And neither do you." I went to get a glass of wine, the first of many that evening, and my face burned with guilt and anger. By the time I turned again to look for her, Lottie was gone too.

I was surprised when I received several offers on the series. I never imagined anyone would want to buy them. My professor told me how rare it was for a young art student to make a profit and had encouraged me to make the sale, but I couldn't imagine it. It would have been like selling my mother's photo albums. Yet I couldn't bear to have the paintings hanging up, either, where Lottie or our father would see them. So I packed them in a box that I stuck in the closet of my bedroom on top of all the old albums that I hadn't returned to our father. When I moved to Boston, I left them in the bedroom closet of this apartment.

And Lottie had found them, either recently or more likely years earlier, and had painstakingly hung them in Mia's bedroom, an homage to the grandmother she would never know, and perhaps also to me, the aunt that Mia had never met.

Lottie

When you have been tricking people your whole life, it's amazing how easy it is to trick yourself. So few knew the truth. Even our father knew only bits and pieces before he got sick. Franci and Whit were the only ones who knew everything, and Franci was on the other side of the country, tired of cleaning up after me. And Whit, well, Whit could not stay to see my implosion.

He knew me too well. Besides Franci, I think he is the only one who has ever really seen me in all my messy shades of color. He tried so hard to convince me that it was not a good idea. He knew what would happen. He knew, and maybe I knew too, but I didn't want to listen.

We tried to convince each other, sitting in a coffee shop on Shattuck, him sipping black tea as I blew the steam from my coffee. His long legs stuck out at odd angles from underneath the little wooden table. At nearly six feet four, he had trouble fitting into small spaces. The rubber soles of his work boots were caked with thick black soil, and his heavy wool socks stopped at his calves. His legs were strong and bristled with soft blond hair, his face sunburned from hours spent on his knees in the dirt making other people's gardens beautiful. Once upon a time he was a lawyer, but he'd given it up years earlier to plant trees and tend flowers and help things grow. It was hard for me to imagine him as a lawyer in a suit and tie every day.

"But why not, Whit?" I asked, for what must have been the hundredth time that month.

"Because I don't want children, Charlotte. You know that. You've *known* that all along. I've always been honest with you about it."

It was true. When we met, Whit told me he never wanted children. For all his love of living things, he had a thick streak of cynicism. He couldn't reconcile bringing life into a world filled with such uncertainty and such pain, suffering, and evil. When he told me he didn't want children, I was twenty-six, electrified by his love. I could have cared less about having babies. But twenty-six is very different from thirty-six. I still secretly hoped he would decide he wanted a baby with me, and this could be an adventure we embarked upon together.

"Charlotte," he said in the serious tone I knew meant business. "I'm not going to change my mind." And for the first time, I believed him and understood that nothing I said or did could change anything.

"I'm going to do it anyway. I'll go to a sperm bank." The words spilled from some secret place. I hadn't even realized I was going to say them, but as soon as I did, I knew it was true. Whit didn't say anything for a moment, and I wondered if he'd already anticipated this.

"It's not a good idea," he said finally.

I blew on my coffee, barely looking up to register what he'd just said. "Why not?" I asked, trying too hard to make my voice casual and light.

"You know why not."

"So you're a liar. It's not that you don't want children; it's that you don't want children with me. You don't think I'd be a good mother." The hurt in my voice took us both by surprise.

"I do not doubt your capacity to love." His words were careful. "I think you have a lot to offer a child. But I also know you have the potential to be an unstable mother. I think you know that but don't want to admit it."

"I'm taking my meds, Whit," I told him, the irritation creeping into my voice. I had been, as soon as I began to think seriously about having a baby.

"Right now," he answered.

"Yes, right now and next week and the week after that."

"And what about the week after that?" His large hands clasped the small paper cup. Each fingernail was rimmed with a sickle of dirt.

"Then too."

He shook his head. "You'll go off them again, Charlotte. You always do. No matter how bad the next time is. You'll go off them again."

"Don't pretend you know everything. You can't see the future," I snapped.

"You also know that bipolar disorder is hereditary," he said.

"There's a higher chance. But it's not a guarantee."

"Charlotte, I'm sorry, but I don't think it's a good idea. And I can't stand by and watch you do it." He shifted his legs under the table so that they were fully extended.

"What are you saying?" I asked.

"I don't know yet." He sipped his tea and looked away from me and out the window.

We talked about other things after that, plants and books and dinner. I'm not sure if we knew it was the beginning of the end. It seems now that it had been too ordinary for me to recognize amidst the bustle of the coffee shop on a typical Thursday. Who could see the end when the late afternoon sun was creeping through the window, and the man I loved was telling me about the orchids he had ordered that morning? I could picture them, a pink so pale they were almost white, stained a deep crimson at the center. Such delicate plants that required such specific and patient care. But if you gave them what they needed, they were stronger than you could imagine. They would bloom for years.

Franci

I was still examining the pictures in the baby's room when the front door opened.

"Hello? Francine?"

"Coming." I hurried into the entryway. Standing in the open doorway was a woman in her early twenties with a sleeping baby in her arms, its head of curly brown hair visible from the end of the hallway.

"Hi, I'm Sally," she said. I stopped in front of her and stared down at the sleeping form in her arms. "And this is Mia."

Her cheeks were round and pink, and she sucked contentedly on a pacifier, the little piece of plastic bobbing rhythmically in her mouth. I reached out my arms, and Sally gently handed her to me. She was a warm bundle against my chest, and she sighed in her sleep.

When I looked up, Sally was taking in the slight differences between Lottie and me—the small space between my front teeth, the missing beauty mark on my left cheekbone, the lighter shade of my eye color.

"I was going to spend last night here with Mia, but"—Sally gestured to the disarray around us—"Charlotte's not usually this messy. It's been a really busy semester for her." I nodded but didn't say anything. "Have you heard how she's doing? Have you been to see her?" Sally asked.

"I just got in a minute ago. I called the hospital last night, and she was going into surgery. She texted to say she was okay, but I don't know anything more."

"I'm so sorry," Sally said. "How awful this must be for you. If there's anything I can do, please let me know. Mia's in daycare a few days a week, but I watch her two evenings while Charlotte is teaching." Lottie was an English professor at Berkeley, and her schedule changed each semester.

Sally and I stood awkwardly in the hallway. All I wanted to do was breathe in the warm baby smell of Mia's neck, press my head into the warm crook of her shoulder and pretend that this was a happy occasion, this first introduction to my infant niece.

"Oh," Sally said suddenly, taking a bag off her shoulder. "Here's her diaper bag. There's a fresh bottle in the bag for when she wakes up."

"Okay. Thank you." I brushed a thumb along Mia's round cheek. "Sally, who is Mia's father?" I asked without lifting my eyes.

"Charlotte went through a sperm donor. I don't really know much more than that. She was always private about it." I nodded. When Lottie didn't want to talk about something, it was like a steel fortress went up around her.

"Can I help you clean up here at all?" Sally gestured with her chin toward the kitchen.

"No, that's okay. We'll be all right."

"Okay." She stood uneasily for another moment. "Well, if there's anything I can do, please let me know. If you need me to watch Mia while you go to the hospital or anything, just knock. I'm right next door."

I thanked her and she slipped outside, leaving me and Mia alone.

I brought Mia into the nursery and settled into the rocking chair. The baby slept soundly, the drunken milk-induced sleep of infants. Her mouth was a heart, her dark hair a curly cap, a miniature pink-and-cream version of Lottie.

I remembered the day I became a mother. Unlike me and Lottie, my girls held on until they were nearly at full term. I was just two weeks away from my due date when my water broke. I was in the kitchen, washing the dinner dishes, and it took a moment to realize that the slick liquid coursing down my legs was not soapy dishwater.

A strange calm settled over me, and I waited a few minutes to call for Mark. I took my time finishing the dishes, wiping down the counters, folding the damp towels neatly over the drying rack. I held my hands tenderly to my belly, enjoying the last moments of having my daughters swimming inside, still truly a part of my flesh and blood, incapable of surviving without me.

Though for weeks I had worried about the pain of labor, I felt no panic, no fear, only the quiet might of motherhood. I would protect these children with every ounce of strength I had, using all of my muscles to push them out into the world, the very force of my love keeping them safe once they blinked in the cold light of day.

In the weeks that followed, I didn't always feel strong. I was tired, beyond exhausted, one of the girls constantly at my breast, the other one sleeping, never enough time to refill my reserves of energy or milk. But I would remember those last moments in the kitchen. "You are stronger than you think," I whispered to both my babies and myself as a mouth latched on to my breast for the fourth time in as many hours. I repeated these words when I felt weakest, most frightened, most overwhelmed by this job that millions of women before me had done but still seemed insurmountable every day. *You are stronger than you think.*

"You are stronger than you think," I whispered to Mia now, so quietly that she didn't even stir. "Remember that."

She slept soundly, oblivious to my presence or, perhaps, comforted by it. Shadows of Lottie caught me off guard every now and then, her presence hovering nearby in Mia's features, in the cushion of the rocking chair, by the well-stocked changing table. Perhaps Lottie wasn't stronger than she realized. Perhaps Lottie's secret knowledge was that she was weaker than she wanted to be.

I went into the living room, sat down on the couch with the baby in my arms, and called my sister. This time she answered on the second ring.

"Franci." Though she sounded tired, I heard the smile in her voice.

"Are you okay?" I spoke softly, so as not to wake Mia, but I was on the verge of tears.

"I'm fine. Well, not fine. I have a broken arm and a fractured ankle. I look like I got the shit kicked out of me, but I'm not going to die."

I took a shaky breath, reassured for the first time since receiving Sally's call. "I'm at your apartment. With Mia."

"Oh good. I was worried." Her casualness was jarring. "Sally's fine as a sitter, but she's not you." Somehow we were able to do this. It had been months since we'd last spoken, but it felt like no time at all.

"Lottie, you have a baby. I didn't even know."

"Let's not do this now, Franci. There's plenty of time for that later. Is she okay?"

I bit back my words and questions. "She's perfect. She's asleep in my arms right now. I'll get her ready, and we'll come by the hospital."

"There's no rush. Let her sleep. I'm going to take a nap myself. I'll see you later though, okay?"

"Okay." I looked around the apartment, readying myself to tackle the mess. I'd closed the door to the kitchen but would have to start in there.

"And Franci? I'm glad you're here. Thank you for coming." She hung up before I had time to answer.

I put Mia to bed and then cleaned the apartment. I wiped down the kitchen and took out the garbage and opened the doors and windows to shoo out the fruit flies. I organized the hundreds of student papers into neat stacks and threw out sour milk and old takeout containers. Lined up on the top row inside the refrigerator were several bags full of pumped breast milk. The date and time were clearly labeled in black Sharpie on each one in Lottie's careful script, the most recent dating back only a few days. When I opened the freezer, I found an entire rack filled with frozen milk. The sight of all those bags lined up neatly, nearly a month's worth, chilled me.

I finally called home.

Mark answered on the first ring. "Are you okay? How's your sister?"

"She's going to be all right. I'm going to head to the hospital soon, but I talked to her and she sounded okay." I settled onto the plush green couch and let my head lean back against the velour cushions.

"What happened?"

"I don't know yet. I'll find out when I see her. I'm just waiting for Mia to wake up from her nap."

"Who?" I'd told him about Mia but not her name.

"Lottie's baby girl, Mia."

"Right." Mark was silent on the other end. "So then Lottie must have been pregnant when you were there last spring."

"Yeah, a few months along."

"You couldn't tell?"

"No, I couldn't." My voice rose, and I struggled to suppress the anger that quickly swelled. "She wasn't even showing then."

"Who's the father?"

"No one. She went through a sperm donor." I thought of the sleeping baby in the other room. "She's so beautiful, Mark. She's like a tiny little Lottie. I forgot how tiny they are. Do you remember when Ana and Autumn were five months?"

"Yeah, I remember. They were pretty incredible."

I lay down on the couch and closed my eyes. We were silent on the line.

"I'm afraid she did it on purpose," I said after a moment.

"What?"

"Lottie. I'm afraid she got hit on purpose."

"Oh, Franci. Why do you think that?"

"You should've seen her apartment, Mark." I began to cry. "It was a mess. It looked like she hadn't cleaned it in months. Except for Mia's room. Mia's room was perfect. And in the freezer she had all this milk stocked up, like she knew she wasn't going to be around." I wiped my eyes with the back of my hand.

"But don't lots of women store their milk? Especially if she's back at work, she'd need to bring it for daycare, right?"

"Yeah, I guess."

"And maybe the house just got messy. It's got to be hard being a single parent, working full-time," Mark went on.

"Yeah." I didn't tell him about the overflowing trash and the rotten food. I wanted to believe him. He knew about her bipolar disorder and understood it on an intellectual level, yet he'd never seen her in the throes of either depression or mania. It was impossible to explain that it was something dangerous and separate from Lottie, yet it was also who she was. Mark had never really known Lottie, had never known what she was capable of. I always choreographed my visits to California during times when I knew he'd be unable to come, and on the few instances when Lottie visited us, I was a careful buffer between them, filling our evenings with activities that wouldn't involve Mark. Easier on everyone to keep them apart.

"How are the girls?" I asked.

"They're fine. They miss you."

"I miss them too."

"Franci, do you want me to come out there? Should we all come to you?"

"No," I said quickly. I didn't want them here, though I didn't know why exactly. The idea of Mark and Ana and Autumn all crowding into

Lottie's neglected little apartment, of Mark's laptop and piles of paper-work scattered across her kitchen and the girls' toys strewn across Mia's room, somehow it just didn't feel right. "No, I'm okay."

"Franci, are you sure? I can help with the baby. I'm sure the girls will want to meet her."

"Not yet." I ached suddenly for my own daughters, for their golden hair to be draped over my shoulder, their strong arms coiled around my neck. "Please, can I talk to the girls?"

"Mommy!" Their voices, suddenly on the line, sounded so close, it was hard to believe how far away they actually were. I listened to them, asked questions, told them I loved them, missed them, would be home soon. And then I was alone again.

The room was silent; Mia slept on.

Lottie

Mia came to me on September seventeenth. I was in the baby's room, folding clothes into tiny little stacks of onesies and sleep suits to put in her drawers. I was forty weeks and two days pregnant, and I'd been having contractions since that afternoon. The late-day sun poured through the window, casting shadows across the slats of the crib. A light breeze blew the mobile, and I took a deep breath as a stronger contraction twisted through my body. I picked my phone up from the dresser and dialed the number of my midwife.

"Hello, Luanne? It's Charlotte Weaver."

"Hi, Charlotte. Is it time?"

"I think so. I've been having contractions since this morning. They're getting stronger." I was suddenly on the verge of tears.

"Okay, it sounds like it's time."

"Oh my god." I clutched the phone against my ear as I eased myself into the rocking chair I'd bought for the room. I was about to have a baby, and I was all alone. Whit and I had broken up several months earlier. I hadn't spoken to Franci since April. I felt more cut off than I'd ever felt in my life, yet at the same time there was something truly freeing about being alone, as if I'd lifted my anchor and set sail. I was both relishing the feeling of being suspended on the open ocean and terrified that I would drown. I had set out for the middle of the ocean, and now I was going to try to swim ashore with a child clinging to my back.

The plan to have a baby had grown more frightening from the day the little plastic stick showed a pink plus sign. A part of me regretted it already. "Oh no, no, you don't understand," I would tell Luanne. "I'm not fit to be a mother. Even my own sister won't trust me with her children anymore." But another part of me still wanted it desperately. I wanted someone to love, someone who would tether me to this world without confining me in the way that Franci and Whit did, someone I could take care of rather than to always be the one in need. But what could Luanne do? What could anyone do? Mia was on her way.

"Oh my god," I repeated.

"Charlotte, are you okay?" Luanne asked. "Are the contractions bad?"

"No." I pressed my palms to my eyes and forced myself to breathe more steadily. "I'm just freaking out a tiny bit."

"Hang in there, Charlotte. I'm on my way. You're going to make a wonderful mother."

At my first obstetrician's appointment, the doctor advised me to continue taking my medication throughout the pregnancy, with a few minor tweaks to dosages and prescriptions. After the appointment with the ob-gyn, I was ushered down the hall to meet Luanne, the midwife. Compared to the sterility of the doctor's office, Luanne's office was warm and homey, with photos of newborn babies and crayon illustrations decorating the wall. Luanne was in her late fifties, and she wore her long, graying blond hair in a loose ponytail. She held my hand while I told her about my bipolar disorder. Even on that first visit, she told me that I would be a good mother. Some days her words were like balm to a burn.

Other days, they were meaningless.

I thought about my own mother, as I had so often during the past nine months. Had she felt like a good mother? *Was* she a good mother? I clasped my hands over my belly and remembered the stories of the Strout girls that she would tell Franci and me at bedtime. She'd sit on a yellow wooden chair between our beds. The room was thick with the smell of the menthol cigarettes she smoked when our father wasn't home, which was often.

"Once . . . in a place that is not here and now, but is very close, once . . . there lived two girls." The stories were always about Louisa and Mirabella Strout. Mirabella had the ability to read minds and to plant new thoughts in other people's brains, while Louisa was able to make herself and others invisible. They lived in a brownstone in Boston with their parents, and in the stories it was always winter, the streets of Boston covered in a thick layer of snow.

Nearly every night the girls were summoned on one adventure or another. They would open the window of their bedroom, join hands, and push off the ledge as if they were in a swimming pool. They would fly through the starry sky above the white city, ready to save small children or animals or old people or just regular grown-ups that were sad.

There was the story where Louisa and Mirabella saved the homeless man who was about to freeze to death and brought him into their bedroom, hiding him in the closet for weeks while they gave him Tupperware containers filled with leftover roast chicken and slices of chocolate cake. Then there was the one where they saved the stray cats that were about to be taken to the pound to be put down. Louisa made them invisible while Mirabella planted the idea in the pound worker's mind that stray cats were a good thing because they kept the city free of rats. The stories were usually dark and involved the downtrodden and the possibility of death. Usually they revealed some sinister irony about life that Franci and I didn't fully understand—how a man could die while sleeping on the sidewalk when there was a house with a warm bed right next to him, or why a city worker would round up a bunch of animals only to kill them. However, Louisa and Mirabella always prevailed and saved the day at the last minute.

Our mother sat between us and told the stories night after night, perhaps emulating what she thought a good mother should do. But did she know that the stories sometimes gave Franci nightmares? Did she know that she often told the same story two nights in a row? Or was she trying to teach us that the world was full of magic and there was darkness behind every curtain, but that light could sometimes be found too? Had she failed terribly as a mother or had she succeeded? I still wasn't sure.

"Charlotte? Did you hear me?" Luanne's voice gently tugged me back to the present. "I said you're going to be a wonderful mother. Now you just need to calm down and breathe."

"Thank you, Luanne. Thank you. I'll see you in a little while." *Help me,* I called silently to Franci, and I wished that I was Mirabella. I wished that I could pluck those two words out of the air and drop them into her mind. But Franci had always related more to Louisa, the invisible twin, and so I couldn't find her anywhere.

Mia was born and Franci wasn't there. It seemed unbelievable that when the most important moment of my life occurred, Franci knew nothing about it.

I wanted to tell her. I had tried during her visit in April, but I kept it to myself for the first few days. I was already a few months along, but no one knew, not even Whit. I was waiting to tell Franci, wanting the moment to be just right. Truth be told, even while I held the secret knowledge of Mia close and waited for that right moment, part of me was already afraid to tell her, just as I was afraid to tell Whit. I knew the doubt and judgment I would see in her eyes when I revealed my news. I couldn't bear to have Franci take that happiness away from me, replacing it with my own misgivings and fear that already lurked nearby. And then the visit went terribly wrong, and she left suddenly, and there was no way I could tell her.

I remember lying in the birthing center the morning after Mia was born, her tiny red body pressed to my skin. Already she had a full head of hair, and she slept peacefully after the fifteen-hour journey it took to find her way into my arms. I examined Mia's exquisite nails, each perfectly formed, her lovely mouth and miniature ears. I watched her sleep and thought of Franci, missing her desperately and wishing she were here.

But another part of me was angry. *See what you've missed?* I wanted to tell her. *See what you've lost?* And then another part of me just wondered, *How did we get here? And will we ever find our way back?* But Franci's answer to that question seemed to reverberate in my brain.

Back to where? she would ask.

Franci

Lottie was always the smart one. In high school she pulled straight As, while my own report card was a mediocre collection of Bs. She worked hard and studied like crazy, but even without the effort, Lottie would have done fine. In college and graduate school she threw herself into her studies with a passion and focus that I envied. Somehow, even during most of her days in the Black, Lottie managed to make it work, rallying to give lectures to groups of a hundred or more undergrads. I wondered if her students noticed her heavy lids and flat affect.

Lottie's expertise was in American feminist writers of the nineteenth and twentieth centuries. Shortly after she was hired as an associate professor, I sat in on one of her classes. That day they were reading a short story by Charlotte Perkins Gilman called "The Yellow Wallpaper." I'd read the story as an undergrad. It was about a woman whose husband brings her to the countryside after the birth of her child to recuperate. Allowed to do little other than lie in bed, the woman fixates on the yellow wallpaper in her room, becoming convinced that there's a woman living in it. The story chronicles the woman's slow and torturous descent into madness. It is both sad and deeply disturbing.

"Nervous breakdown," Lottie addressed the class. "Depression. Anxiety. A temporary nervous condition. Postpartum depression." She paused, scanning the class for understanding. "What is wrong with the woman in 'The Yellow Wallpaper'?"

The class shifted in their seats. Several students muttered under their breath, "She's crazy." Lottie knew the names of every single person in each of her classes, even in this lecture with over one hundred students. I knew that if no one raised a hand, she'd choose a student at random, and I prayed she wouldn't call on me as a joke. Finally, a student a few rows back raised her hand. Lottie nodded at the young woman.

"She starts off just tired, and she's not interacting with her baby. She's probably suffering from postpartum depression?" Her voice went up at the end, indicating she wasn't certain of this, looking to Lottie for confirmation, though Lottie didn't respond. "But then she becomes obsessed. She thinks there's a woman in the wallpaper."

"A sign of madness?" Lottie asked. It must have taken courage to stand before this packed lecture hall, yet my sister was utterly in control.

"Well, no," the student conceded. "Not on its own. But the narrator convinces herself there's a real woman in the wallpaper, alive and trapped behind bars." The student tapped a pencil on her text.

Lottie nodded. "Is this a reliable narrator?" There were murmurs of "no," and I watched most of the students shake their heads. "When do we learn that we can't trust this character to tell her own story accurately?" Lottie waited, raising her pencil and getting ready to call on someone. A blond guy raised his hand before the pencil fell.

"When she first describes the wallpaper. That's when you start to know that something's not quite right with her. By the end of the story, she's become the woman in the wallpaper, and she escapes. She's finally free."

"So is she free, or is she crazy?" Lottie asked. The question hung unanswered in the hushed lecture hall.

I thought of Lottie during her spells of depression, staring blankly at the water stains on the ceiling. I wondered what it was she saw there.

~

Afterward we ate lunch in the student union.

"You were amazing." I placed a tray between us on the table.

"Thanks." Lottie reached for one of the yogurts.

"Really. You seemed so . . . confident. So sure of yourself up there. Don't you get nervous?"

Lottie looked up in surprise. "Why would I get nervous? I've read the stories; I understand them."

"I know, but I would be intimidated in front of such a big group of people."

Lottie shrugged. "You get used to it," she said, removing a turkey sandwich from her canvas shoulder bag and giving me half.

"What do you think actually happens at the end of the story?" I asked.

"She commits suicide." Lottie's tone was matter-of-fact. Peeking out from the sleeves of Lottie's blouse were a few of the pale white flecks on her arms, the faint scars from the night I'd accompanied her to the ER. The sandwich felt thick in my mouth, and I forced myself to swallow it.

Around us the union hummed with students and professors relaxing between classes. People sat in small groups or alone with books spread across tables. Lottie and I met here for lunch most afternoons, though during this particular week my supervisor was taking vacation, which allowed me the time off to sit in on Lottie's class.

Lately I found myself dreaming of moving to Boston, the city our mother had left so many years earlier and never found her way back to. I knew I was being overly romantic, but I pictured brownstones and oak trees covered in red and yellow leaves; wide streets dotted with white colonials, their shutters painted forest green; and sidewalks dappled with the sunlight that flickered through thick foliage.

I had only been to Boston once, on a trip with my father and Lottie the autumn after Mother's death. Our father was presenting his research at Harvard, and Lottie and I wandered through Harvard Square and

Harvard Yard. It had been a damp, gray October morning, and the leaves lay scattered upon the grass. Despite the rush of city life just beyond, the Yard had been quiet and serene, as if even the tourists knew better than to disturb the serious hum of academia that went on within the redbrick walls.

We stayed in a hotel in Back Bay that overlooked the Public Garden. In the mornings while our father was in the hotel hunched over his notebooks, Lottie and I bought cups of hot chocolate and donuts from a street vendor and ate breakfast in the garden. We sat on a bench and watched the ducks and tourists, the businessmen and vagrants, as they each made their way through the sanctuary of the park toward Downtown Crossing.

I pictured our mother here, walking through the garden, dressed in the red-and-orange wool that conjures a New England autumn. I missed her intensely, and I leaned against Lottie, my head falling on her shoulder. Neither of us said anything, but I knew she was thinking of Mother as well. I reached for Lottie's hand and squeezed it, silently promising our mother I'd return here someday.

But that was before. Before Lottie's first episode, before the spells in Lottie's life, and by extension my own, were broken into Black, White, and the calm of Gray. Sitting in the union, talking about suicide so cavalierly, I tried to summon the courage to tell her I wanted to move.

"Do you like teaching?" I asked instead.

"I do." Lottie was thoughtful for a moment. "It's kind of a rush, having everyone in the room focus on you like that. It sounds kind of twisted, but there's a neat sense of power." Lottie flashed a wicked grin and took a sip of soda.

The year before, I'd applied to art school without telling anyone, not even Lottie, not when I applied or when the four programs rejected me. I'd taken art classes throughout high school and college, yet I chose not to major in art once at Berkeley. It felt too impractical, too self-indulgent, too much like something Lottie would have done. So I majored in journalism instead, taking art classes on the side. But when I looked back on my best memories of college, most of them had taken place in the early evening hours at a studio, light filtering through the plastic blinds, a bouquet of flowers propped at the center of the room and the whole class silent as we focused intently on the thick piece of canvas before us. I could easily conjure up the slightly musty odor of the room, the smell of charcoal dust, paint, and linseed oil mixed with the rich scent of coffee that came from the numerous paper cups that sat beside our easels.

The memories always filled me with a deep sense of contentment and optimism, and it was with great trepidation that I put together my portfolio and sent out the applications.

It shouldn't have been a surprise when I didn't get in. An art major was a prerequisite for most of the programs. My portfolio was thin, considering I'd only taken one class a semester, and though my recommendations were solid, behind each lay what wasn't written, what I'd been told in all of my classes: I needed to take more risks in my work.

I hadn't expected the crushing sense of disappointment when the slender envelopes arrived in the mailbox, one after the other, or the heavy sense of defeat that followed each rejection. I threw the letters out at work, afraid Lottie would come across them in our apartment. I continued in my job, determined that my days of art were behind me, even as it became clear that they'd never been in front of me.

It took me almost a year to muster up the courage to apply to grad school again, though I stayed away from art this time. I could become a teacher, I decided. Safe and predictable, a good schedule for when I got married and had children. I scrutinized the prerequisites for the teaching programs before getting my materials together; though again, I didn't tell Lottie that I was applying. The week before, a fat yellow envelope arrived at work with a return address of Boston University.

"I've been thinking that maybe I'd like to teach too," I said.

"Really?" Lottie's thin eyebrows raised in surprise. She leaned forward, reaching for my hand. "You'd be great, Franci. What are you thinking of teaching? Journalism?"

I shook my head. "No, I was thinking high school. English, probably."

"That's fabulous!" Her enthusiasm was so real; I hated to ruin it. "You could probably even start on your master's this spring. I don't think Berkeley typically accepts students for the second semester, but they might make an exception for you, considering how long you've been here."

"I don't want to go to Berkeley," I said, looking down at my hand still clasped gently in Lottie's.

She tilted her head to the side. "No? They have an excellent education department. But maybe you want a change? Dad might be able to help get you in to Stanford. It's kind of a long shot, but you never know. And there's always USF or San Francisco State."

I shook my head, staring down at the plastic table. "No. I don't think I want to go anywhere in California." I forced myself to continue. "I want to go to Boston." I looked up. She frowned at me in confusion, her eyes narrowing slightly behind the black frames of her glasses.

"Boston?" Lottie asked skeptically. "You do realize it's freezing there, don't you?"

I attempted a small smile. "I know. But I've always wondered what it would be like to live through a real New England winter." I waited a beat before adding, "And I was accepted at Boston University."

"You already applied?" she asked, clearly taken aback. I nodded, swallowing my guilt. "But, Franci . . ." Lottie trailed off, a frantic look suddenly in her eyes. "What about me?"

What about Lottie? I didn't have an answer.

I was silent.

"But . . . Franci." I felt her panic as it descended. It shivered in the pit of my own stomach, a small abandoned bird. "What about me?" she asked again.

I hadn't let myself believe in the idea. Like my instructors had said, I didn't know how to take risks. I shook my head, a foolish smile spreading across my face, assuring Lottie this was all a misunderstanding. In my mind I was already sliding the acceptance letter from BU into the recycling bin by my desk.

"Forget it. It was just an idea. You're right. Berkeley has a great education program." I shook my head again, as if shaking the remainder of the idea away.

Lottie eyed me warily. "Really? Just like that?"

"Yes, really. It was just a thought."

"You were accepted at Boston University? When?"

"Last week. It doesn't matter, though; I have plenty of time to get my application in here." I began to gather our garbage on the tray, eager now to end the conversation.

"You were really thinking about moving?"

"Just for a minute. But not anymore."

Lottie looked at the clock on the wall. "I need to get going. I have office hours in fifteen minutes. I'm going to grab a cup of coffee first."

Lottie got in line, and I finished clearing our table. It had been a silly idea, I tried to convince myself. I would probably have hated the cold winters, and I'd heard the summers were sweltering. Better off staying right here in sunny, mellow California. I ignored the lump that had formed at the back of my throat as the half-hatched plan cracked from its egg. A moment later Lottie appeared with the cup of coffee.

"Maybe it's not the worst idea in the world," she said, handing me a chocolate chip cookie wrapped in a napkin. I reached for it without speaking, waiting for her to continue. "Maybe it would be okay if you tried a new city. It's not as if I'm helpless here, right?"

"Of course not," I said quickly.

"I've been good, right? I'm taking my meds. I haven't been off them in almost a year. And I'm not going to," she said firmly. I nodded. "And things with Whit have been great. He's really supportive. Not that he's responsible for me. He shouldn't be. That's not fair." Lottie paused, realizing what she was implying. "Not that *you* should be responsible for me, either."

"It's okay. I don't mind." We walked toward the stairwell, and I linked my arm through Lottie's to show her that I really didn't mind. Did I? Most days I wasn't sure. "I can't imagine being so far away from you. It would be too weird."

Lottie's heels clicked along the stairs, and my clogs made a heavy scraping sound. I tightened my grip on her arm. It *would* be strange to be so far away from her. It would be terrifying. But part of me had looked forward to that rootless feeling and the exhilarating freedom I imagined came with it.

I pushed open the heavy metal doors and stepped out into the afternoon. It was mid-November, but the sun still carried heat. Along the wide swaths of green, students sat cross-legged, bent over textbooks, or they lay in the grass, backpacks tucked under their heads as makeshift pillows. This was where we parted most afternoons before making our way toward our respective departments. But Lottie stood on the pavement, her book bag slung across her body and her coffee in her hand. She looked deep in thought, but she turned to me.

"You should go." Her voice held an air of finality, as if she'd been thinking about this for a long time and not just during the walk through the cafeteria and down the stairs. Lottie closed her eyes and tilted her face up to catch the warmth of the sun's rays, and her pale skin was bathed in the vivid light of the afternoon. She nodded again, her eyes still closed. "You should go," she repeated.

I was silent, waiting for her to take it back. But she didn't. Not then and not ever, though I'm sure she must have wanted to many times. For once, I didn't protest.

"Thank you," I whispered instead, leaning forward to embrace my sister, planting a clumsy peck on her parted lips.

Later, when I thought about my decision to move to Boston, I remembered that afternoon and the generous and selfless gift Lottie had bravely imparted to me. I pictured my confident, brilliant, terrified, and changeable sister, and how she had looked up at the sky that afternoon, ready to face any uncertainty. She looked like an angel, her hair around her face, the white glow that her skin gave off, the serene look of calm as she braced herself for whatever might come next.

In the weeks before I left California, our apartment was filled with boxes to be shipped and bags to be donated. The furniture in my bedroom would stay; Lottie had decided not to take a roommate and to convert it into a guest room. "For when you come to visit," she said.

The evening before my flight, we ate dinner with our father in a small Italian place in Palo Alto. Lottie had been chattering away all night in an effort to distract us from the reason we were out. When she went to the bathroom, the table took on an awkward quiet.

"You all ready for tomorrow morning?" my father asked, stabbing a squiggly calamari from the appetizer plate we were sharing.

"I think so."

I was ready to leave, tired of imagining all the reasons why I should stay.

"You'll keep an eye on Lottie, won't you?" I asked.

"Of course."

Though he knew of her diagnosis, Lottie and I had worked hard to keep the ugliness of it from touching our father. As far as he was concerned her little mood disorder was fully under control with the medication that she took daily without complaint. There was no reason for it to be otherwise.

"We'll have to plan a trip. For you both to come visit," I said. My father smiled and nodded noncommittally. A slight sheen of olive oil clung to the stubble of his beard.

"Your mother would be proud of you," he said. I looked down at my plate, unsure why the words left me feeling so empty.

When I arrived in Boston, I was surprised how at home I felt right away. It was late August and the trees were still green, though here and there leaves lay in scattered brown clusters on the sidewalks. The temperature was a comfortable seventy-five, much like Berkeley when I'd left.

My new roommates, Heidi and Jan, were friends from the University of Massachusetts and several years younger than me, and I liked them immediately. Within a few weeks, we developed systems for cleaning the house, buying groceries, and splitting the cost of the bills. At night we gathered around a secondhand table in the kitchen, drinking cheap red wine from ceramic mugs. For the first time in a while, I felt young.

Winter approached quickly, and I wondered how I would endure the bracing New England cold. But again, I was surprised at how easily I adapted. Heidi and Jan were skiers, and they invited me to New Hampshire over winter break. Never having been on skis before, I assumed I would be clumsy and embarrassed, but I loved the thrill of the icy air on my face as I rushed down the mountain alone.

I spoke with my father once a week and with Lottie nearly every day. She, too, seemed happy, at peace, her intense nature possibly mellowed by my absence.

I met Mark at the registrar's office one morning in late February. It was a bitterly cold day, and I was wearing several layers, but after standing in the long line I was sweating and light-headed. Perspiration prickled at my neck in the overly heated room, and I began to strip the winter clothes off slowly. First the hat, then a few minutes later

I unwound the scarf from my neck. Mark was ahead of me, and he smiled as I took off my heavy coat, stepping out of line to put my pile of clothes on an empty chair. There were still several students in front of us, one of whom had been speaking with the sole assistant at the window for nearly ten minutes. I smiled back at Mark, who looked cool and comfortable in a fleece jacket.

"You got to love February in New England," he said with a grin.

"It's my first," I told him.

"Oh yeah? Where are you from?"

"California. Berkeley."

His eyebrows went up in amusement as they often did when I told people I was from Berkeley. People in New England assumed that everyone in Berkeley grew their own wheatgrass and fueled their cars with vegetable oil. One girl I met had asked me if it was true that you were allowed to go to class topless at Berkeley.

It took another twenty-five minutes before it was Mark's turn, and by then he'd asked me out for the next night.

We went for Chinese food, and the night after that we went to a movie. A few nights later he cooked dinner for me at his apartment, and I surprised myself by sleeping with him. There was something about Mark, like Boston, that allowed me to be free. I wanted to call Lottie the next morning to tell her, but I kept it to myself, worried that she'd accidentally ruin it with her automatic criticism. As far as Lottie was concerned, no one was ever good enough.

Lottie met Mark for the first time when she came to visit that June. I wanted her to love Boston as I did, for her to see just how quaint and charming it could be. Though it was only the third week in June, the temperature was in the low nineties, and Lottie had been complaining about the heat since she arrived. My apartment had no air-conditioning, and the small window fans did little to relieve the thick humidity.

We made plans to meet Mark for dinner at one of his favorite Italian restaurants. The train had no air-conditioning and with transfers, stops, and wait time, it took over an hour to get from Allston to the North End. I was relieved that the restaurant was air-conditioned, and Lottie collapsed into the booth in a sticky heap.

Mark joined us a few minutes later, kissing me before acknowledging Lottie. I felt a secret thrill to be the center of his attention, aware of Lottie watching the kiss.

"You must be Lottie," Mark said, turning and extending his hand.

"It's Charlotte, actually. Franci's the only one who still calls me Lottie."

"It's nice to meet you, Charlotte." He settled into the booth beside me, letting his hand rest on my bare knee under the table. He looked from Lottie to me and then back at Lottie. "You two really do look identical. It's kind of weird."

Lottie shrugged and raised her eyebrows. She wore a black sundress, and the skin of her chest was flushed pink. Her hair was in a frizzy pile on top of her head, and her upper lip was damp with sweat. Unlike me, Mark had a car, and he'd driven from work. He looked comfortable and handsome, and I felt a ripple of pride to be with him.

"Franci tells me you're from around here," she said, holding her glass of ice water to her forehead.

"New Hampshire originally. And then Framingham, not far from here."

Lottie rolled her eyes to the ceiling. "I can't imagine living in a place where it was this hot."

Mark raised his eyebrows. "Doesn't it get hot in California?" The waiter came, and Mark ordered a bottle of wine.

"I live in *Northern* California. We rarely get temperatures like this," Lottie corrected. "And I'll have a gin and tonic first, please," she told the waiter. I fought the urge to question whether that was a good idea. Lottie wasn't supposed to drink with her medication, but she often did. A glass of wine here or there wasn't usually a problem, but the doctor had been stern when he talked about hard alcohol. And Lottie was never able to do anything in moderation.

"When Franci said she wanted to move here, I didn't understand it," Lottie continued. "I know our mother was from here originally, but I've never had much of an interest in living in a place where it's freezing cold for half the year and a hundred degrees the other half."

"That's not true, Lottie," I objected. "Fall is beautiful here. Remember when we were here with Dad?" Lottie shrugged her shoulders. "And there's spring."

"Isn't it spring now?" Lottie asked, with a slight sneer. Our drinks came and Lottie squeezed the lime into her cocktail, taking a large slug. I sipped my white wine, and we silently studied the menu.

Over dinner, Mark asked Lottie about her job at Berkeley. Lottie answered him perfunctorily, not going into much detail. "Franci tells me you're getting your MBA?" I detected the note of distaste in her voice.

"I actually just graduated." I'd attended the graduation the previous month and sat beside Mark's mother in the stadium seats. She had leaned over and squeezed my hand when they called Mark's name.

"Planning on ruling the world, are you?" Lottie asked.

"*Lottie.*" I shot her a look across the table.

Mark frowned at her with an amused smile on his face. "Excuse me?"

"Well, that is why people get MBAs, isn't it? To make enough money to squish the little guy?" Lottie pressed.

Mark didn't take the bait. He shrugged and tilted his head. "I assume people get MBAs for many different reasons. I got mine because I've always been interested in business and because I didn't want a job where I was always worried about how I was going to pay my rent." He could have told Lottie that he'd watched his mother do that after his father died, that his family was forced to sell their house and move in with his grandmother, and that he'd shared a bedroom with his sister in high school, but I knew he didn't want to give Lottie the justification for his decisions. As he told me later, his choices were ultimately none of her goddamn business.

"A job like teaching, you mean?" Lottie asked, signaling to the waiter for another drink.

"I imagine that you probably do all right as a professor at Berkeley."

"*Associate* professor," Lottie interrupted.

"On the tenure track, from what I hear. Which is pretty impressive for someone your age. But if not, you can always consider going back for your MBA. Berkeley has a great business school." I knew he was teasing. He was baiting her, as she was baiting him, but Lottie didn't get the joke.

"I love my job. I would never give it up just for more money. For some of us, how we make our money is just as important as how much we make," Lottie snapped. I cringed inwardly at her self-righteous tone. Had she always been like this, I wondered. Was she louder, brassier, more outspoken than usual, or had I just forgotten?

The rest of the dinner passed in an awkward silence interrupted by meaningless small talk. Under the table, Mark kept his hand on my knee, only removing it to take a sip from his glass. Its warm presence steadied me enough to get through the meal without bursting into tears or throwing something at Lottie. Finally, our plates were empty except for a few strands of noodles and the pink tails of shrimp.

"Do either of you want dessert?" Mark asked. Both Lottie and I shook our heads, and Mark signaled to the waiter for the check. He paid with his credit card, and I didn't know if I was relieved or ashamed that for all of her mockery of Mark's financial ambitions, Lottie didn't once reach for her purse.

He drove us back to my apartment and kissed me slowly, deliberately, even though Lottie was waiting impatiently on the sidewalk.

Later, while Lottie was showering, I called him.

"I'm sorry about dinner," I apologized. "I don't know why she acted that way. She's not usually like that." I wondered if this were true.

"It's okay. It seemed like she'd made her mind up about me before I actually sat down."

"I really wanted you two to like each other." I pulled my knees to my chest and leaned back in bed. In the bathroom down the hall, the water turned off.

"I'm sure we will. First impressions aren't everything."

"I know. But she's my twin sister. She means a lot to me," I persisted. "It's important to me that you like her. I just wish she hadn't been such a jerk."

"At least she lives in California, right?" Mark said lightly. I tried not to let the comment rattle me. Seemingly innocent, it contained so much—an assumption that I belonged here and would stay, that this was only the beginning for us, but also that Mark was relieved that Lottie wouldn't be around very often.

"I guess." A shadow moved in the slant of light under the bedroom door. Outside, raindrops began to fall. "Anyway, I'm sorry about tonight. Maybe we can try again before she leaves."

"Maybe." He paused, and when he spoke again his voice was softer, more serious. "But you know it doesn't really matter, Franci. I may never be best friends with your sister, but I know she's important to you. And I love *you*. That's what matters." He'd never told me he loved me before, and I actually felt my jaw drop just as Lottie opened the door to the bedroom. She stood in a towel, dripping water onto the floor.

"Okay," I whispered, wanting to say the words back to him but not wanting Lottie there for it. Mark was silent on the other end. "Me too," I managed. "Lottie just came in," I explained. "We're about to go to bed."

"Okay. I'll talk to you tomorrow, Franci," he said and then hung up. I held on to the phone, willing myself back to the place just moments before. I looked up at Lottie, ready to tell her, but her eyes were dark.

"Were you apologizing for me?"

"What?" I asked, though I'd heard the question clearly.

"You said you were sorry about tonight. What are you sorry about, Franci?" Lottie's eyes were narrow and beady, and I wondered if I looked the same when I was angry. Normally Lottie's temper had the ability to jar me, but it was hard to take her seriously when she was wearing only a ratty old towel. And Mark's words had made me suddenly untouchable.

"For the way you behaved," I said, getting up off the bed and pulling pajamas from the drawer. "You acted like a spoiled child."

"A child? Why, because I wasn't immediately impressed by him?" Lottie threw the towel on the floor and walked naked across the room. She was beautiful in her fury, all curves and perfect posture, totally unabashed that people could likely see her through the flimsy white curtains. Lottie rummaged through my dresser until she found a tee shirt and shorts. "Give me a break, Franci. You're the one who's acting like a child, all doe-eyed and in awe of Mr. MBA and his potential earnings."

"You're drunk," I said with mild disgust. Outside, it had begun to pour, and I closed the curtains. Down below, people were hurrying through the streets, trying uselessly not to get wet.

"Jesus, Franci, I am not. I had a few drinks. Will you relax already?"

"You shouldn't be drinking," I said quietly.

"Spare me the lecture." We both stood by the bed, but neither of us made a move to get in.

"You shouldn't. It's not good for you. You know what the doctor said about drinking while on the medication."

"Yes, Franci, I know what the doctor said. He's *my* doctor; I should know what he said."

"You are still taking the medication, aren't you?" I asked, the thought filling me with dread.

"Yes, I'm still taking it!" Lottie's cheeks were pink with anger. "My god, you know nothing about it."

"I do too." I felt my own face growing hot. "I've been there, Lottie. I've seen you. I know a thing or two about it."

"Well, you're not there now and I'm managing just fine. You're relieved of your duties, remember?" The statement cut me to the quick.

She let out a sigh and got into bed, scooting over to make room for me. I got in beside her and quickly turned out the light. We lay for a moment without talking.

"I'm okay, Franci. You don't need to worry all the time. I can take care of myself." Her voice drifted in the dark. *No, you can't,* I was tempted to say, but I stayed silent, because if I really believed that, how could I ever have left? "And Mark seems like a nice guy," she continued. I wasn't sure if she was telling the truth, but I appreciated the effort that I knew it took. "He's not my type, but he seems to really care about you."

"He told me he loved me," I said.

"Oh, Franci, that's so good." She was quiet. "You like it here."

"I do. Even more than I expected."

"It suits you," Lottie said, her voice already heavy with sleep. "It's nice to see you so happy." As we talked, our bodies moved closer. With the rain, the heat had broken and a damp breeze drifted in the windows. I remembered the bedroom we'd shared for so many years in the old house, the one with the embroidered curtains and pale yellow carpet.

"I'm glad you're here," I whispered.

"Mhmm," Lottie murmured, nearly asleep. I lay awake, listening to the sounds of the city outside my window and beside me the steady sound of Lottie breathing in the noisy night.

Lottie

Franci has always been cautious. She has always been scared to let the messiness of life get too close to her. But the one place in her life where she is strong and confident is in her mothering.

While it took me a long time to realize I wanted to be a mother, Franci has known since she was a little girl. As a child I was more interested in my easel and paints, my musical instruments, and my soccer ball than in dolls or pretend kitchen sets. But Franci spent hours with Lucy, her plastic baby doll that came with a cloth diaper and a real bottle. She put Lucy to bed in her cradle, all the while singing lullabies and whispering who knows what into her ear. Lucy had a pink stroller, and on nice days Franci would take her for walks around the yard. Some days Lucy was better taken care of than we were.

Growing up, Franci didn't really have boyfriends. She dated a little, but even in high school Franci was ready to get serious in a way that boys could sense. It scared them, and after a few dates they'd stop calling. In college Franci fared a little better, but even then her desire to settle down was obvious. It was as if she had "Marriage Material" tattooed on her forehead. By then she was already skilled at taking care of me, and why she wanted more responsibility, more burden, I could not understand.

Then she moved to Boston and married Mark. It wasn't that I didn't like Mark. He seemed nice enough, if a bit stuffy and traditional. I'd always hoped Franci would end up with someone more creative and daring, someone who'd push her outside her comfort zone when her desire to live safely was so strong. But the truth is no one would have ever measured up, because while I wanted Franci to be happy, a selfish part of me wanted her all to myself. Even as an adult, I wanted to be the center of her world.

Then Ana and Autumn came. And in that instant, everything changed. Franci had been living in Boston for four or five years, and we'd adapted to not seeing each other often, though we still talked on the phone nearly every day. With the arrival of Ana and Autumn our calls grew less frequent. Franci was nursing, or resting, or giving the girls a bath, or just too tired to talk. As they got older, Franci was at the playground or going to music class or a playgroup. When we did manage to squeeze in a few minutes, all she wanted to talk about was the new word that Autumn said, the funny thing that Ana had done, or some new mild concern she'd brought up with the doctor.

It was boring to listen to, but that didn't bother me. What was so surprising was that Franci hardly ever seemed worried about me anymore. Every now and then she'd ask how I was feeling or if I was still taking my pills or about the medication's side effects. But she didn't seem as concerned about the answers to the questions as she once had; she merely seemed to be asking out of habit. I knew that Whit still called her every month or so to check in, but I suspected that even those conversations had become perfunctory and automatic, if Franci even answered the phone.

In many ways it was a good thing. Franci was letting me live my life; she was finally living her own life without the constant obligation of caring for me. I knew if I needed her, she'd always help. But what I didn't know was if she would drop everything and come immediately.

She had other responsibilities now. She had other loves. And those new loves usurped ours.

It wasn't exactly envy that I felt. It was a separation like when Franci played with Lucy. I was welcome to join them, but it didn't matter to her if I did or not. She would have fun playing without me. I was always invited, but I wasn't necessary to their game.

Franci

"I'm here to see a patient," I told the woman at the front desk of the hospital.

"Name, please?"

"Lottie—Charlotte—Weaver," I corrected myself.

Our mother had such high hopes when she named us. Charlotte and Francine Weaver. Proper-sounding Bostonian names, even though we were born in California. We were only on the West Coast temporarily, Mother always said, although that turned out not to be the case.

Our parents moved to Palo Alto the year before Lottie and I were born, when our father accepted a job at Stanford. He was a cancer researcher, one of the top in his field, and though Mother admired his work, the move was difficult for her. How could she complain about living so far from her own home when the work her husband did had the potential to save so many lives? She didn't, but she raised us with the belief that we would move "back east" someday soon. By the time I was in middle school, I no longer believed we'd ever leave California, but Mother never gave up, so the roots she put down in California were tenuous, only reaching a few inches into the ground.

Charlotte and Francine: strong, proud, formal names. Francine became Franci almost immediately, and I have stayed Franci for my whole life. To Mother's dismay, Charlotte was Lottie throughout high school. In college she became Charlotte again, though by then

Mother was gone and not there to appreciate the conversion. And with Charlotte's given name came other far more drastic transformations.

"She's in room 308," the woman said.

I took the elevator to the third floor, holding Mia's carrier carefully, the heavy bucket seat swinging as I struggled down the hall to Lottie's room. I entered the room so slowly that my sister was revealed to me in pieces. First, I could make out the slight shape of her body under the hospital blanket. She was propped up in the bed, and her right arm was in a bright white cast that rested awkwardly against her body. The left side of her face was pale, her skin nearly as pallid as the sheets, but the right side bloomed a florid red and purple, a dark and swollen wound that took up nearly half her face. Her eyes were open, but they looked sunken and hollow, her cheekbones protruding too sharply.

We both heard my quick intake of breath.

She stared vacantly at the wall, but when she saw me, she tried to smile. Her eyes were red and moist.

"You're here." Lottie's voice was hoarse and raw. I hurried to the bed and settled beside her, placing the baby carrier on the ground. She reached for me with her one good arm, and I held her in an awkward embrace.

"Oh, Lottie. Are you okay?"

"I'm fine. Though I know it looks bad," she murmured into my hair, pulling away and catching sight of the baby carrier on the floor. "Mia," she breathed. Her eyes filled with tears.

I gently took Mia out of the carrier, laying her on the bed between us. I found Lottie's hand. Our heads touched. "You have a baby," I whispered. Lottie nodded, resting her hand on Mia's cheek.

"I should have been here," I said. I'd begun to cry, my fear finally cracking with relief at the sight of Lottie alive. Even though she'd told me she was okay, I didn't really believe it till I saw her with my own eyes.

"It's okay, Franci." Lottie squeezed my hand lightly.

"I didn't realize. You were all alone. I didn't know you and Whit had broken up. I didn't know you had no one to help you. I should have been here." My cries came harder, turning into full-blown sobs—the kind of uncontrolled, hiccupy crying that I did so rarely, only when I was alone or in front of Lottie.

"Franci, it's okay. *Really*. I understand now." Lottie caught my gaze and held it. I forced myself to look at her swollen face.

"You do?"

She looked down at Mia. "I do. Now I understand." Mia began to whimper, and Lottie reached for her with her good arm. I carefully placed Mia against her chest.

"I think she's hungry," I said, pulling out a bottle and positioning Mia on a pillow in a way that Lottie could feed her. "What happened?" I asked after they were settled.

Lottie rolled her eyes. "Fucking asshole driver. I was in the bike lane during rush hour. The bastard pulled right out without even looking or signaling." She didn't meet my eyes as she told the story, instead gesturing with her good hand.

I waited a moment. The words were stuck in my throat like a chicken bone, sharp and dry. "Were you wearing a helmet?" Lottie and I had argued about this before. She preferred to ride around town without one, while I thought anyone who would risk the city traffic without a helmet had a death wish. I always knew depression was creeping in when she'd accidentally leave it behind, and though she never said so, I suspected she was testing fate on those days, leaving her life in the hands of unknown forces.

"I forgot it." She shrugged on one side. "I was already late, and I was down the block before I realized I wasn't wearing it. It was stupid." She tried to smile, though she winced and brought her hand to touch her swollen cheek. "How terrible do I look?"

"Um." I grimaced. "Not great." I looked away and down at Mia. She was falling asleep as she drank the bottle, her eyelids getting heavier and heavier, then fluttering open for a moment before closing again. "You just forgot the helmet?" I asked quietly.

"Franci, of course I forgot. It was an *accident*," Lottie said, and her tone was full of exasperation, but I knew what a good actor my sister could be. "Do you have any idea how many biking accidents there are in this city every year? I should have gone back for my helmet. But the driver should have been looking where he was going. I should sue him."

I remembered the rotting fruit and the dizzy flies. "Your apartment was a mess."

"Well, call in the Merry Maids," Lottie said bitterly. "We can't all afford a live-in housecleaner, Franci."

"I don't have a live-in housecleaner." I did pay a woman once a week to come clean for four hours. I still felt guilty about this, and my defensiveness briefly took me away from my line of questioning. "I mean, your house looked really bad. Like you were depressed." For a moment she looked at me. Her blue eyes held on to mine, and she seemed about to say something. But then she looked down at Mia.

Lottie shook her head. "It's hard being a single parent. Harder than I realized. Harder than you can imagine. Especially when you also have to work full-time." The last sentence was a direct jab at me, and though only minutes earlier I'd worried she was dead, for a second I wanted to inflict pain on her.

"I called Whit."

"I know." She looked away. "He came by last night."

"I needed someone to check on you."

"Why?" Her voice was suddenly full of anger. "We broke up months ago. He's never even met Mia. He wanted nothing to do with her."

"Is he her father?" Part of me still wanted to believe the sperm donor was just a story Lottie had made up.

"No," she said. "He made it very clear that he didn't want any children with me. I went to a sperm bank. Mia's father is a twenty-eight-year-old Caucasian nonsmoker with no history of mental illness, heart disease, or cancer. That's all I know about him." She looked down at Mia who was sucking hungrily at the bottle. "Whit has nothing to do with us. There's no reason for him to get involved now."

"I'm sorry. I didn't know who else to call."

"To help you fix me?" There was an ugly sneer on her face; she looked like some sort of ghoul with her awful bruises and dark under-eye circles. They'd shaved away a patch of hair just above her ear, and a thin track of stitches ran several inches.

"I just thought he should know. I'm sorry."

Lottie closed her eyes for a moment, and when she opened them the anger was gone, replaced with a dim fatigue. She shook her head. "I just need you to take care of Mia for me, okay, Franci?"

"Of course I will. I'll stay for as long as you need me. Do you know when you'll be out of the hospital?" I asked.

"Apparently, it's not as serious as it looks. I have a concussion and a broken arm and a fractured ankle; cuts, bruises, and stitches here and there. Knowing health care in this country, they'll probably kick me out today." She rubbed her eyes. "Though the doctor said they want to monitor me for internal bleeding, so maybe not for another day or two."

"What about your meds?"

"Don't worry, the docs have it covered." I looked at her closely, trying to gauge her levels. "*Relax*, Franci, I'm in a hospital. Is there any safer place for a nutcase like me? They're taking care of it."

I sighed. It was always like this with Lottie—trying not to ask too much, not to accuse. Mia had finished the bottle and fallen asleep in the crook of Lottie's arm. "Are you in a lot of pain?" I asked, mostly just to change the subject.

She smirked. "They've got me so doped up, I can barely feel my head." She stifled a yawn. "All I want to do is sleep."

"We'll let you get some rest. I'll call you later, and we'll be by again tomorrow."

"Okay." Lottie extended her good arm out to me, and I came closer. She clutched my hand. "I missed you, Franci."

"I missed you too."

I moved away so that Lottie could plant a kiss on Mia's cheek and inhale her scent. Tears dripped onto Mia's face, faster than I would have expected, her fat round cheek suddenly shiny with water. Lottie sat back and wiped at her eyes. "Just take good care of her, okay?" She looked drained and tired, sapped of the fight that had been in her just a few minutes ago.

"I will. You know I will."

Lottie fell back against the sheets and closed her eyes, releasing a heavy sigh like air being let out of a balloon. Before Mia was back in her carrier, Lottie had fallen asleep. Or maybe she just didn't want to look at the two of us together anymore, me clear-minded and healthy, holding her near-orphaned daughter tightly in my arms.

Lottie

I started to fall apart in December. Mia had been with me for three months by then, a miraculous and challenging three months where I fumbled through everything from daycare to midnight feedings to breast pumps. I was a mother. This reality shocked me every day. I'd been dutifully taking my medication, each morning swallowing down my handful of brightly colored pills.

But they weren't working. At least not the way they were supposed to. When Mia was born, I'd switched to a different combination, one that allowed me to breastfeed her. But the pills weren't right, and I was still experiencing symptoms. Not the full-blown Black or White, but glimmers of each. Before the hospital released Mia and me, the obstetrician, knowing my history, made me set up an appointment with a psychiatrist to monitor the new concoction of medication. The psychiatrist had tinkered with the dosage and sent me on my way, booking me for another appointment in two weeks to see how things were. Two weeks later I was still wobbly, depression creeping in around the edges in the dark hours of the silent house when it was only me and Mia. But the night before the follow-up appointment, Mia was up five times in seven hours. I turned the alarm off in the morning before it could wake her again, and I overslept, missing the appointment. Between getting ready to go back to work and trying to adjust to my new life, I hadn't rescheduled.

My maternity leave would run out after the winter break, and I was both dreading going back to work and dying to return. I knew the isolation of being alone with Mia all day wasn't good for me, but I wasn't sure how I would manage to juggle both the job and Mia. It wasn't only the hours of teaching, it was the pile of papers that I came home with and corrected each week, staying up late into the night with a stack of essays, then sleeping late the next morning since my first classes rarely started before eleven. When she wasn't waking me to feed, Mia mewed like a kitten until I held her. I didn't know how I'd ever keep on top of my classes and her needs. Sleep deprivation, difficult for all new mothers, was even more dangerous for me.

It was nearly Christmas, and I'd promised myself and Mia we'd get a tree. Not that a three-month-old cared about a Christmas tree, but it seemed symbolic somehow, a promise that I could raise her on my own and fill our life together with happy memories. Though still functioning, I had the high-flying transcendence that often preceded the full-blown White. Yet instead of rescheduling an appointment with the doctor, I drove to a Christmas tree lot and picked out the tallest, fattest tree there. The man at the lot helped me tie the tree to the roof of the car.

When we pulled up in front of our house, I got out of the car and stood staring at the enormous tree strapped to the roof. It hadn't occurred to me how I would get it up the stairs of my house and inside, all the while struggling to get Mia and her diaper bag inside as well. *What an inane ritual,* I thought, *to chop down a perfectly healthy, growing tree and bring it into a house for a few weeks, only to decorate it with plastic crap and feed it tiny sips of water until it withered away before your eyes.* Three weeks from now the streets would be littered with dead trees, their green carcasses lining the sidewalks, waiting for the garbage truck. And here I was, participating in this disgusting tradition, teaching Mia that it was okay to treat living things like disposable commodities.

I drove back to the lot. Getting out of the car, I smelled the rich scent of evergreen trees in the cool night air. "Frosty the Snowman" was playing over the speakers, and the lot was lit with strings of colored lights. Somewhere in the back of my mind, I recognized a hint of nostalgia. I vaguely remembered a morning when Franci and I sat cross-legged under a tree and unwrapped matching pink bathrobes with furry high-heeled slippers. The living room smelled of pine needles and the oranges poked with cloves that Mother put out at Christmas. We'd put on the bathrobes immediately, dancing through the living room while Mother and Daddy watched us, Mother sipping her coffee, a small smile on her face as she watched us dance.

It was a good memory, though like all memories of my mother, it was always laced with something else. So I pushed it aside and found the man who'd sold us the tree.

He was young, in his early twenties, perhaps a student at the university, maybe even someone who'd taken a class with me. He wore a Cal baseball cap and protective gloves to keep his hands from getting stabbed by the sharp needles.

"Hey, you're back again. You need another tree?" He gave us an easy grin.

"No, I want to return this one." I gestured to my car parked in the lot. Mia was strapped to my chest in her BabyBjörn.

"You want to exchange it for a different one?"

"No, I want to return it."

He frowned. "Is something wrong with the tree? Is it damaged?"

"It's dead," I told him.

He let out a short laugh. "Well, yeah. I mean, they sell live ones that you can take home to plant, but we don't sell those here." He looked at me closely. He had green eyes and a beautiful mouth. I wondered briefly if I could take him home with me.

"It's wrong. It's a disgusting practice that should be outlawed." Mia rested her head against my chest. It was well past her bedtime. "What a thing to expose a child to."

The man shrugged. "I just work here. I didn't chop the tree down, I didn't create the tradition of Christmas trees, I didn't make you buy a tree. I just work here."

"You should be ashamed of yourself," I said.

He rolled his eyes. Even in the dim light I could see that they were framed by long lashes. "Do you want the tree or not? We don't usually take returns, but since you bought it just a few minutes ago, I'll take it back if you don't want it."

"We don't want it."

"Okay." He walked toward the car, untying the rope and hauling the tree down.

He handed me several twenties. "Here you go."

"I think you should replant it," I told him. He let out another short laugh. "I think you should replant them all. I'll help you," I said earnestly.

"Are you out of your mind? The trees have already been chopped down." He turned away, holding the tree firmly by the middle. I could almost make out the muscles beneath his sweatshirt, and I had a sudden yearning to hold his bicep between my palms. "Next year think about buying one with the roots attached. There're plenty of places in Berkeley where you can get those."

"Wait." My desire was banging against my indignation. He turned back, and I reached for him, catching the sleeve of his sweatshirt between my fingers. "You can come home with me." He looked down at my hand, his expression an awed mix of disbelief and disgust. "We'll plant the trees in my yard." I glanced down at Mia and lowered my voice into what I imagined was a smoky whisper. "Then you can stay with me. I'll put her to bed. It will be fun."

He was already backing away, his sweatshirt out of my reach. "I don't think so. Go home and put your kid to bed. It's almost ten o'clock." He turned away from me, shaking his head, dragging the dead tree behind him.

I stood there watching him and then walked toward the car. I bundled Mia back into her car seat. Her head was heavy with sleep. I felt the weight of my embarrassment and fury, my helplessness and terror. It would only be a matter of time before I directed it all at Mia, and this sudden realization hit me with a frightening clarity.

In the bathroom at home I brushed my teeth. The overhead light cast a greenish tinge on my skin, exposing every wrinkle, pockmark, and blemish. I pictured the look of disgust on the man's face when I offered to bring him home. The shame rose up my body like a blush, familiar and toxic.

I opened the medicine cabinet and found jumbled rows of lotions, oils, prescriptions, and other pills. Behind a bottle of Excedrin, I found what I was looking for: a small box of razor blades.

I made sure Mia was asleep before I securely closed the door to my bedroom, the box in my hand. I sat up in bed, my legs pulled into my chest. Slowly I rolled up the leg of my pajama pants, revealing a flesh-colored bandage on my upper calf. I loosened the tape of the bandage, pushing back the corners with my fingernail until I'd eased off the flap. I peeled back the bandage, revealing three neat lines that had crusted into scabs. Rubbing the pad of my thumb along the rust-colored scabs, I felt the thin ridge of dried blood where the wounds were mostly healed; if I left them alone with a daub of antiseptic, they'd be gone within a week or two.

I looked around the bedroom before I started, as if someone might have snuck in without me knowing it, as if the worst part about a prowler in the house would be getting caught doing this. But the room was empty and quiet, and so I began the sick habit I'd reacquired in the months since Franci stopped speaking to me.

It was a habit I found more embarrassing than disturbing. As a professor, I had girls who did this. Cutters, we called them. The term always conjured up pictures of saw-wielding young women in lumber jackets and plaid flannel shirts cutting wood. In the Health Services offices, I once picked up a glossy pamphlet on the subject. "Warning Signs" it read in bold black letters, but I could no longer remember if the cutting was a warning sign for something else or if we were supposed to be looking for warning signs of cutting.

With the edge of the razor blade, I methodically sliced off the first scab. A thin line of blood rose up immediately. With the blood, I felt my air passages opening more widely, my breath coming more easily. I inhaled deeply, as the pain began its slow and pleasant burn, and then I moved on to the second stripe, less hesitant this time, the slicing more controlled.

The pamphlet had taken a clinical view on this behavior, but I've always understood the allure. It was like lancing a blister. There was so much that hurt below the surface that adding a little more pain actually made the wound feel better. It released the pressure that burned below.

I brought the blade down one more time, harder, and the blood came thicker. One more time, one more stripe.

I closed my eyes as I finished off the last scab. When I opened them there were three lines of fresh blood, much like the marks left by a cat's claws, a tattooed kiss to my daughter, the pain taken out on myself instead of her. I replaced the bandage, the calm settling over me.

Franci

As we grew into adults, I became Lottie's guardian, but it wasn't always that way. From birth through high school, she shielded me from the world.

On Saturday nights in high school, Lottie went out and I stayed in, watching TV well past when our parents had gone to bed. The evening would pass quietly, and during commercials I'd wonder what Lottie was doing, who she was with. I never joined her and her friends, choosing the solitude of our darkened living room over my own social awkwardness at a party. Just as *Saturday Night Live* came on, Lottie would make her curfew. We'd watch the first few skits together and then go upstairs to the bedroom that we shared.

This was my favorite part of the night. Lottie would usually be breathless and excited from the party she had been to, occasionally a little boozy, but this just made her more talkative. We turned off the bedroom light, talking until we both fell asleep.

One particular night has always stuck out sharply in my memory: it was our junior year, the final night of our school's production of *Bye Bye Birdie*. Lottie was the female lead. I'd attended opening night with our parents, and I was struck silent by how she transformed herself onstage.

On the final night of the show the cast was going to a party at Marty Leighton's house. Marty was a senior and the leading man opposite Lottie in the play. He was tall and broad-shouldered, with thick black eyebrows that framed a pair of eyes so blue it was rumored he wore colored contact lenses. Lottie had developed a huge crush on him, and she'd been looking forward to the party even more than the final production of the show.

Though our curfew was eleven thirty, neither of our parents was ever up to enforce it. The night of Marty's party, I watched all of *Saturday Night Live* by myself and nearly fell asleep on the couch waiting for Lottie to come home. As I watched television, I developed an achy nausea that started in my belly but seemed to spread throughout my body, reaching all the way into my throat and down into the tips of my toes. I blamed it on the popcorn, though I knew better, and eventually went upstairs to get ready for bed.

When Lottie finally opened the bedroom door, I'd fallen asleep. The sick feeling hadn't disappeared, but it had settled some and now just hung there, heavy and woolen in my stomach. The bedside clock read 2:22 a.m.

"So how was it?" I asked through the grogginess of sleep.

"Oh, Franci, you scared me." Lottie's voice sounded odd and high-pitched.

"What happened with Marty?" She was making strange sniffing noises and kept her back to me as she undressed. In the dim blue light she hunched her shoulders and unbuttoned her sleeveless top, letting it fall to the floor. She stepped out of her skirt and sandals and pulled on a tee shirt. "What happened?" I asked again.

"Nothing." Lottie peeled back the covers on her bed and climbed in. I reached out and turned on the bedside lamp. Lottie winced at the brightness, bringing her hand up to her mouth. But she wasn't fast enough. Her lower lip was a swollen, purplish red. I brought my hand to my own mouth, my body suddenly throbbing in sympathy as it often did when Lottie was hurt.

"What happened?" I asked again, getting out of bed and going to her.

"Nothing. I mean, it was an accident." Lottie tried to smile at me, but the pain in her lip made her cringe instead. "Do you want to hear about Marty?" She tried to look excited, but her eyes were dull.

"Yeah, what happened?"

"Get back in bed," Lottie ordered and I obeyed. She turned off the light. "I did it."

"Did what?"

"I did it. I slept with him." Lottie sounded giddy, but her voice verged on the hysterical.

"Oh my god, Lottie. Really?" I asked, incredulous. "You really slept with him? What happened?"

"Well, the show was great. It was a packed house, our biggest audience all week. And then we went to the party at his house."

"Uh-huh."

"We just kind of hung around together all night. I had a few drinks, and eventually Marty asked if I wanted to go upstairs, and I said yes. I mean, that's what I wanted to happen all along."

"You'd been planning on sleeping with him?" Though I didn't understand either emotion, and I tried to suppress them both, I found myself fighting both envy and sympathy.

"Well, no. But I wanted something to happen. I just hadn't figured out how much." She was quiet.

"Okay . . . ," I said slowly, my voice urging her to continue.

"So we went up to his room. It all just happened so fast."

"Tell me."

"I wasn't planning on sleeping with him, but I could tell he wanted to. I mean, of course he wanted to, he's a guy," Lottie joked, but her voice was false.

"What happened to your mouth? Did he do something to you?"

"No. I mean, not on purpose. We were moving positions a lot, and it was dark in the room. Somehow his head ended up hitting me in the mouth. That's what happened to my lip. And then . . . I don't know. Then we were doing it. And it hurt, but it's supposed to hurt, right? It just hurt more than I thought it would." She was quiet for a moment. "And then it was over. We went back down to the party, and Marty got me an ice pack for my lip, which was kind of embarrassing. It had already started to swell and people kept asking me what happened, and what was I supposed to say? Marty hit me with his head while we were having sex?" Lottie tried to laugh. "I just told people I'd had too much to drink and tripped. Somehow that sounded better." She was silent, waiting for my reaction.

"Oh, Lottie." I didn't know what to say. I wasn't sure if I should congratulate or comfort her. "Did you want to sleep with him?" The twin beds in our room were only a foot apart. Lottie lay on her side, toward the open window so I couldn't see her face. Her back rose and fell lightly as she breathed.

"What?" Lottie stalled. "Oh, I don't know. I guess so."

"Did he make you do it?"

"No!" Then again, more softly, "No. It really wasn't like that, Franci. Don't go all after-school special on me, okay?" She shifted in her bed, and in the inky darkness I saw that her eyes were closed. She spoke without opening them. "It all happened so fast. We're not even going out. I just figured my first time would be with a boyfriend." I was silent. What was there to say? "It's not a big deal," she said brightly. "It had to happen sometime. Why not with Marty Leighton? I could lose my virginity to a lot worse, right?" Lottie reached out and held on to my fingers. She squeezed them tightly. "Right?" she asked again.

"Right," I assured her. Lottie didn't let go of my fingers, not even after we both fell asleep. I woke up later that night, and our fingers were still entwined, both of our hands clammy and warm.

I thought about it all the next week, each time I saw Marty in the hallway at school, leaning against the shiny purple lockers and fawning over girls with too much makeup and short skirts. Though Lottie claimed not to care, I knew she was hurt. There was something underhanded in what he'd done. He looked so cocky and confident each time I saw him, thick black brows like furry caterpillars creeping across his face and those blue eyes that may or may not have come from a box. For her part, Lottie seemed to have moved on, and if nothing else, Marty was discreet. No one at school seemed to have heard about what happened at the party.

The only time that I ever got close to confronting him was on the afternoon that our whole world changed, just a week later. It was a Friday, and I was hurrying to French class. We were having a test on the conditional, and I recited the different forms aloud in my head, the verbs looping through my brain so quickly that I almost didn't see Marty leaning on his locker. He caught sight of me and quickly turned away, and then realizing that I wasn't Lottie, turned back again, relaxing.

I hated him in that moment, and I narrowed my eyes at him and squared my shoulders, ready to face him. He didn't give me the chance. Within seconds he'd slammed his locker shut and yelled ahead to another senior boy in a red-and-blue varsity jacket. He disappeared into the emptying hallway before I even had a chance to open my mouth. The giant clock in the hallway said that I was four minutes late for the exam.

As I arrived at French class, still berating myself for my failed efforts to redeem Lottie, I heard the loudspeaker summoning Lottie and me to the office. Already in Madame Loisel's classroom, the other students were bent over the test, furiously trying to remember how to conjugate the irregular verbs that Madame had thrown in just to check if we'd studied. With my hand on the door, peering through the glass, I was grateful that I'd been given a reprieve from the test, even if only for a few extra minutes. I would always feel bad about being relieved, as if I might have been able to change something had I intuited the danger more quickly.

∼

Lottie was already in the principal's office, sitting anxiously in one of Mr. Lombeck's comfortable chairs. I hadn't seen my sister since that morning when we parted ways in the hall. Lottie's hands were busy in her lap, twisting and untwisting together, and it was the nervousness in her fidgeting that gave me my first flutter of anxiety.

Mr. Lombeck looked up from his desk and motioned me into the room. I took the seat beside Lottie. We didn't speak, but Lottie reached out and grasped my hand, squeezing it tightly. I looked from her to Mr. Lombeck in confusion. Already Lottie's eyes were wet.

"There's been an accident," Mr. Lombeck said, breaking the silence.

"What kind of accident?" I asked.

"Mother," Lottie whispered.

"Is she okay?" I directed the question at Mr. Lombeck, not Lottie. He was the adult. He would reassure us.

"Your father's on his way." Mr. Lombeck didn't look at either of us and instead stared down at a pile of paperwork on his desk, a pen poised in his hand. He never wrote anything, just stared blankly at the page. His office wasn't particularly hot, but I noticed his brow perspiring, and every few minutes he wiped his forehead with the back of his hand.

Later we speculated whether Mr. Lombeck knew that she was dead. Lottie didn't think he knew anything more than that there'd been an accident, but I maintained that he knew all along and didn't want to be the one to have to tell us. I held those long minutes of not knowing against him through the rest of high school, even after he wrote me a college recommendation.

Our father arrived soon after. He looked oily and ragged, his graying brown hair sticking up in funny little tufts around his head, his checked shirt coming untucked from his pants. Mr. Lombeck got up quickly then, leaving us alone in the office.

When I heard "accident," I'd immediately assumed a car accident. What other kind of serious accident did people have? But what our father told us, as he got down on his knees and grasped our hands as if we were small children, as if he were in a church rather than our principal's office, was that it was not that kind of accident. In a bone-weary voice, our father told us that Mother had fallen. The stairs in our house were steep and narrow, and when we were little Mother frequently told us to slow down, warning that someone was going to break her neck on those stairs if she kept running up and down at such outrageous speeds.

And that's exactly what happened. As Mother carried a basket of laundry downstairs, the sheets and pillowcases and towels blocking her view, she slipped and fell down those steep stairs. She landed at the bottom, dirty laundry scattered on the floor, her neck snapped cleanly in half.

Lottie

Our mother was beautiful. She was slender with long black hair that fell in waves down her back, and she had excellent posture. Before Franci and I were born, she was a dancer, a ballerina in a small company in Boston.

The story we'd been told many times by our father was that one night he was dragged to a dance performance—a benefit for the university in Boston where he was working. Our mother was one of the ballerinas onstage in a pale pink tulle skirt and white tights, her hair pulled into a shiny black bun. Our father sat in his seat, mesmerized by the leaps and pirouettes Mother performed across the stage. He watched, nearly breathless, through the entire performance, trying to figure out how to talk to her after the show.

When it was over, he made excuses to his colleagues and hung around the lobby near the dressing room where the ballerinas were changing. Finally Mother emerged. She'd taken off her costume and wore a cotton skirt and wool sweater, her long black hair unpinned in loose waves around her face. He told her how much he loved the performance, how beautiful she was on the stage.

They talked for a long time in the lobby of the theater, and then he walked her home. On the way out, he hunched in the doorway and lit Mother's cigarette for her. That was how he knew he was done for. Our father, the cancer researcher, lit the cigarette of the woman he'd already fallen in love with. He followed the burning ember all the way back to Mother's apartment.

That was the story our father told us while we were growing up, and Mother smiled patiently when he told it, rolling her eyes every now and then. In each telling there was a new embellishment, or some tiny detail was different. The color of Mother's skirt was sometimes gray and sometimes purple. Her hair was down or, other times, it was held to the side with a butterfly barrette. In one version he walked her back to her apartment and kissed her good night. In another they stopped at an Italian restaurant and shared a plate of spaghetti and meatballs. In yet another version she invited him upstairs and made them both grilled cheese sandwiches and tomato soup.

Franci and I loved each story, and we'd press him for more. We were never concerned that the story always changed. In my mind, they fell in love in all of the versions our father had created.

Not until high school did Mother tell me the truth.

It was a Thursday evening, and I'd just gotten home from soccer practice. Our father was still at work and most likely would be for another few hours. Franci was upstairs doing homework. Mother sat at the table with me while I wolfed down the plate of macaroni and cheese she'd kept warm on the stove. She sipped a glass of white wine and smoked a cigarette while I ate, turning her head to blow the smoke away from my meal.

I could tell she was sad. Unlike Franci, I was better able to read our mother's moods and sense when a change was coming. Yet I was also still naive enough to think we might be able to control the course her moods would take. I tried to engage her in the story of meeting our father, prompting her to tell it. She was never the one to tell the story; it was always our father. She let out a thin sigh and looked just past me without answering. I urged her on.

"What was the performance that you were in? Did you see Daddy in the audience? Could you tell that he was watching you?" I pressed.

The cigarette burned between her fingers, untouched for several moments. She seemed deep in thought, as if she were trying to remember. When she spoke, she didn't answer my questions. I realized later, she was debating whether she should tell me at all.

"That's not how it happened, Charlotte. Your father and I met at the party of a mutual friend. He didn't even see me dance until we'd already been dating for several months." She raised her eyebrows and waved the hand that held the cigarette in the air. "Your father prefers his story. It's more romantic." After a moment she stood and began tidying the kitchen.

I sat heavily at the table, the half-eaten bowl of macaroni still in front me, holding up to the light Mother's story against the many versions I'd heard over the years. At the time I'd felt a sadness over the mundane and simple truth. It wasn't until years later that I wondered if perhaps our father's was the truer one after all.

My mother taught me that every story has a hundred versions. Within each one exists a hundred lies. The trick is to find the kernel of truth tucked into the center. If you can find that, cup your hands gently around it. Don't touch it, because it can burn you. Just know it's there; keep that secret knowledge to yourself and follow it home, like a glowing ember in the quickly darkening night.

Franci

Saturday morning Mia woke at six. I stumbled into the kitchen to make a bottle and then brought her back to bed with me. After sucking down the milk, she dozed for another hour. Instead of sleeping, I watched her, the healthy pink cheeks, the bow of a mouth, the thick dark hair. Lottie may have been struggling to hold her life together, but Mia was perfect.

I put Mia in the infant seat on the floor and made coffee, sitting down at one of the tall stools as I tried to figure out what came next. Sometime soon I would visit my father in the nursing home in Palo Alto. The thought of visiting him left me with an anxious dread, as each time his decline was more dramatic. He'd been diagnosed with Alzheimer's four years earlier, and though I called him every week, most times he didn't know who I was. We'd had more than one conversation that ended with him putting the phone down and wandering off while I kept talking. I pushed the thought of him aside for the moment. There were too many other things to worry about.

From the living room my cell phone rang. I knew it would be Mark before I even looked at the display, but when I answered it was the girls, their voices nearly identical as they prattled away about the movie Daddy had rented for them and the pizza they ordered for dinner with just pepperoni, no vegetables—exactly the way they liked it—and when was I coming home: "Mommy, when are you coming home?" Their voices pulled me back, an invisible cord stretching across the miles between us, and I ached with missing them. Mark got on a few minutes later, and I brought the phone into the kitchen and sat on the floor beside Mia.

"How are you?" he asked.

I felt my daughters' absence deep in my throat. I held Mia's chubby hand in my own, fingering the baby smoothness of her palm.

"I'm okay." It was nearly ten o'clock in Boston. I pictured him sitting in the kitchen with his own mug of coffee, with cream and two sugars in his favorite Red Sox mug. "Are the girls all right?"

"They're fine. They miss you and want to know when you're coming home." He paused. "How's your sister?"

"She's fine. Well, not fine, but she's going to be okay." I handed Mia a set of plastic keys from the counter, which she began to chew on. "She has a broken arm, so she's going to be in a cast for a while, and she might have one on her foot too. It's a miracle she's alive. She wasn't wearing a helmet." This still nagged at me, despite Lottie's protestations.

"Why not? Goddamn bikers think they're untouchable." Mark frequently came home with complaints about the bike messengers downtown who zoomed in and out of traffic, ignoring all road rules.

"*Mark.*" Though I felt the same frustration, I didn't like his criticism of Lottie.

"So . . . what's . . . your plan?" His words were tentative, waiting for me to snap at him.

"My plan?" I forced myself not to sound exasperated. "I don't really have one right now. I'm just taking this day by day."

I hated the cautious way we spoke to each other, both of us trying not to start a fight, both of us always hovering around the edge of one. I wasn't quite sure what it was that had come between us over the last year or so. Somewhere around the time that the girls entered kindergarten, things had changed.

Since then, my days had taken on a tedious routine. I went through the motions of being a good wife and mother—school drop-off, grocery shopping, dinner preparation, dealing with endless piles of laundry, but I was detached from each task. There was both so much and so little to do, and I'd be surprised when it was time to pick up the girls, yet amazed by how little I'd actually done all day. Lottie would have said I was depressed, and maybe I was, but not in the throes of Blackness that she experienced. I knew deep down that part of my malaise was because I was empty without her.

Without Lottie, I didn't have anyone to confide in about how I was feeling. Instead, I tried to talk with my friend, Beth. Recently she'd gone back to work full-time, and I missed the long morning coffees we used to share after dropping the kids at preschool. We still talked on the phone a few times a week.

It was during one of these conversations that I told her I'd been feeling restless and that Mark and I weren't connecting lately. It was a Tuesday, and Beth was home with Elijah, who had the flu. The phone was tucked under my ear as I folded laundry.

"I'm telling you, Franci, you're fucking miserable and just don't even realize it," Beth said.

"How do you know?" I asked, both insulted and intrigued at how Beth could peer inside of me and be able to spot something so easily.

"Because it was the same way for me. I didn't realize how unhappy I was until I got back to work. I'm telling you, going back was the best thing I could have done. For Elijah, for my marriage, but most importantly, for me."

"You weren't miserable. I used to see you every day. I would have known if you'd been miserable."

"Franci, I was a fucking mess. You didn't always see it, but at least two days a week, I would go home and cry my eyes out while Elijah was napping. Never in front of him, or you or Thomas, because god forbid I actually tell my husband how fucking unhappy I was, but at least two days a week I would go home and cry." I was stunned. I couldn't imagine it.

"Well, maybe you should see someone," I suggested. "That sounds pretty serious."

"I did see someone. I saw a shrink who told me that I didn't need antidepressants. She said I had too much time to think, and it was making me unhappy."

"Too much time? I don't have any time," I argued. I could barely form a complete thought without being interrupted by one of the girls or by some unfinished chore—crumbs that needed sweeping or a meal that needed to be prepared.

"Too much time to *think*," she clarified. "You need to get out of your own head. Her prescription was to go back to work." I imagined the therapist scribbling the word *employment* on a prescription pad.

"That's ridiculous," I said, because it was easier than sifting through the emotions brought up by this advice.

"Maybe, but since I've gone back to work, I haven't cried once. Well, once, when I watched this terrible movie on TV about a mother who was dying, but you know what I mean."

"Well, that's you, Beth. I'm not coming home and crying every day," I said, which was true. "When it's time to go back, I'll know."

"But you won't, Franci, that's my point. I didn't know. I was crying like a baby, but I didn't know until I actually paid a woman to tell me what the hell was wrong with me. I could have gone on like that for another three years, carpooling and doing laundry and wiping snotty noses."

"But you still have to do all of those things," I said, carrying a stack of clothes into the girls' bedroom. "It's not like by working, you get out of all that."

"No, but it's about having something else in my life that doesn't revolve around taking care of other people."

I didn't say anything. Instead, I smoothed out a green corduroy jumper of Ana's, rubbing the wrinkles with my thumb.

"Franci? Are you there?" Beth asked.

"I'm here."

"Oh, Jesus, I'm an asshole. Listen to me, back at work for barely three months and acting as if I've discovered the answer to life."

"No, it's fine," I said.

"Hon, if you're happy being home, don't even listen to me. Some women are cut out for that. I wasn't. I overstayed my time as a stay-at-home mom for, like, three years. I should have gone back to work as soon as Elijah was off the boob. But if you're happy doing it, don't even listen to me."

"It's okay," I said. "You're probably right."

"Oh shit, Elijah just woke up. I think he's starting a new round of puking up there. I'm telling you, if I have to wash one more load of vomit-stained sheets, I'm going to lose my mind." She hung up before I had a chance to say goodbye.

The thing I wasn't able to explain to Beth or Mark was why the idea of going back to teaching filled me with such fear. I'd never told anyone about Caitlin.

I'd been an English teacher for five years before I became pregnant. I taught four classes—two sections of freshman English, a senior course in world literature, and a junior honors elective in creative writing.

The winter I was pregnant, I gave my creative writing students a memoir assignment. Each student had chosen a memoir to read, and then they had to write their own. This was the type of writing that was most enjoyable to read. With twenty-five kids per class, I hardly got to know the students at all. The memoirs were an opportunity to see them in a deeper and more multidimensional light.

They were due the week before Christmas vacation. Once I began grading a section of papers, I'd usually knock the whole stack out at once, and so the students were used to getting assignments back within a week. Since I'd become pregnant, however, I'd lost my usual stamina. I no longer had the energy to stay up till eleven at night after a full day's work. By the time I got home from school, it was all I could do to pull on pajamas and eat the dinner Mark had cooked before collapsing into bed. Thus a week after turning the memoirs in, as we were getting ready to go into the Christmas break, the papers were still sitting in a yellow folder in my schoolbag.

The Friday before vacation was a half day. Students dropped into my classroom between exams to bring Christmas cookies and boxes of chocolate. I was six months pregnant, hungry all of the time, and I'd been attacking a tin of sugar cookies when Caitlin came to see me.

"Hey, Ms. Weaver." Caitlin stood hesitantly in the doorway. She was a slight, dark-haired girl who didn't speak up in class often but usually had something valuable to say when she did. Though the desks were set up in a horseshoe, most of the time Caitlin still managed to appear as if she were sitting in a back row, folding her body in on itself so that she was nearly removed from the semicircle. When I'd see her in the hallway, she typically had on headphones. She was the type of student I usually sought out, though this year I'd made fewer connections with my students, perhaps because I knew that in a couple of months, after the twins were born, I would be gone indefinitely.

I wiped the crumbs from my mouth and swallowed the mouthful of sugar cookie with an embarrassed laugh.

"Hi, Caitlin. Come on in." She hovered at the door for a moment before entering.

"I was just wondering if you'd graded our memoirs yet." Bringing a finger to her mouth, she chewed vigorously on the already ragged nail. There was an ugly pocked sore on the back of the hand she held to her mouth.

"No, I'm sorry, I haven't gotten to them yet. I'll get yours back to you after break."

"Oh, okay." She looked disappointed.

"Would you like a cookie? A piece of chocolate?" I gestured to the mound on my desk.

"No, no thanks." Caitlin stood by the desk, eyes darting anxiously around the room.

"Are you ready for break?"

She shrugged. "Yeah, I guess."

"Do you have any plans for the vacation?"

She shrugged again. "Not really. Just hang out, I guess. My parents want to go skiing."

"That should be fun." Caitlin nodded but continued to stand by my desk. "Is everything okay? Anything on your mind?"

For a moment she looked as if she might say something. There was a split second where I recognized the girl's desire to connect. But just as quickly, it was replaced by the detached and indifferent façade she'd developed during her years of adolescence.

"Nope. Just wondering about the grades." She gave a half smile and met my eyes for the first time since she'd come into the class. She began to back out of the classroom, but when she got to the door, she paused. "When are the babies due?"

My hand automatically came to rest on my stomach. "March tenth."

She nodded and was quiet for a moment. "You'll be a good mom," she said finally. She held my gaze for a moment before looking away.

"Thank you." I was surprised how grateful I was for the words. "I hope so."

She gave me a small smile. "Have a nice vacation, Ms. Weaver."

"You too, Caitlin. Have fun skiing."

She turned and was gone.

I meant to pull Caitlin's memoir out right then, but another student came by and then I had an exam to proctor.

We spent Christmas with Mark's mother and sister, and the folder was still unopened in my bag when the call came from my principal. On Christmas day, Caitlin Underwood swallowed a bottle of pills and killed herself.

The first thing I did after hanging up the phone was to pull out the yellow folder. My heart pounded in my chest, and I was crying as I flipped through the stack of papers until I came to Caitlin's. I read the title and my stomach turned over. She'd written a collection of poems for the assignment. The first one was called "Drowning." I began to read, my eyes travelling so quickly that words and snatches of phrases bounced off the page.

> *feel like I'm being pulled underwater . . . stole an X-Acto knife from art class last week . . . wrote my initials on my forearm. no one even noticed . . . beads of blood rise like mercury . . . no one sees . . . water in my nose and mouth, eyes in the hallway pass over me, never seeing . . . the water keeps rising . . . where's the life jacket? I think I'm going under . . . wonder how much longer I can keep treading water.*

I felt the pit of my stomach rising up into my mouth, and I dropped the papers and ran for the bathroom. As I vomited into the bowl, all I could think about was my last conversation with Caitlin. "You'll be a good mom," she'd told me, and I'd been so grateful for this small gift the girl had given me.

The funeral was on the last Saturday of vacation. I sat in one of the back rows of pews in the overflowing church beside several of my coworkers. Even from that far back, I could see the bobbing head of Caitlin's mother as she cried into her hands. I sat through the funeral with my own hands clasped tightly across my belly as if asking my unborn children to never subject me to such pain. I listened as Caitlin's family and friends described a quiet young woman who loved to read and write. The word *suicide* was never mentioned. Instead, they referred to how she was "lost" or "gone." *Drowned,* I kept thinking. She was drowning, and now she had gone under.

After the funeral, I didn't speak to the family or go to the house where people were gathering. Instead, I sat in my car and cried, rocking back and forth in the driver's seat, the girls slipping silently up and down inside me.

I never told anyone about Caitlin's memoir. At my next doctor's appointment I learned that I'd developed high blood pressure. The doctor put me on bed rest for the last two months of the pregnancy for fear of preterm labor. I was relieved not to have to go back to the classroom, not to have to be reminded of my last conversation with Caitlin, and not to have to wonder if every journaling exercise or creative writing assignment had the potential to unearth what it did in Caitlin.

I thought about throwing the memoir out. Rightfully it belonged with Caitlin's parents, but I couldn't bring myself to give it to them for fear of what they might say to me upon reading it. And it seemed cruel to show them evidence of their daughter's misery after it was too late. I considered burning the poems, getting rid of the proof of my oversight. I couldn't bring myself to do that, either. It seemed important to keep them somehow—to remember Caitlin, this complex young woman that too few of us had tried hard enough with, or to remind myself of the absolute necessity of vigilance at all times. In the end I put the folder on a shelf in the back of my closet. Sometimes I'd stumble across it when looking for a misplaced sweater, and I'd have to sit down for a few moments and take several deep breaths before I could return to whatever I was doing. Every time I thought about returning to work, Caitlin's face shimmered before me, and I was gripped by a paralyzing fear and shame.

And so it was easier to stay where I was. Stagnant, yes. Stuck, maybe. But culpable to another mother? Never again.

Talking to Mark now, sitting in Lottie's living room, I remembered Caitlin. She was the first secret between us, the first thing I'd withheld. I'd kept it from him as self-preservation, not realizing it would be the beginning of so much unspoken between us.

"I'm sorry," I said, though I wasn't even sure what I was apologizing for. "I don't know when Lottie's getting out of the hospital. Even once she's released, she's going to need help. She'll be in a cast, and I'm not sure if she'll even be able to walk. It's not as if I can just leave them here." I lifted Mia from her seat, and she blew spit bubbles at me and smiled. "I'll probably be gone for at least a week. Maybe more. You might want to call your mother and see if she can come help out with the girls. If there's any way you can cancel your next trip to New York, I think you should."

"Okay," Mark said. He sounded tired. "Just call me when you know anything more."

"I will," I promised. As I hung up the phone, I extracted a lock of hair from Mia's tight grasp. She leaned against my chest, and I closed my eyes, resting my chin on her seal-like scalp.

When Mia and I arrived at the hospital later that day, Whit was already there. He sat in a chair by Lottie's bed and watched her sleep. With her eyes closed and the bruises on her face, I had a moment of panic where I thought she was dead. And then I watched her chest rise, and I was able to breathe again.

"Hi, Whit," I said softly so that I wouldn't wake Lottie. He looked up, startled from the intimacy of the moment. As often happened, his eyes took several seconds to register that I was Franci, the other sister.

"Franci." His voice was full of emotion as he stood up and came to me. "How are you doing?" I planted a kiss on Whit's cool and bristled cheek, and then let my eyes close for just a second as his broad shoulders and arms enveloped me. It felt good to be held, and I leaned my full weight into him.

"She's been asleep since I got here," he whispered. Then, noticing the baby carrier at my feet, he looked down at Mia. "Is this . . . ?" He squatted on the floor beside her.

"Mia," I said.

He didn't take his eyes off her. Mia yawned, her pink mouth stretching into an *O*. I'd seen Whit during my last visit. He came for dinner, and Lottie made a chicken curry. We stayed up late drinking red wine. Lottie had placed tea candles all around the room, and we'd watched the shadows flicker off the walls.

"Lottie told me the two of you had a falling out," Whit said, his eyes still on the baby.

"It's complicated. But we haven't spoken since last April." Lottie had left dozens of messages for me in the first few weeks, sending texts that I deleted without reading. She stopped calling after that first month. I knew we would speak eventually. I couldn't ever cut her out of my life completely. It would have been like cutting off my own head and expecting to live. Even when I wanted to the most, I knew I couldn't live without her.

Lottie opened her eyes, and for a moment something like fear flickered in her face as her eyes darted back and forth between us. But then her face relaxed and she gave a wry grin.

"Hi, kids."

"Hi," we said in unison. Whit and Lottie looked at each other. So many unspoken things hovered between them.

"I'll give you guys a few minutes. Mia and I will be outside." I reached for the baby carrier.

"Leave her here," Lottie said. "Whit, can you hold her?" Her face was clear of all manipulation, or maybe it was just masked beneath the injuries to her face. But I knew my sister. We both knew what she was doing.

Whit knew her too and he should have known better, but he reached for Mia. I reluctantly placed her in his arms. He looked awkward and unsure, and I wondered if he'd ever held a baby before. Lottie didn't seem to notice. She patted the empty spot on the bed and smiled up at Whit. I closed the door quietly behind me.

~

Returning from seeing Lottie in the hospital, back at Lottie's house with Lottie's baby girl, I experienced a strange slipping feeling. I unpacked the groceries I'd bought, sliding them into Lottie's empty cupboards, and I had the unnerving sense that I was moving silently into Lottie's life, leaving my own body empty and unattended as I stepped into hers. I was reminded of the paper dolls we cut out of books when we were children, carefully maneuvering scissors around the page, clipping the legs of the doll, the ruffles on the skirt, the flip in its hair. At the end, I'd hold a doll in one hand, and in the piece of paper where the doll had just been, her perfect silhouette would stand empty.

It was nearly five thirty in Boston, and though Mark would not normally be home at this hour, I figured he would be tonight. I dialed his number.

"We're cooking dinner. We're having spaghetti. Right, girls?" Mark said after he picked up. I heard murmurs of approval in the background followed by the excited cries of "Mommy!" I pictured Mark in our kitchen, the sleeves of his dress shirt rolled up, his tie loosened, and the top two buttons undone. The girls would be sitting at the kitchen counter, and Mark would be filling plastic cups with milk. He'd probably forget to cut the noodles, and Ana would get mad when he tried to shake Parmesan cheese on hers, and Autumn would have to remind him to cook a vegetable. For a moment, I missed the easy domesticity that normally enveloped us all.

"I'm making spaghetti tonight too," I told him. "For Whit." I carried Mia in one arm while holding the phone in my free hand. I walked around the kitchen, jostling her in a steady rhythm. "I saw him today at the hospital and invited him to dinner." Whit and Mark had never met. Lottie and I were good at compartmentalizing our relationships. "He and Lottie broke up."

"Oh, really?" From the tone of his voice, I knew he was distracted. The girls chattered in the background, and Mark murmured back to them in acknowledgment.

"About a year ago. About the time I stopped talking to her." My eyes welled up for what felt like the hundredth time in just a few days. "She was all alone, Mark. She had no one."

"You had every reason to stop speaking with her. She *endangered* our children. She shouldn't even have a child of her own." He spoke quietly so the girls wouldn't hear, but the anger was real. "This baby, Mia. Is she okay?"

"She's fine."

"Do you think your sister is capable of taking care of her?" he asked. I finally had his full attention.

"I think she really wants to be a good mother."

"I asked if you thought she was *capable* of taking care of her," he said.

"Well, not right now. That's why I'm here," I said, stalling.

"In general."

It took a while for me to answer. "Some days," I finally said.

"Franci." Mark's voice was heavy. "What about the other days?"

"What am I supposed to do? It's not as if I can take the baby away from her. Lottie's her mother. How could I do that to her?"

"How can we not?" he asked. I heard the girls calling in the background.

"I've got to go," I said.

"Franci. We need to talk about this."

"I'll call you later. Give the girls a kiss for me," I said and then hung up the phone.

I thought about what Mark had said. Clearly, Lottie loved Mia. I knew that from just the few short interactions I'd seen. But I also knew that love wasn't enough. I wished I lived close enough that I could see them every day, pay attention to how Lottie handled the pressure of all the banal tasks that having children involved. But then I'd be right back where I started, taking care of Lottie all over again. Neither of us wanted that. I pushed Mark's words aside. There would be time to think about the future. Right now I just needed to put one foot in front of the other and take care of what was in front of me.

I put Mia down for a nap and pulled a load of laundry from the dryer, making my way down to Lottie's room with the basket. Lottie had tons of clothes, and she didn't shop at places like the Gap or any other store that issued thousands of the same skirt to women all over the country. Lottie shopped in boutiques and consignment stores, and each item looked unique and made just for her. I'd always envied her sense of style. I tended to gravitate toward jeans and wool sweaters and tee shirts, all in inoffensive, muted tones.

As I pulled each beautiful and carefully chosen item from the basket, I wanted to wrap myself in Lottie's clothes like a second skin. I quickly stripped out of my jeans and sweater and slipped into a purple silk dress with beading at the collar that I found hanging in her closet. I took the dress off and replaced it with a pair of tight jeans and a sparkly tank top. I slipped out of the jeans and tank and put on a long white sundress that tied at the shoulders with red silk ribbons. I never wore clothes like these, and there was something thrilling about seeing myself dressed not only as Lottie but as a different version of myself.

The house in Palo Alto where we grew up had an attic filled with trunks of Mother's old clothes. I never understood why she kept them. Some of the clothes were winter gear she hardly ever had a chance to wear, but most of them were from when she was younger, in another life that Lottie and I never knew. In most of my memories, I picture her wearing slim black slacks or linen skirts, but in the attic there was a heavy black trunk filled with fancy clothes in rich textures and another box full of high heels, some with straps and rhinestones. Our mother would pull scarves and white-fringed shawls from boxes, draping them over us.

"Beautiful," she'd remark as Lottie stepped into a cream-colored silk dress with a long pink sash. "You're gorgeous, darling," she'd say as I zipped up a purple pencil skirt and matched it with a ruffled button-down.

"Beautiful, lovely," Lottie and I remarked to each other as we tottered around the rickety attic floor in high-heeled sandals.

"Mother, will you put on our faces?" one of us would eventually ask, borrowing her expression. She'd bring us into the bathroom and kneel before us, carefully applying blush and lipstick and eye shadow from her own bag of expensive cosmetics.

Our father hated it.

"They're too young for all this, Katherine," he'd say, turning his frown from Lottie and me to our mother.

"Oh, stop it, Leo," Mother would say, shushing him. "Stop overreacting."

"But the makeup," he protested. "It's just too much on little girls."

"Don't be silly. Little girls like makeup," she would say, pressing her cool fingers to his mouth. She'd kiss him tenderly until he blushed, and Lottie and I gazed in admiration through sticky mascaraed eyes, both at our parents' love and at our mother's subtle skills of manipulation.

Still wearing Lottie's long white sundress, I peeled back the quilt and slid under the covers of her bed. Thoughts of my mother often left me tired and depleted. My bare legs were smooth against the cool, unused sheets, and I lay down, breathing in Lottie's distinctive scent.

I tried to clear my mind, to stop the endless spiral of thoughts and find quiet. I imagined a white piece of paper, a clear blue sky. But as soon as my mind was blank, Lottie's face would appear, the thin lines of stitches, the battered cheek, the image of her helmetless head, the sour milk in the fridge, and the overflowing garbage in the kitchen. *You can try to pretend she's okay*, I thought, *but you'll never convince yourself.*

Franci

The year we were seventeen, the months after our mother died, was a season suspended in time. It was after the worst thing we could imagine had happened but before Lottie's own mind turned in on itself.

We watched our father withdraw. He'd always been a quiet man, but he possessed a warm and naked love for the women in his life, made clear in the moments when he would wrap his arms around his wife's waist or squat down on the floor to be closer to me or Lottie. But after Mother's death, he became silent and absent, working even longer hours than usual, returning home too rumpled and exhausted to talk with us.

Within three months, he'd sold the small Arts and Crafts home where we'd grown up. Lottie and I were too stunned by it all to even object. He moved us into a three-bedroom condo closer to the university. It was the first time Lottie and I had our own rooms, but most nights we ended up squeezed into one of the twin beds together.

Pretty soon we realized that if anyone was going to pick up the pieces of our home life, it would have to be us. In the first few weeks after Mother's death, the house was filled with casseroles and pasta salads, blueberry cobblers, lasagnas, and quiches, the offerings brought over by neighbors and friends. Lottie had the sense to put them in the freezer, and we slowly made our way through the food in the weeks that followed. But once we moved, there were no longer neighbors to keep watch over us, and the cupboards remained empty. The toilet bowl took on a pale yellow tint and the acrid scent of urine. The kitchen counters were sticky and oily. The refrigerator was bare except for milk, butter, cheese, and a variety of condiments and sauces. In the closet were saltines, a loaf of bread, a can of oyster stock, and a jar of beets. How these items made their way from the old house to this one, we didn't know, but it became clear that our father had no plans to grocery shop, cook, or clean anytime soon. This had always been our mother's domain. Our father mowed the lawn and took out the trash, but she took on the daily management of the house herself. She cooked and cleaned and helped us with our homework, expecting little of our father other than his steady presence and good humor. I wondered if my father even knew how to operate the vacuum.

One evening, he returned home with a greasy paper bag filled with burgers and fries from a diner in town. He'd been staying later at work, getting home just at dinnertime with a rotation of takeout—pizza, Thai, Chinese, Indian. The pantry was filled with miniature packets of soy sauce and ketchup. That night Lottie and I were waiting for him, already seated at the kitchen table.

"Dad," Lottie began, as he unpacked the burgers. He didn't even bother putting out plates, just poured the fries onto one of the wrappers in the center of the table and unceremoniously plopped a burger in front of each of us. "Daddy," Lottie tried again.

"Eat up before it gets cold," he said, taking a bite of his own burger. Orange cheese hung from the soggy bun.

"We've got to do something," Lottie said. "The house is a mess, and there's never any food." He didn't look up or answer, and I nibbled anxiously on a fry. "This isn't what she would have wanted. We need to do better than this."

He looked at Lottie, really seeing her for the first time in a while, and something seemed to pass between them. Lottie held his gaze, but then he dropped his eyes back to his meal, his hand groping for his wallet. He withdrew several twenty-dollar bills and placed them on the table.

"Here. You and your sister can buy a few groceries tomorrow. Pick up some cleaning supplies too. It's getting a bit untidy in here." He ate several fries at once.

"We'll go now," Lottie said, standing up. She held her hand out for the keys. Mother had taught us how to drive the previous winter. They were terror-filled sessions with her clinging anxiously to the armrest or door handle as she barked out orders, but the end result was that we'd each passed our driver's license test on the first try. Our father fished the keys out of his pocket and handed them to Lottie.

"Don't you want to finish your dinner?" he asked. Lottie sat back down reluctantly, ate several bites of her burger and a few fries, and then stood up again, waiting for me to finish. We drove to the Safeway, where we filled the cart with pasta, deli meats, cereal, and cans of soup and then added bleach and toilet cleanser.

Our father began to leave money underneath the sugar bowl on Friday mornings, and together Lottie and I would do the shopping. We struggled home from the store laden with bags. As most of our friends were making plans for the weekend, we tackled the house, changing the sheets and doing laundry. Our father began to return home from work early enough that we could eat together in the kitchen—quiet, simple dinners of pasta or soup and grilled cheese. By the time summer came around, we'd learned how to make the household run without our mother, and this knowledge filled me with both pride and the hollow understanding that we'd actually survive without her.

The summer arrived without the usual excitement that typically accompanied the last few days of school. Lottie and I had gotten jobs in downtown Palo Alto: Lottie as a waitress at an upscale diner in town, while I would be working at the candy shop several stores down the street.

The Apple Shack was a bustling restaurant that hired attractive college girls each summer. The uniform was a khaki miniskirt and pink polo shirt that the manager seemed to only buy in size small. Lottie was the youngest of the waitresses, though that didn't stop her from making friends with the older girls with an effortless agility.

Sweetland was a far less glamorous establishment, and I worked with only two other people: Tanya, the baby-faced owner whose round hips and waist were evidence that she sampled too much of her product, and Kevin, a thin, gangly boy who'd just graduated from our high school. I could wear whatever I wanted to work, but once I arrived, I had to put on a bright red Sweetland apron and a white paper cap.

Lottie and I both worked the evening shift. Most nights I worked alone in the small sugar-scented shop, and I'd bring a book to read as I perched on the stool by the register. On Friday and Saturday evenings, Kevin would be there too, and those nights usually passed faster. Despite Kevin's somewhat goofy appearance, he was surprisingly loud and funny. He didn't seem to harbor any of the self-conscious embarrassment over his looks that I would have assumed.

Lottie's shift didn't start till five, and she'd often stop in on her way to work to say hello and buy a piece of butter crunch. Kevin, who had no problem chattering on endlessly to me, always became tongue-tied and inarticulate around her. He'd find something to keep himself busy—sweeping the back room, lining up the chocolate turtles in perfect rows, wiping down the already-clean counter. When she left, Kevin would come back to the register and prop himself on the stool, resuming his continuous stream of chatter as if we'd never been interrupted.

That night I asked him about it.

"What's the deal? Why do you act so weird when my sister comes in here?"

"Dude, your sister's hot. I always get nervous around hot girls," Kevin answered.

I held my tongue. I didn't say, *We're identical twins, you moron.* It was true the apron and paper hat gave me a lumpy, genderless look, especially when compared to Lottie's minuscule uniform. We were flat-chested and petite. We were pale with unmanageably curly hair and could be called either button-nosed or snub-nosed, depending on whether you were trying to be cruel or kind. Yet Lottie possessed a self-assurance that rendered her hot, while I was still just "cute."

Kevin was suddenly busying himself with the jelly-bean display, and I realized Lottie had come back into the shop.

"Some of us are going to a party after work if you want to come. Some guys that my coworkers know from school." Lottie nodded her head at Kevin. "You can come too, if you want."

"What time?" I asked.

"Well, we get off close to eleven. Around then." Sweetland closed at nine. I was usually curled up in front of the television by eleven.

"Come on," Kevin urged, suddenly more talkative now that his chance with Lottie was emerging. "Why not?"

"I don't know," I said. Parties made me uncomfortable. Lottie tended to go off on her own and leave me standing alone by the keg, unsure of whom to talk to.

"I've got to get to work," Lottie said. "If you change your mind, come by the restaurant." She turned to leave, and Kevin reached out and squeezed the skin on my forearm. Hard.

"Ow!" I yelped, turning to him. He was giving me an intense stare. "Oh, fine," I grumbled under my breath. "We'll come," I called to Lottie.

"'Kay," Lottie said, not even bothering to turn around. Instead, she lifted up her hand and waved, waggling her fingers. Kevin gave me a thumbs-up sign, his knobby thumbs sticking foolishly in the air. I turned back to my book with a sigh.

~

After work we walked over to the Apple Shack. I watched Lottie and the effortless way she joked with the other waitresses as if she'd known them her whole life and not just a few weeks. They were the type of girls who'd always intimidated me—tall, tan, with an easy poise that came from years of dance classes and sporting events. California girls, though technically I, too, was a California girl.

When Lottie got off work, we piled into the car of one of her coworkers. A few minutes later we pulled up in front of a large brick house several blocks from the Stanford campus.

Kevin and I followed Lottie, who was already marching up the front steps of the house as if she lived there. One of the girls carried a case of Heineken, passing out beers to everyone once inside. The house was large and would have been beautiful if anyone other than college boys had been living in it. Instead, the living room was decorated with beer advertisements and glossy posters of bikini-clad women lounging on sports cars, and a giant pool table was set up off to the side of the room. There were couches, but they looked at least fifty years old, and in all likelihood they were probably picked up off the side of the road for free, or passed down from tenant to tenant. The party was already in full swing, and as I had suspected, Lottie soon disappeared, leaving me with Kevin.

"Cheers," Kevin said, clicking his bottle against mine.

"Cheers." I took a swig, forcing myself not to make a face as the flavor hit. I didn't like beer, but I didn't drink very often, and Lottie said it was an acquired taste, like coffee. I didn't particularly like coffee, either, and didn't really see the point of acquiring a taste for something you didn't like, especially if it wasn't good for you to begin with, but I drank the beer anyway.

"Cool party," Kevin said, glancing around. I nodded, drinking more, figuring if I drank faster, then maybe I would acquire a taste for it sooner. Kevin seemed to be looking for Lottie, and I was tempted to tell him to give up, it would never happen, but I kept my mouth shut.

"So what's it like being a twin?" I forced myself not to roll my eyes. People always asked us this.

"It's okay. Good, I guess." After seventeen years, I had yet to come up with a pat answer.

"It must be cool. Did you guys play tricks on your parents and stuff when you were kids?"

"We could sometimes trick my dad, but my mother always knew."

Kevin suddenly looked serious. "She died this year, right?" I was surprised that he knew this; we weren't friends at school. I nodded. "I'm really sorry, that's got to be awful." I nodded again, finishing the beer in one long swallow. "Sorry, I didn't mean to . . ." He trailed off, and I held up my empty bottle. Someone had left the case of beer at our feet, and Kevin grinned as he opened another one and handed it to me.

"I gotta take a leak," he said, and suddenly I was left alone, always my biggest nightmare at a party like this. But somehow it didn't terrify me quite as much with the beer in my hand. The second one went down easily, and I *was* acquiring a taste for it. I didn't mind the dull tang anymore, and holding the cold bottle was like a prop—I didn't have to worry about what to do with my hands. Maybe I'd start smoking too.

I sank into one of the couches, trying not to think about how many people had probably spilled beer or vomited or had sex on it. The couch was soft and squishy, and I was tired. As predicted, Lottie was nowhere to be found.

With the two beers taking the edge off my shyness, I observed the party as it unfolded. In one corner, a tall brunette was talking with a thick boy in a baseball cap. The brunette was fingering her beaded necklace as she talked to the boy. In another corner, a busty redhead with freckles was talking to two tall boys in khakis and plaid shirts. She fiddled with her hair while she talked, throwing her head back to laugh every few minutes. As I scanned the room, similar scenes were playing out all around me. If I went looking for Lottie, I'd most likely find her talking to some boy, twisting her bracelet or pulling on an earring, reaching out to touch his wrist every few minutes to make a point. It was as if all of these girls spoke some secret language I'd never learned.

"What's up?"

I looked beside me on the couch, expecting Kevin, but instead a boy in a maroon Stanford cap and pale blue oxford was sitting beside me. He was handsome in a way that high school boys were not, and dark hair peeked out from underneath his hat.

"Hi. I mean, nothing," I faltered.

"You look bored." He grinned at me.

"No, not bored. Just watching."

"Watching what?"

"People watching. No one in particular."

"Kind of like your own anthropological experiment?"

I'd heard of anthropology but couldn't remember if it was the study of stars or some other science, so I just nodded.

The boy held out a hand. "I'm Jonas."

"Franci." His handshake was firm and solid. I suddenly wished, not for the first time, that I spoke that instinctive language of flirting. I brought a finger up to my hair, in an attempt to play with it in the easy way I'd seen other girls do, but my ring ended up getting snagged on a curl.

"These yours?" he asked, gesturing to the case at my feet.

"I guess."

"Can I have one?"

I nodded and Jonas reached in and pulled out two more beers, handing one to me. I realized my bottle was empty. "So do you live on campus?" he asked.

"Um, we live in town."

"Who's we?"

"Me and my sister." I looked around, wondering where Lottie was now. I wanted her to see me with Jonas. "Where do you live?"

"Right here." He nodded to the room. I told him my major was science, and he asked what type of science, which stumped me. I said biology since that was the only science class in which I'd gotten an A. He told me about the advertising agency in San Francisco where he was interning. I caught sight of Kevin standing alone in the doorway watching me, though he didn't say anything. Jonas was asking me a question.

"Sorry, what?"

He laughed. "People watching?"

"Yeah." My head was beginning to throb, and I wanted to lie down. But not here.

"I asked if you wanted to go sit outside on the porch," Jonas said.

"Um, okay, I guess," I mumbled, getting to my feet. Someone had lowered the lights, and as I made my way through the living room and kitchen, I was aware of Jonas's hand resting on my back. Kevin stood awkwardly by the stairs, intently examining the label on his beer. Lottie was in the kitchen, talking to a shaggy-haired guy by the refrigerator. When I stumbled past, I nodded blearily and she eyed me with concern but didn't stop her conversation.

The porch was actually a small back deck set up with plastic lawn chairs and a wooden swing just big enough for two, an out-of-place piece of furniture in this setting. I was about to sit in a plastic deck chair, but Jonas caught my hand and pulled me onto the swing. He was a large boy with thick quads, much bigger than the boys I knew from high school, and the chair was a tight squeeze. Jonas didn't seem to mind. He handed me another beer, which I accepted even though I didn't want it. This one was in a silver can, and it tasted stronger.

Before I realized it, Jonas had brought his hand to my chin and was turning my face toward his, bringing his mouth close to mine. He smelled of beer and shaving cream, and his tongue was slippery like a fish. I had kissed boys before. Four, to be precise, but none of them had moved with the ease that Jonas did, none of them had the hands of a man, and I felt a thrill of pleasure and fear zip down my spine. Even as we kissed, I was thinking about telling Lottie later when we got back home. But when I pictured telling her, I imagined us in our old house, in the room we once shared, our parents asleep down the hall despite the steady thump from the water heater. The idea of going back to the condo, into my own bedroom, filled me with a tired sadness.

"My mother's dead," I said, between kisses. Jonas had managed to work his hand inside my bra.

"I'm sorry," he breathed, his fingers working steadily against my nipple. I felt a rush of warmth shoot through my stomach and groin.

"She fell down the stairs," I persisted. I suddenly wanted to talk. I wanted to tell him about Mother, about how beautiful she was on the nights that she dressed up to go to a fund-raiser with our father, about the heavy scent of her face cream that she smeared on before bed, about the weeks when she wouldn't come out of her room. I suddenly wanted to tell him everything.

"That sucks. I'm sorry," Jonas whispered, pulling my hand toward him and guiding it to the crotch of his jeans. I felt the hard warmth through the denim. I didn't know what he wanted me to do so I just let my hand rest there, atop the bulge in his pants. Jonas let out a soft groan that made me wince slightly. There was something too primal about the noise.

My bra was unclasped, and now he was trying to get my shirt off. Even through the dull haze of alcohol, I was aware enough to know that I didn't want to get undressed on the deck of a crowded house party. I held on to the hem of my tee shirt and shook my head.

"Why not?" Jonas asked, still tugging gently on the shirt.

"Too many people," I said.

"We could go upstairs to my room," he suggested. I shook my head again. "Okay." Jonas resumed rubbing his thick fingers inside my shirt, and I let my hand rest where it was. He brought his free hand on top of mine, putting pressure on it so that the hardness was pressed firmly into my palm. He moved my hand back and forth in a steady rubbing motion and let out another groan, this one louder. I was aware of a wet warmth between my own legs even as the sound of his noises filled me with a mild revulsion.

He stopped playing with my breasts, all attention now focused on the bulge in his pants. At one point he tried to undo the button and zipper of his jeans, but I shook my head again, murmuring "No." This time it was not so much out of modesty but out of a fear at what I would see. Even in the dark, I knew I didn't want to see what I was holding. His breath came in short gasps, and I felt detached from my body. It wasn't me sitting here, doing this. I was somewhere else, back in our old bedroom, Lottie tucked in across from me, Mother asleep down the hall. I rubbed faster, harder, somehow convincing myself that if I could do this one thing that other girls did all the time, easily, casually, without a second thought, if I could do this one thing, then when we left the party, Mother would be at home. We would go back to our real life, and everything would be okay. All I needed was to do this one thing right.

He came with an abrupt groan and grunt and released my hand, leaving it motionless on the quickly deflating denim.

"Fuck," he whispered in a low breath, his head resting on the back of the wooden swing. With his eyes closed, I could see him more as the boy he was just a few years ago, a Marty Leighton or another popular guy at school. I felt a flash of pride and self-loathing roll together at once, a feeling that would only grow stronger over the next few days.

"Fuck," he whispered again, and then, "thanks." He turned, his eyes focusing on me for the first time since we'd come outside. His arm fell casually around my shoulder, and I rested my head against his firm chest, breathing in the comforting smell of laundry detergent. I closed my eyes for a moment, wondering if I might just fall asleep right here.

"I'm going to get a beer," Jonas said, straightening up so that I had to lift my head. "You want one?"

"No thanks," I whispered. My mouth was dry.

"Okay." He walked into the house, the back door slamming behind him. Inside the party was loud, the sounds of laughter and bottles clinking and jokes spilling out onto the deck. I sat on the swing, the hard wooden planks digging into the back of my legs. Five minutes passed. Then ten. Then fifteen. I'd assumed he was going to come back after he got his beer. He'd asked if I wanted one. I wondered if he would have come back if I'd said yes.

The beginning of tears pushed forward, but I squeezed them back. This was no reason for tears. Giving a hand job to a boy whose last name you didn't know was no reason to cry. Your mother dying, *that* was reason to cry. Knowing you would never see her again, *that* was reason to cry. Imagining her smashed and broken body amidst a heap of strewn clothes, *that* was reason to cry. But not this.

I sat on the swing, pushing myself back and forth slowly with one foot. After what must have been twenty minutes, I heard the door slam shut and the sound of footsteps making their way toward me.

"Franci?" It was Lottie, not Jonas, and I was flooded with disappointment and relief. "Are you okay?" She settled beside me on the swing.

"Yeah, I guess. I don't know." I let my head rest on her shoulder. "Not really."

"What happened?" she asked, but I didn't answer. "What's wrong?"

"Nothing. Everything."

Lottie picked up my hand and squeezed it. "I know," she sighed.

"I want to go home."

"Okay. We'll see if we can get a ride." She straightened up.

"No. I want to go home, Lottie. Our real home."

"Oh." She slid back onto the swing. "I know. But we can't. We can't go home, Franci. It's too late for that."

Soon we would go back to the party. We'd find Kevin, probably sitting alone somewhere, drinking his beer. We'd find the girls we came with, and maybe one of them would drive us home. More likely we'd end up having to walk several miles back to town. We'd go into the sterile, silent condo where our father was asleep alone. And Mother would still be dead.

The tears did come then, heaving sobs, and Lottie held me tightly. She wrapped me in her arms and rocked back and forth as if I were a child and she was my mother. But it wasn't the same.

Lottie

After Mia was born, I was good. For a while.

Franci and Whit have never understood why I go off the medication. It is a hard thing to explain, an unfair thing to try to rationalize, as they were often the ones who were left to pick up the pieces of my shattered self and put me back together again. Humpty Dumpty sat on a wall. Humpty Dumpty took a great fall. I felt like Humpty, an egg shattered into a thousand pieces, lovingly taped back together again, but still never quite right.

After Franci left, after Whit left, after Mia was born, I realized how few friends I actually had. There were coworkers from the university who came by bearing casseroles and baby blankets, but no one I was particularly close to. I saw Whit a few times while I was pregnant, but after Mia came along, I stopped returning his calls. He had made his choice, and I didn't want to watch him judge me as I mothered; I couldn't stand to see him scrutinizing my moods, my appearance, waiting for some clue that I was unfit. It was easier to ignore him and pretend I'd never wanted to spend the rest of my life with him.

The medication has tricked me so many times. Too many times have I thought that the handful of pills has cured me, as if I am swallowing a two-week course of penicillin and not medications I'm expected to take forever. If pain has no memory, then my roller-coaster ride through the Black and White suffers from amnesia. While I have patchy memories of the despair, it is with detachment, as if I'm hearing someone else's story. It is nearly impossible to remember that I make it through the day because of the pills I take each morning. And so when I don't take those pills one morning, I'm surprised how quickly the descent begins.

On one particular morning, Mia sat in her bouncy chair by my feet as I drank my third cup of coffee. Trying to battle my exhaustion with coffee was like using an umbrella in a monsoon and thinking you could stay dry. The exhaustion rained down on me like a storm throughout the day, letting up for an hour here or there, and then returning in full force. I ran a brush through my hair, hurriedly put on lipstick, and reached for the first bottle of pills. There was never just one; it was always a combination, a "cocktail" as the doctors called it, bringing to mind images of brightly colored drinks with umbrellas sticking out. As I uncapped the bottle, I paused. Had I taken the pills the day before? I couldn't remember.

And suddenly the idea was there again. Maybe I didn't need them anymore. Even as the thought wound its way around my brain, I could feel the room begin to tilt. I had been so good. I had been on all of my medications since Franci left the previous April. Every night, after I tucked Mia into her crib, I prayed for the strength to continue taking the pills. When my mouth became dry from the dehydration the medication caused, when a prescription-induced headache would overpower me, or when insomnia would keep me awake night after night, I would pray—to God, to Franci, or to whoever might be listening—to give me the strength to keep taking my medicine.

But I could be a better mother without all of the side effects of the pills—without the insomnia that descended unpredictably and unbidden and that left me exhausted the next day, without the restless energy that left me unable to sit still for more than a few minutes, without the tremors in my hands that made me worry I would drop Mia. I would be a better mother without the pills.

"Liar," a ghost whispered in my ear, the heat of his words damp on my neck. I heard the harsh rasp of his breath as he reminded me of the Black, the days to come when I would not be able to get out of bed. "What kind of a life is *that* for a child?" the ghost asked. Or the White—those moments when I was caught in the grip of flight, so high up and away from everyone else that I was untouchable. "What kind of mother will you be on those days?" The ghost was angry; we'd been here before.

But this time it would be different, I pleaded. *I* would be different. I *was* different now; I was a mother. Mia had already changed me. *Please,* I begged him. *Please, let me try once more.* But the ghost just laughed.

I have always imagined the pills in my body as a gunmetal-gray liquid. Steely and silver, they flow uninterrupted through my bloodstream. Within a few hours of missing my medication, the steady stream would turn to beaded drops of mercury while my blood raged red. By that evening, I would already feel the difference. My body would twang and jangle in its hyperalert state.

"Just take the pills," the ghost ordered.

But I refused. This time I would beat it, I told him. This time *I* would win.

"This time I can do it," I told Mia, who looked up at me serenely.

"Stupid Lottie," the ghost said, and then he turned away.

I should have known better. Since the disease took over, my whole life has been this way. And yet I keep finding myself back there: one leg straddling the White, the other straddling the Black, in constant pursuit of some nonexistent shade of gray.

Franci

I awoke with a start. The small clock on the nightstand said it was nearly six o'clock. I'd fallen asleep still wearing Lottie's soft white sundress. Down the hall I heard Mia's high-pitched cries, and I struggled out of bed, grabbing a yellow cardigan from the pile I'd made on the floor.

I changed Mia's diaper and fed her, and then I strapped her into the pink swing in the kitchen while I put water on to boil. A little after seven the doorbell rang.

Whit stood smiling uncertainly on the landing. The top of a bottle of wine stuck out from a brown paper bag.

"Hey." A day's worth of stubble covered his face, and I had the urge to run my hand over it, to feel the roughness against my palm.

"Come on in." I opened the door, and he followed me into the kitchen.

He crouched on the floor beside Mia, reaching out a finger. She grabbed it in her fist and held on tightly. He stayed beside her for a moment, watching her, looking at her, perhaps imagining what might have been. Finally he stood up, rubbing a hand over his short hair, a gesture I remembered. Appraising me, his eyes narrowed slowly. "Are those Charlotte's clothes?"

"I was going through some of Lottie's things earlier. Doing laundry." I wrapped the thin cardigan around myself.

Whit frowned. Uncorking the bottle of wine, he poured two glasses, handing me one. "I bought her that dress when we were in Carmel a few years ago."

"Oh." I looked awkwardly down at the outfit. "I'll go change," I said, putting the wineglass down on the countertop.

"No, no." Whit waved his hand, brushing the idea away. "It looks nice on you." He fingered the swollen cork he'd removed from the wine bottle. Its end was stained a lurid red. "You look like Charlotte," he said quietly. The kitchen was cozy with the water steaming on the stove and the air fragrant with the smell of fresh basil. Being here, in Lottie's kitchen with her daughter and former lover, it fit too easily, too comfortably. I reminded myself of my own husband and children waiting for me on the other side of the country, my own life, so very different from this one. We stood in a self-conscious silence until Mia finally let out a whimper. When I looked down at her, she was rubbing her eyes with a fist.

I shook my head. "I don't know her schedule yet. She woke up not that long ago, but that looks like tired to me. Can you make a salad while I get her ready for bed?"

By the time I finished putting Mia to bed, Whit had drained the pasta and mixed in the sauce. A green salad was on the table in the living room. Lottie's apartment was small, with no dining room. When she had guests over, she pulled pillows out of a closet and set them on the floor. So Whit and I ate at the coffee table, sitting on red silk cushions.

"When was the last time you spoke with Lottie?" I asked him over dinner.

"We broke up last May. I talked to her a few times over the summer. Mia was born in September, and I called a few times to see how things were going, but we didn't see each other. Charlotte didn't want me to meet her. She was angry. The last time we spoke was probably late November." He buttered two pieces of bread and placed one on my plate.

"How did she sound?"

"Good. She took the first semester off. She was getting ready to go back to work, trying to figure out childcare." Whit shrugged. "The usual new mom stuff, I guess."

"She was pregnant when I was here last year. Did you know?"

Whit shook his head. "I didn't know for another few weeks. I tried to call you when I found out."

"I thought you were trying to convince me to speak with Lottie." I'd deleted the messages from him and Lottie, not even listening to the words. I knew if I heard either of their voices, I wouldn't be strong enough to keep Lottie at bay.

Whit shook his head. "I didn't even know that the two of you had stopped talking. Lottie never told me. You know how secretive she can be."

I nodded. Lottie could have a different version of the truth for each person. Sometimes it was hard to tell which one she actually believed.

"Neither of us wanted it to end the way it did, but I suppose I didn't really give her a choice," he said. "You know what Charlotte's like when she gets an idea in her head. I knew there was no arguing with her. But I couldn't. The bipolar, it's . . ." He gestured emptily with his hands. "It's not something you bring a child into. Even when she's doing okay, it's unpredictable. And then every now and then she'll go off her meds." Whit shook his head, and I could see the pain he'd endured over his long relationship with Lottie. "It hadn't happened in a long time, a few years. But it infuriated me every time she did that to herself. And to me. I knew it would happen again, someday. I couldn't watch her do that to a child, whether it was mine or not."

"But why didn't you try to stop her from having Mia in the first place?" I asked.

"What could I do? Charlotte doesn't listen to anyone. It was hard enough to walk away."

Would she have listened to me, I wondered. *Probably not.*

"I was always surprised that you and Lottie never got married," I said.

"I wanted to. I asked her many times, but Charlotte wouldn't marry me." He let out a frustrated laugh. "Do you know how ridiculous that is? I own a house ten minutes from here. We were together for ten years and spent almost every night together. But she wouldn't even move in with me."

I looked at him in surprise. Lottie had never told me this. "Why not?"

He was quiet for a moment, perhaps mulling over Lottie's reasoning in his mind. "She thought that if we got married, I'd stay with her out of obligation. She said if we got married, then I wouldn't be able to leave if I wanted to." He leaned back, resting his head against the couch and staring at the ceiling. "The irony is she was right. It did make it easier to leave." After a moment he snapped back up, reaching for his wineglass. He drained it and then refilled it.

I knew Lottie's other reason for not wanting to move in with Whit. If they lived together, he'd watch her even more closely. He could count her pills each morning and night. He would see the dip before the drop. Lottie hated such scrutiny, from me and from him. What I suspected she really wanted was freedom from us both.

"I never imagined that things would end with us the way they did, not after so long. But we were a couple. You two . . ." Whit gestured to me. "You two are family. You're *more* than family. What happened?"

"She didn't say anything after my last visit?" I sat on the couch, pulled my knees up, and spread an afghan over my legs.

"No. Nothing."

Mark knew the whole story, but with him I'd defended Lottie, even though I didn't want to. We'd hardly spoken about it since, but it was always there, the absence of Lottie between us.

Whit was the only other person in the world who loved Lottie the way I did, the only other person who could see past the Black.

"During my last visit, I realized I couldn't trust her with my children." He waited for me to go on. "I should have recognized it as soon as I got here," I continued. "You'd think after all this time I'd know. But it's been a while since I lived with her. I don't see her every day." In truth, part of it was that I wasn't watching for signs of decline. I'd relinquished that job to Whit long ago.

The visit had started off well. Lottie picked us up at the airport that afternoon and drove us back to Berkeley. The girls sat in the backseat, leaning against each other as they fought off sleep. Once we arrived at Lottie's apartment, they napped in the guest room while Lottie made cups of tea.

"So I've taken almost the whole week off. What would you like to do?" Lottie asked, her tone nearly giddy. "We can go to San Francisco one day and take the girls to Golden Gate Park. We can go to the farmers' market. We can poke around bookstores. We could go down to Monterey to the aquarium. Whatever you like," Lottie said, spreading her arms wide. "I'm just so happy to have you all here."

We ended up doing all of those things and more. We took the girls to the farmers' market and filled green canvas bags with mangoes, avocados, and fat, ripe tomatoes. We drove to Sausalito and ate fried clams and calamari in a restaurant that overlooked the water. Ana and Autumn nervously tried the squiggly, battered seafood dipped in cocktail sauce. Lottie and I laughed when they each reached for seconds.

During the visit I tried not to scrutinize my sister. It was too exhausting to constantly check Lottie's mental state. She was a little too animated in the first few days, talking quickly, her face flushed pink with a nervous energy. But I was preoccupied, too busy being a mother to be Lottie's keeper too.

On the fifth day of the weeklong visit, we went to Monterey and Carmel for a night. We drove down Highway 1, the scenic road that wound its way along the jagged Pacific coastline. Lottie was driving, and she'd been unusually silent since we'd gotten on the road that morning.

"Are you okay?"

"I'm fine." Lottie flicked her eyes off the road for just a moment and briefly locked eyes with me. "Why?"

"You're just quiet. Are you feeling okay?" I asked cautiously.

"I'm just a little tired." Lottie's tone was guarded. *Leave it alone,* she was saying.

We rented a room at a lodge in Carmel-by-the-Sea. The room was spacious and airy with a cathedral ceiling and a balcony with a view of the ocean; the water was a pale blue sliver in the distance framed by cypress trees, their dark trunks arching away from the sea like slender dancers holding a pose.

On the first day we wandered through the picturesque town. We ate dinner at an outdoor café with heat lamps and a large fire pit in the center of the patio. I was overcome by a rush of love and gratitude for this bounty as I watched my sister and daughters around the table.

On our second day we went to Monterey. Lottie took the girls to the aquarium while I met up with an old college friend for lunch. By the time I left to meet them at the aquarium, I was nearly twenty minutes late, so I called Lottie and left a message.

When I arrived at the outside area where families waited in line with strollers and cameras, I didn't see Lottie or the girls. I peered through the tinted glass windows into the lobby and nervously fumbled in my purse for my phone. I called Lottie and left another message. I was getting ready to walk back to the car when I saw Lottie running toward me. Her eyes had a wild, frantic look to them, her cheeks flushed pink. She was alone.

"Thank god you're here," Lottie said, breathing heavily as she clasped my upper arm.

"Where are Ana and Autumn?"

Lottie's eyes immediately filled with tears. "Oh god, Franci. I don't know. I can't find them."

"What do you mean you can't find them? Where are they?" I felt a stab of fear in the center of my chest as my heart rate sped up.

"I don't know. We were all together, and then I turned around and they were gone."

"Jesus, Lottie, weren't you watching them?"

"I was watching them. I only turned around for a second. We were at the jellyfish exhibit, and it's dark. They were just ahead of me, but when I came out of the exhibit, they weren't there."

"Have you told security?"

"No. I was looking for them. And I was waiting for you."

"How long ago was this?" I pulled her with me as I ran toward the entrance of the aquarium, past the groups of tourists waiting in line to buy tickets.

"I'm not sure. Less than twenty minutes?"

"Twenty minutes?" I turned on Lottie, not even trying to hide my fury. "How could you not tell security? They're probably terrified." I didn't dare speak aloud my real fear—that someone had taken them and they were already in a car on the freeway, miles and miles away by now.

"I thought I could find them. I just figured they'd wandered off," Lottie pleaded. "I'm so sorry."

I turned to the attendant at the door who stood collecting tickets. "My daughters are lost. Do you have a security office?" He directed us inside, and we pushed through the doors. The aquarium was warm and humid and smelled of an unpleasant mixture of fish food and stagnant water. In a tank that stretched floor to ceiling, giant silver tuna and speckled sharks swam in slow circles.

I hurried to the information desk, Lottie trailing behind me. While I explained the situation, Lottie looked on, chewing violently on a fingernail. The man at the desk picked up a telephone, his back toward us.

He spoke softly into the phone and then hung up, swiveling around in his chair so that he was facing us again.

"Did someone find them? Are they okay?" I asked.

The man held up a hand without answering and looked toward the escalator. I followed his gaze and saw an older man in khakis and a navy-blue polo shirt standing between Ana and Autumn. The girls each held one of his hands, and they were both talking at once to the man, who was smiling and nodding. Neither of them looked scared. When they reached the bottom of the escalator, they both jumped from the shrinking step onto the landing at the same time as I rushed to greet them.

"Hi, Mommy. Hi, Aunt Lottie," both girls said.

The man smiled at me and released them, pushing them gently toward where I crouched with arms open.

"Are you guys okay?" I asked, inhaling the soft scent of their hair.

"Mommy, Norman took us to see the scuba diver feed the sharks!" Autumn answered.

"Where did you go?" I asked, stroking Ana's cheek. "We were so worried."

"I don't know. We turned around and Aunt Lottie was gone. So we went to the guard like you told us when we went to the museum last time," Ana said. I remembered taking the girls to the Boston Children's Museum over Thanksgiving, and I'd given specific instructions on what to do if they were ever lost.

Norman studied me as I stood up. "We paged you several times," he said, frowning slightly. Then his expression lightened, and he shook his head. "You'd be surprised how easy it is for kids to wander off in a big place like this."

"Thank you so much," I said, firmly grasping each girl. "Say thank you to the man for taking care of you."

"Thank you, Norman!" they called in unison. I thanked him again and began walking toward the exit, holding tightly onto the girls, Lottie trailing behind.

In the car, I buckled Ana and Autumn's seat belts, even though they were old enough to do it themselves.

"I'll drive," I said, and Lottie offered up the keys without a word. I plucked them from her outstretched palm and adjusted my sunglasses so I wouldn't have to look at her. I couldn't recall ever being so angry with her, but I couldn't unleash my fury. Not with the girls in the backseat.

"He said it happens all the time," Lottie said weakly.

"I'm sure it does."

"I'm sorry, Franci. Really. I don't know what happened. I swear, I took my eyes off them for only a second." *That's all it takes,* I thought, but managed to bite my tongue.

"I know. And thank god they're fine. Let's get back to the hotel."

"Please, Franci. I know you're mad."

"Jesus, Lottie, give me a minute, will you? My heart rate's not even back to normal."

"It was an accident."

"Of course it was."

"Please, I can't stand to have you mad at me. Do you forgive me?"

I let out a long sigh. "Yes, I forgive you. I just want to go back to the hotel." I started the car and backed carefully out of the spot. We drove slowly through the parking lot, and I gripped the wheel, letting the tight dread drain from my chest. *Thank you,* I breathed silently. To whom? God? My sister? Norman? The girls for having the good sense to get help? Maybe I was just thanking my good fortune and luck for having stepped out of tragedy's path this time.

Lottie

I should have known that day in the aquarium. I should have told Franci.

I am always surprised by how fast it can happen. One moment I'll be in the dull state of medicated regularity, and the next I'll be soaring in the White or plunging headfirst into the Black. Sometimes it happened a little more slowly, a steady drip of White or Black before the total wash. That was the way it happened during Franci's visit.

Franci doesn't understand it; no one does, even when I try to explain that living with the medication is often like not living at all compared to the highs of White and the sweeping vistas of that state. It's hard to explain to Franci that I never feel fully like myself on the drugs. It's too frightening for her to truly comprehend this, to acknowledge that I might be the most like myself amidst the unfurling tendrils of madness.

The week before, I'd sat in my doctor's office in a paper robe while she talked to me about the need to switch prescriptions to accommodate the pregnancy. I gripped the plastic cushioned exam table while she warned me that many women with bipolar disorder have an episode at least once during pregnancy, even while on medication.

I almost told Franci. As I felt the first flutters of the Black, as I sensed the symptoms clawing their way through the haze of medication, I almost asked her for help. But I was so tired of needing help, and I was trying to find the nerve to tell her that I was pregnant. I couldn't tell her I was going to become a mother in the same breath that I told her I was already falling apart.

As I brought Ana and Autumn into the aquarium, I was certain I could hold on. I would be okay. I held their hands and tried not to think about motherhood. But then we entered the jellyfish display. The room was dark and filled with giant tanks that were lit from behind, and Ana and Autumn ran ahead to press their faces to the tanks, their hands leaving shadowy imprints on the bright glass. The jellyfish bobbed in electric shades of pink and white and orange, their stingers streaming behind like the strings of party balloons. Their bloated bodies pulsed like fat hearts beating.

The girls wandered a few more feet ahead of me. To them it was just another exhibit, but I was transfixed.

As always happens, I couldn't control the spin of my mind. I started by thinking only how beautiful they were, these delicate sea creatures that moved like women in an old-fashioned synchronized swim dance. But then I began to think about how sad it must be for all these fish, used to the vast waters of the Pacific, to be kept in the tiny tanks. I wondered if the fish were able to sleep with the artificial lights shining inside. Did fish sleep? I wondered what the life span for a jellyfish might be, and if it were shorter for those who were held captive in these glass cells.

And then I began to think about the afternoon my mother and I came across a dead jellyfish in the sand on a visit to San Diego. We were walking along the shoreline, searching for sea glass. I walked slowly, my eyes peeled for the bright shards of green and blue that dotted the sand, and Mother reached out a hand to tug me away from the gooey mess of the dead jellyfish. The fish was clear, its body nearly smeared and melted into the sand, and I wanted to reach out to feel its thick gelatinous form, but Mother squeezed my hand and pulled me along the beach.

She wore a red bathing suit with a little skirt that tied on the side. Her long black hair was held back with a polka-dotted headband, and she tilted her head toward the sun, exposing the long white expanse of her neck, graceful as a swan's. In my memory she was the most beautiful woman I could imagine.

"Ma'am? Please don't touch the tanks," a voice said. I looked up to see one of the aquarium workers beside me and realized I was leaning against the tank, my hands splayed wide against the cool glass. I hurried on through the rest of the exhibit, my head down, embarrassed to have been discovered in such a private moment.

It wasn't until I was on the other end of the exhibit that I remembered the girls. I could never tell Franci, but I'd forgotten about her daughters. It was probably a full ten minutes before I even remembered that they should have been with me.

It was all I could do not to get down on my knees right there in the lobby of the aquarium when they came sliding down the escalator, placid and glowing. It was all I could do not to beg Franci in the moment, *Please help me.* But I knew I couldn't stand her silent reproach, the weight of all that judgment, the tight look on her face when she was worried or frustrated with me. So I didn't say a word. I only looked away for a minute, I promised. It happens all the time. I let her believe that I was well. I let her believe I was safe.

By then I could feel the dark hazy fog as it settled in, tucking itself into the crevices of my body, plugging my ears, my mouth, my nose, making it impossible to breathe naturally. The fog was dense and oppressive, and as always, there was nothing to do but submit. The only option was to try to steel myself for the descent. But no matter how many times it happens, no matter how much I try to gather my strength and optimism and goodwill around me like a protective cloak, there is no preparation for the fall.

Franci

On the drive back to Berkeley that April afternoon, Lottie was quiet. Several times I looked anxiously at my sister with her head resting against the glass. Instead of Highway 1, we'd taken the more direct route home, and the highway was thick with giant trucks and tankers.

"I'm not mad," I offered, but there was an edge in my voice. "Really, it could happen to anyone. I'm just glad the girls knew enough to get help. I'm not mad, okay?"

Lottie nodded.

"Are you all right?" I asked in a hushed whisper. "You haven't gone off your meds, have you?" I hated to ask. I no longer wanted to know the answer.

"No, Franci. I haven't." Since we'd left the aquarium, she seemed to have been overcome with a heavy lethargy. It had been a long day, I rationalized.

By the time we got back to the apartment, it was nearly seven. I hauled the single suitcase and backpack from the car. The evening was overcast and rainy, and inside the apartment was dim, the only light coming from the leaky gray that peered through the drawn curtains.

Ana and Autumn settled on the couch to watch television, and I unpacked the clothes from our trip, repacking them for our flight to Boston the following morning.

"Are you all ready to go?" Lottie asked. Her eyes were dull and flat, the lids ready to slide closed at any moment. The bridge of her nose and her cheeks and forehead were sunburned, giving her a feverish look.

"Just about." I was ready to go home. I always forgot how much Lottie exhausted me. The afternoon at the aquarium had left me anxious to get home to Boston and to Mark, to the stability and safety of our life. Lottie lay down on the bed and extended her arm across her face, blocking out the overhead light.

"Are you okay?" I asked, for what seemed like the tenth time that day.

"I have a headache. I just took some aspirin."

Ana appeared in the doorway. "I'm hungry, Mommy. What's for dinner?" She, too, looked tired and disheveled, her blond braids unraveling around her shoulders, her tee shirt stained with chocolate.

"Dinner. That's a good question." I looked at Lottie, who hadn't moved from her spot on the bed. "Pizza? Does that sound good?"

Ana nodded, without any enthusiasm or distaste, an indication of the fatigue that was threatening to overtake us all.

"Okay. Is there a place around here that delivers?"

"Mmm," Lottie murmured. "There's probably a flyer on the fridge."

I went into the kitchen, returning a minute later. "There's not. Would it be somewhere else?"

"I don't know." Lottie lay motionless, the crook of her elbow blocking any view of her face.

I let out an exasperated sigh. "Is there a pizza place nearby?"

"There's one on Telegraph."

"Go put your shoes back on," I told Ana. "We're going to go get a pizza."

"I'm tired, Mommy. Can't we stay here?" Ana whined.

I looked at Lottie motionless on the bed. "No, honey. Aunt Lottie doesn't feel well."

Lottie struggled to sit up. "Franci, I'm fine. Leave them here. The place is just around the corner."

"They can come with me," I said, pulling my coat on. "Come on, honey, you can help me pick the toppings."

"I don't want to come. I want to stay and watch TV." Ana looked close to tears.

"Franci, just leave them." Lottie sat all the way up and smoothed the hair from her face. "They're tired. It's been a long day." She looked more alert. "I'm so sorry about this afternoon. But are you never going to leave them with me again?" I could see the hurt in her expression.

"Of course not," I said, trying to convince us both. "You just seem really tired. You could take a nap while we're gone."

"The aspirin's starting to kick in. I'm already feeling better." I still didn't answer. "Franci, we'll be fine. Just go get the pizza."

"Please, Mommy?" Ana asked. She looked so tired.

I hesitated another moment before giving in. "Okay, but after dinner you guys need to have a bath, okay? We've got an early flight tomorrow." Ana nodded, returning to the living room to watch more television.

"I'll be back in a few minutes," I said to Lottie. "They're just watching TV. You guys will be okay, right?"

Lottie nodded. "We'll be fine, Franci. I can give them a bath for you so you don't have to do it later," she offered.

"No, it's fine, just let them watch TV. I'll be back in fifteen minutes."

The trip to the pizza place took more than fifteen minutes. Telegraph Avenue was congested with people; students and beggars and street vendors lined the colorful strip of downtown Berkeley. I had to stop at an ATM to get out cash for the next day, and I'd forgotten that it was Friday night—the line at the pizza place was jammed up against the door.

I sat on a stool and waited for our order to be ready. I reached into my purse to check the time, but realized I'd left my cell phone back at Lottie's. Already I'd been gone for nearly a half hour.

When the pizza was finally ready, I walked the four blocks back to the apartment, the cardboard box held in front of me and a plastic bag of salads strung precariously around my wrist. The scent of melted cheese and broiled onions wafted from the container, and I suddenly realized how hungry I was, relieved to finally be away from the crowded restaurant. But as I turned up Lottie's street, I felt the hunger drain out of me. In front of Lottie's apartment, an ambulance and a police car were parked, their lights flashing silently in the night, casting red and blue shadows against the yellow house.

I broke into a run, still awkwardly trying to carry dinner; the plastic bag bounced steadily against my thigh. As I neared the house, time seemed to stand still. I felt it splitting in half, and though I didn't know what I'd find inside, I already knew that I was standing in the slender, pearl-shaped space between before and after.

In front of the house, a police officer held a hand out to stop me.

"Slow down, ma'am," he instructed.

"What's going on? My sister lives here. My daughters are with her. Are they okay? What happened?" The words tumbled from my lips.

"There was a call to 911. There are EMTs inside taking care—" I didn't hear the rest of what he said because I dropped the dinner at his feet and ran around him, up the stairs and through the front door. I heard him half-heartedly trying to stop me, but he seemed to realize that he wasn't going to keep me away.

The first thing I heard was Ana's wailing. Both girls were crying, but Ana's came out in a high-pitched keening. The sound reached somewhere deep inside of me. It was the sound of pain and suffering, my babies in distress, and I knew it was somehow Lottie's fault.

I stepped into the bathroom, my sandal nearly slipping on the tiled floor that was slick with soapy water. For all of the noise of the girls' crying, the room felt unbelievably quiet. Autumn and Lottie were huddled in the corner of the bathroom. Autumn was wrapped in a towel, and her hair hung dark and dripping down her shoulders. She was crying softly but appeared unhurt. Lottie stood behind Autumn, an arm wrapped protectively around her, her sundress drenched in water.

Ana sat on the closed toilet seat, naked except for a towel draped awkwardly across her body, and there were two EMTs crouching on the floor beside her. Her face was covered in blood that seemed to course in rivulets from some unknown wound. Beneath the blood her skin was whiter than I'd ever seen it, as if she'd been bathing in milk. One of the men was talking quietly to Ana while holding her hand. The other one was unwrapping gauze and bandages.

"Ana," I whispered. My own voice was foreign to me. It came out in a warbled whisper.

"Mama!" Ana screamed and lurched toward me, but the man with the bandages held her still. I kneeled down beside her and wrapped my arms around her thin waist. I could feel Autumn behind me, her head pressed against my back.

"What happened?" I sat up and put my arm around Autumn. I directed the question to Lottie, but it was Autumn who answered.

"We were playing in the tubby, and Ana had to go to the bathroom. When she got back in, she slipped. She bumped her head on the faucet. Really hard." Autumn's voice came in jagged breaths. "She went under the water, and I couldn't get her up. She was so heavy. I couldn't get her out of the tub, Mommy. I tried, but she was too heavy."

Autumn buried her face in my shoulder, and I shivered as cold drops of water trickled down the back of my shirt. "I held her head up from the water. I thought she was dead." Autumn's voice cracked, and she burst into tears again. My whole body had gone still, envisioning this scene as it played out. My baby girl, holding her twin sister's head out of the water, praying for her to breathe, brave and helpless all at once. "Aunt Lottie came and we got her out," Autumn continued. "She spit up a lot of water and was coughing. There was blood all over her face and in the bath." I looked into the tub and noticed that the water was tinted pink. I looked away, feeling as if I might throw up.

"Where was Aunt Lottie when you were in the bath?" I asked Autumn, though I was looking at my sister. Lottie stared at the floor and closed her eyes again.

"I don't know." Autumn turned toward Lottie, her eyes darting anxiously between us. I knew Autumn was wondering if she should be blaming or protecting her aunt. "The phone rang and Aunt Lottie went to answer it. She didn't come back until Ana got hurt." Ana whimpered softly as the EMT affixed the bandage to her head. I saw now that the wound was just above her eye. Autumn let out a deep breath and inched around me so that her face was right next to Ana's. "It's okay, Ana. You'll be okay. Mommy's here now. Don't cry. It will be okay," she crooned softly into her sister's neck.

"She's going to be fine," said the EMT with the bandages. "She needs a few stitches, and she needs to be checked for a concussion, but she'll be fine." There was a bandage at the top of Ana's forehead, just above her left eye and reaching into her hairline. "I've put on a butterfly bandage for now, but we'll have to take her to the hospital to get that cut stitched up. You can ride in the ambulance or follow behind us in your car," the man said. He wrapped Ana in a thick gray blanket and gathered her in his arms, holding her like one would cradle a newborn.

Lottie finally opened her eyes and met mine. Just for a moment. But it was a moment when I was almost certain that telepathy could exist between twins. *Please forgive me,* Lottie said. And in that split second, I answered her. *I will never be able to forgive this.* I broke my gaze first.

Franci

The room had grown completely dark as I spoke, and the candles on the mantel had burned out. During the time it took to tell the story, Whit had barely moved at all. He sat completely still, his attention focused on me, hands still clasped in his lap. He hadn't even touched his wineglass.

"Ana was only at the hospital for a few hours," I said. "She was fine. We left the next morning as we'd planned."

"How did you leave it with Charlotte?" Whit asked.

"I barely spoke to her." I looked down at my lap and picked at a loose thread on Lottie's white dress. "She wouldn't even admit she'd gone off her meds. Not that it would have made a difference to me. I wouldn't let her drive us to the airport. We took a cab."

I remembered Lottie's face when the cab pulled up, and I ushered the girls inside without saying goodbye. "I can't talk to you for a while. Don't call me," I'd said. Lottie had looked stunned and empty, as if the full realization of what was happening had finally settled in.

I looked up and met Whit's eyes. "When I got home, I told Mark what happened. I've never seen him so angry. At me more than Lottie. He told me he never wanted the girls around her again." I paused to take a breath. "Even though I was madder at her than I've ever been in my whole life, part of me wanted to defend her to him. It doesn't make any sense." I reached for my glass. The wine had lost its flavor long ago—it tasted bitter and tart now, but I was enjoying the hazy disconnected feeling it brought with it. Maybe it was the wine, maybe it was Whit, but I felt a palpable relief at having told him the story.

"I keep thinking about that week. She must have been pregnant. I can't believe she didn't tell me." I fingered the stem of my wineglass. "Maybe she tried. She probably knew that, even before what happened with Ana, I wouldn't have thought it was a good idea." I leaned back against the couch, letting my head rest on a pillow.

"It wasn't," said Whit.

"Maybe not. But I can't blame her for wanting a child. And now that Mia's here, it's hard to imagine that she shouldn't be." Only half realizing I was doing it, I extended my legs on the couch so that my toes nearly touched Whit's legs. "I'm so tired of being afraid for her. I was so tired of trying to save her."

Whit reached out a hand and placed it on the arch of my bare foot, his fingers encircling it like a fitted slipper. His hand was warm and solid, and I closed my eyes. His other hand moved slowly up my calf till it reached the sensitive skin behind my knee, and I arched my back, surprised to realize what we were about to do.

I had never been unfaithful to Mark. But somehow here, with Whit, it didn't have the same illicit feeling that I imagined. I was far from home. I'd known Whit for over ten years. Our lives had been inextricably tangled in our messy and treacherous love for Lottie for so long. All of these circumstances were stacked upon one another like a child's wooden block set. The higher the tower grew, the easier it was to imagine sleeping with Whit, even though I knew the tower would ultimately come crashing down.

When Whit pushed up Lottie's white sundress, his hands were rough against the smooth skin of my inner thighs. I kept my eyes closed as he lowered his torso down, bringing his face close, his lips finding mine.

It was the kind of kiss that Mark and I rarely shared these days. It was hungry and hard, and I felt the tip of his tongue, the scrape of teeth. I kept my eyes closed tightly, afraid that if I opened them, I might break some spell.

His fingers found the thin straps of my underwear, and he eased them down my legs. His lips were by my ear, his breath making the hairs on my neck stand on end as I fumbled with the heavy metal buckle of his belt.

"You're beautiful," he whispered. I paused, my fingers still on his worn leather belt. I had an uncanny vision of us from above, laid out on Lottie's couch, me wearing Lottie's dress with her lover of so many years. It wasn't me Whit wanted. It was Charlotte. And that was enough to stop me.

"Wait," I whispered, pushing myself up from underneath his body. "Hold on."

"What?" He looked sleepy, as if he'd just woken up, and my face tingled from where his beard had chafed my cheeks.

"We shouldn't be doing this." I pulled the dress down to cover my nakedness, tucking my feet beneath me.

Since I first met Whit, we'd been united in Lottie's care, complicit in the steady regulation of her moods as we tried to pull her back from the lure of the White or the pit of the Black. There was an undeniable intimacy in that, a shared responsibility and power. I wasn't Lottie, yet I was. I was the steady and healthy version of the woman he loved, and though I might not have burned as bright, I didn't start fires, either. The connection between us had always been there, but we'd been careful not to cross that line.

Whit sat up and looked at me intently for a moment, probably trying to gauge the likelihood that I would change my mind. Whatever he saw in my face, it was enough to make him rebuckle his belt. I wiped my wrist along my mouth, cleaning my lips of wine and his kisses. He rubbed his hand along his bristled scalp, smoothing down the quarter inch of hair.

"I should go," he said when I didn't speak. He stood up and so did I, following him to the door. I pulled Lottie's dress over my knees and felt like I was wearing a costume hours after the party had ended. I was embarrassed and drunk, and I wanted to go home. We stood awkwardly at the door.

"Whit . . . ," I began, unsure of what I needed to say, but he shook his head.

"Forget it. Call if you need anything, okay? Otherwise, I'm sure I'll see you at the hospital." I nodded and watched him step outside into the night.

I closed the door behind him, flipping the dead bolt and chain. As soon as I shut the door, I wished he hadn't left. Whether I wanted to sleep with him or not, it meant that I would be forced to spend the night alone in Lottie's silent bedroom with the implications of what I'd nearly done. For a moment, I considered calling him back.

But the moment had passed, and I heard his car as it started up and backed out of the driveway. I leaned against the door, the tiny glass peephole digging into my spine, my head resting against the wood. After a moment I flipped off the hall light, double-checked the locks, and went to bed alone.

Franci

I awoke the next morning with a splitting headache, a dry mouth, and a piercing sense of shame and humiliation. I lay in bed feeding Mia a bottle and tried to imagine what Mark would say if he found out.

Besides Mark I'd only slept with one other man, a boyfriend I'd had at Berkeley. In the nine years that Mark and I had been together, neither of us had been unfaithful, as far as I knew.

It was easy to blame the wine, the intimacy of the evening, the mutual struggle over Lottie. But Mark felt so far away, even before there were thousands of miles physically between us.

I wondered what Lottie would do if I told her. She was as likely to slap me across the face as she was to laugh and roll her eyes. I decided never to tell her, even while I knew how impossible it was to keep things from my sister. It was as if a secret between us emitted a strong and unpleasant odor, some pheromone of the soul that Lottie would be able to sniff out as soon as I entered her room.

I strapped Mia into her car seat and drove to the hospital, sipping strong coffee from Lottie's Cal mug. In the backseat Mia sucked contentedly on her pacifier, oblivious to the drama that unfolded around her. She stared out the window at the treetops and telephone wires overhead, a placid expression on her face.

In the parking lot of the garage I secured Mia into the BabyBjörn, and she burrowed against my chest, seeking my warmth. I felt nauseated in the pit of my belly—a combination of the hangover, the coffee on an empty stomach, and the heavy layer of guilt that covered everything.

On Lottie's floor I walked slowly toward her room, peering through the glass door first. Whit sat at the foot of her bed, and Lottie's face was obscured from the angle where I stood. I took a step back so neither of them would see me, but Whit had already lifted his head and caught my eye. I opened the door and stepped inside.

Lottie's bruises were beginning to turn yellow and green around the edges. Her hair was clipped back away from her face, and though there were still dark circles under her eyes, she looked better than the day before.

"Hi, sweet girl," she said to Mia. I began to unbuckle the straps on the carrier, but Lottie shook her head. "She looks so comfortable in there. Leave her be." She looked up from Mia to me. "What's wrong?"

I felt myself flush. "What do you mean? Nothing."

"You look weird. Your face has gone all blotchy."

I shrugged my shoulders and fussed over Mia, making every effort not to look at Whit.

"Did you bring me some clothes?" The previous day she'd asked me to bring some things from home.

"Shoot. I forgot."

"Franci." She rolled her eyes. "It would be nice to get out of this stupid gown. I don't even have any clean underwear."

"I'm sorry. It just . . . slipped my mind. I'll run back and get you some things."

"I should get going," Whit said. He'd gotten up from the bed and was zipping up his vest. "I've got a job in Marin this afternoon."

"Oh." Lottie looked disappointed. "Will you be back later?"

"Probably not today." He looked at me and then away.

"Okay." Lottie looked down at the bed. "The doctors tell me I'll be getting out of here tomorrow," she said, brightening. "You can come see me at the house. Or maybe you could pick me up. Franci's got her hands full with Mia."

Whit smiled but lowered his eyes. "Maybe. I'll see what I can do." Lottie pursed her lips together, a gesture that always indicated she was close to crying. I inched awkwardly toward the door.

"I'll be back in a few minutes," I told her. "I'm just going to run back to your house to pick up a few things."

"I'll walk you out," Whit said, and I looked at him in surprise.

Lottie eyed the two of us together. She knew something was up; she just hadn't figured out what exactly. Whit leaned over the bed and cupped her chin in his hand. "I'll try to come by tomorrow," he said and leaned down to kiss her cheek. She tilted her face upward, offering him her mouth instead. I looked away as he kissed her lightly on the lips. She clung to his hand for a moment, searching his face.

I slipped out of the room. I couldn't stand to see the desperation in her gesture and the disappointment that I knew would follow. It was only a matter of time. I was halfway down the hall when Whit caught up with me.

"Hey," he said.

"Hey." We walked in silence to the elevator. I pressed the down button and the doors opened; we stepped inside. "I'm sorry about last night," I said finally.

Whit shook his head, holding his hand out, as if to keep my words from touching him. "Let's forget about it." I nodded. The elevator opened, and we stepped into the parking garage. "Where's your husband?" he asked.

I looked at him in surprise. "He's at home. With the girls."

"They should be here. To help you."

I let out a harsh laugh. "You obviously don't have kids. Five-year-old girls are not a huge help." The bridge of his nose was lightly freckled, and he had the weathered pink skin of someone who spent a great deal of time outdoors. It was hard to imagine Whit as a lawyer in a shirt and tie in an office every day. I wondered where he had gotten the courage to decide he could change his life and if he ever regretted it. But Whit was cut from a different cloth than me, something sturdier and more resilient. Regret seemed unlikely.

"It's not going to be easy," he continued. "Taking care of Lottie and her baby. How long are you planning on staying?"

"I don't know. As long as I need to, I guess." I shook my head in exasperation. "Nothing's ever simple with her, is it?"

"Who are you mad at?" he asked, instead of answering. The question seemed genuine, as if he really were trying to figure it out. "Yourself or her?"

I smiled at him through closed lips. "Both, obviously."

"Do you wish you'd stayed to take care of her? Made your life here instead of in Boston?" We were standing by Lottie's car now.

I shrugged. "I left her with you."

"But you're her sister. Her twin. No one could know her, could love her, like you. Right? That's what you're thinking." There was an edge of meanness to his words.

"I guess. Yeah." I put the key into the lock of the door, but Whit caught my wrist in his hand.

"She doesn't want to be taken care of the way you take care of her," Whit said. "She doesn't want to be helpless the way you make her. She isn't helpless. She's strong."

"Strong?" I could hear the anger in my own voice. "Whatever she's told you, there's more to this accident than a negligent driver. You should have seen her house when I got there. There was rotten food in the fridge. There were flies in the kitchen, the same kitchen where she would warm milk for Mia. Does a strong person let her house fall down around her?" I asked. "Does a strong person stop taking medicine that makes her better, over and over and over again?"

"A sick person does those things." He dropped my wrist and looked away, breaking his gaze from mine. "You've always connected sick with weak, Franci. And Charlotte can't stand that. She has always been stronger without you. Whenever you came back, it was just an excuse for her to fall apart all over again. She knew you would be there to pick up the pieces. It was your job. It's what you're good at." He shook his head, and I could see the quiet rage smoldering behind his eyes. "I swear, sometimes I think she did it to please you."

"That's sick," I said, though there was a tiny part of me that had wondered the same thing myself. I thought back to the many visits with Lottie over the years. During a few of those trips, Lottie went off her meds right before or after my visit. I'd never wanted to connect it to my presence. I hadn't considered that the visits might be as emotionally intense for Lottie as they were for me.

Whit shrugged. "She just wants you to respect her."

"What are you talking about? I've idolized her since we were children."

"That's not the same thing," Whit said, shaking his head, dismayed that I still didn't get it. "Franci, she wants your approval. She wants to know that you think she's okay. That you think she can do this, raise this baby and be a good mother."

"But that's crazy, Whit, and you know it. Don't put that on me." I was furious all of a sudden. "*You* didn't think she could do it. That's why you left. She *can't* do it. Everything will fall apart. It's already started to fall apart." I was shouting, my words reverberating off the walls of the garage. A woman hurried to her car, glancing in our direction.

"If you tell her that, then it will be true," Whit said in a quiet voice.

"What can I do?" I finally asked him. "I don't see how she can do this alone." I met his eyes. "Are you going to be there? Are you going to help her?"

He looked away. "She's not my baby, Franci."

"That's not the point!" I nearly shrieked at him. It was suddenly so clear to me, the difference in our roles. Whit was with Lottie by choice, while I was bound to her by something thicker than blood. Whit could walk away. Try as I might, I would never be able to do that to my sister.

I looked down at Mia. She had Lottie's dark curls, her long lashes and pale skin. There was nothing of Whit in this child, but she looked just like me. I unlocked the car and lifted Mia out of the carrier and into the car seat. Somewhere between Lottie's room and the parking garage she'd fallen asleep, not even stirring during our argument. I closed the car door gently and then turned back to Whit.

"You know she wants to get back together with you. You can see that, can't you?" I waited, but he didn't answer. "You need to tell her it's not going to work out the way she wants. There is no happily ever after with this story." As soon as I'd uttered such a callous and yet undeniably true sentence, I was close to tears. I got into the driver's seat and started up the car, rolling the window down to look at him again. He stood by the car, his hands hanging uselessly by his sides. He looked as broken and tired as I felt. "You need to tell her," I said again through the open window. He didn't answer.

Lottie

When I awake, the idea is there: if I fail, Franci will succeed.

Suicide attempt. Such a deliberate phrase. But does it cover not wearing your seat belt while on the freeway? Does it cover walking home alone at night through a bad neighborhood? Does it cover closing your eyes for just a moment while you're driving, just to see what it feels like to have the thick black night hurtling toward you? Does it cover this superstitious brand of risk, as if Fate and I are playing a game together, and Fate will decide how hard I fall?

Does it cover not going back for my helmet?

Franci wants me to be able to answer yes or no. She wants the lines drawn clearly.

How do I explain that the answer is not so simple? That I didn't try to get hit by the car, but that I wasn't paying attention? Instead, I was looking at the people getting on the bus. I was struck by the faces of the people standing in the back, holding on to the metal bar inside the bus for support, staring blankly out the windows. I only saw them for a second, but I held on to the image, and I was so saddened by the nothingness that I saw, the hopelessness and emptiness that had been breeding for years. When I finally dragged my eyes away from the gray gloom inside the bus, the car was already pulling out in front of me. And then it was upon me, and I didn't even have a moment to wonder if I should have worn the helmet.

I didn't have a moment to think about what could be lost.

Franci

"Careful," I said to Lottie, opening her car door.

"I'm *being* careful." She gingerly twisted her body so that her feet were on the sidewalk. The giant plastic boot looked like a costume out of a science fiction film, but it meant that Lottie would be able to walk while the fracture healed. Her arm would be in a cast for up to ten weeks.

Lottie's neighbor, Sally, had offered to watch Mia for a few hours while I picked up Lottie from the hospital. It had taken much of the afternoon for the paperwork to be completed, and it was nearly four o'clock by the time we arrived back at the apartment. Lottie began the slow and awkward journey up the front steps. Her boot clicked against the asphalt, and she winced with each step. I tried to hold her good arm, but she jerked my hand away. At the top of the steps she paused, panting slightly.

"How are you going to do this with Mia too?" I asked.

"Just open the door, Franci," Lottie demanded, leaning on the railing.

I unlocked it and held it open for her. "I'm just saying. You can barely make it up here by yourself. What would you do if you had Mia with you right now?"

Lottie hobbled into the living room without answering.

"And what about driving? Can you drive with that thing on your foot and one arm? Is it even legal to drive with it?"

"Jesus, Franci, I don't know."

"Well, whether it's legal or not, it can't be safe. You can't drive with Mia. And it will be another few weeks, at least, before you get the boot off." I heard the shrillness in my voice, yet I couldn't stop. All of the anxiety that I'd kept to myself while Lottie was in the hospital poured out now. "How are you going to get around? How are you going to get to work? How are you going to get Mia to daycare?"

"I was planning on riding my bike," Lottie said sarcastically. She looked tired but managed a grin as she collapsed on the couch. "I don't know. I really don't know how I'm going to do any of it. It's not your problem, though. You should think about getting back to Boston."

"Oh, shut up," I said, rolling my eyes. "It's not as if I'm going to leave you here totally helpless. I'll talk to Sally. Maybe she can help out, with some extra babysitting and driving and that sort of thing. Mark and I could pay her."

"I can pay her, Franci. I have money. I do have a job, you know." She began to thumb through the mail on the coffee table.

"Fine."

"And Whit might be able to help out a little," she said, without looking up from the stack of mail. "They're finishing up a job this week, so his schedule should be more flexible." I didn't answer. "Can you get me the phone so I can call Sally to tell her to bring Mia over?" Lottie asked. She stretched herself out onto the couch and flipped on the television. "Do you think you could make me a cup of tea? And some toast? I'm starving. They didn't even give me lunch today." I stood where I was for a moment, watching her. The swelling in her face had gone down, and she'd arranged her hair to cover the stitches above her ear. "Please?" She smiled sweetly, the same grin she always gave when she was trying to gain a favor.

In the kitchen I put on the kettle and made toast. As I fixed Lottie's snack, Sally came into the apartment with Mia. When I returned to the living room with a plate and mug of tea for Lottie, Sally was sitting on the couch. Mia fussed as Lottie tried to hold her with one arm.

"Hi, Sally. Do you want a cup of tea?" I asked.

"Oh, no thanks. I've got to get to class soon." She turned to Lottie. "My god, so scary! You're lucky to be alive."

"I know." Mia whimpered and struggled to get comfortable. Sally adjusted her on Lottie's lap.

"Seriously," Sally continued. "This could have been so much worse. You really need to be careful when you ride your bike. Weren't you wearing your helmet?"

"I forgot it," Lottie said, taking a bit of toast. Toast crumbs fell in Mia's hair. "Mmm, real butter. You should have tasted the nasty processed crap they fed me at the hospital."

Sally met my eyes, likely distraught by Lottie's cavalier attitude toward her brush with death. She wasn't really cavalier, I knew, but she wouldn't show anyone how much she'd scared herself. "So how much longer will you be here, Franci?" Sally asked when it became clear that Lottie was done talking about the accident.

"I don't know. Another week, at least. I want to make sure that Lottie gets settled." Sally nodded, her ponytail swinging against her shoulder. "I was hoping we could talk about you helping out a bit for the next few weeks or months, with driving and babysitting, that sort of thing. We'd pay you, of course," I said, careful not to look at Lottie.

"Oh, sure. I'd be happy to help. Anything I can do," she said quickly.

"Great. We can talk more about the details later." We were quiet for a moment, some new awkwardness having descended over the room.

"We should go out for a drink!" Sally said suddenly. "To celebrate Charlotte being home and being okay."

"Now?" I asked. Lottie and I locked eyes and a silent laugh travelled between us. Going to a bar with the baby and Lottie in casts was preposterous. The age difference between us and Sally was glaringly apparent.

"Well, no. I have to go to class now, but maybe we could go out later?"

"Probably not today," I said. "I don't think Charlotte's supposed to drink on all of the pain medication she's on. Just getting in and out of the house is difficult. And Mia will need to go to bed soon." Mia squirmed in Lottie's lap, rooting against her shirt with puckered lips.

"Oh, right. Sorry," Sally said. She looked disappointed. I realized that Sally was another Lottie fan. My sister had collected admirers her whole life like other people collected stamps or knickknacks.

"You could go, Franci," Lottie said.

"I don't think so. I have to be here to help you," I said, wanting to let Sally off the hook. She wanted Lottie, not me.

"Whit's coming over to help," Lottie said.

"He is?" I felt a flutter in my stomach that I didn't want to identify. "You didn't tell me that."

Lottie shrugged. "We talked this morning before I left the hospital. He said he'd come over tonight."

"Did he say he was coming over to help with Mia?"

"Well, no, not explicitly. But what else does he think he's coming over for? You should go, Franci." Lottie brought Mia's fist to her mouth and kissed it. "Are you hungry, baby?" she asked Mia.

"So, what do you think?" Sally asked without enthusiasm. "Drinks around eight?"

"I don't think so," I said. "I'm pretty tired. It's been a long couple of days."

"Oh, go on, Franci," Lottie said. "Whit and I don't need a chaperone. We'll be fine."

Sally looked at me expectantly. I knew the only reason Lottie wanted me to go was so she could be alone with Whit. Much as I didn't want to go to a bar with a near stranger, I had no interest in staying home with Whit and Lottie.

"Okay, I guess so."

"Great." Sally stood up from the couch. "I'll come by around eight. See you then." After the door slammed behind her, I turned to Lottie.

"What on earth are we going to talk about?" We both looked down at Mia who'd snatched the rattle from Lottie's hands and was shaking it in jerky motions.

"She's nice. Young, but nice." Lottie shrugged. "You'll spend the whole time talking about me." I looked away guiltily because she was probably right.

"God, I can't even remember the last time I went out for a drink," I said. "Actually, that's not true. It was in October. The weekend of Mark's high school reunion."

"You need to get out more, Franci," Lottie said.

"I know." I sighed. "So Whit's coming over tonight."

"Yup." Lottie looked at me, waiting for me to go on. I faked a yawn.

"I'm going to go lie down for a little while. Will you two be okay here if I bring you a bottle?"

"Sure," Lottie said.

I prepared the bottle and brought it to them. I felt Lottie's eyes on me, waiting for me to tell her about Whit, to identify the chord of tension that jangled between us. I kept my eyes on Mia, the bottle, the brightly colored rattle that she clutched in her chubby fist. I focused on anything other than my sister's eyes, which had always been able to root out the truth.

Lottie

I stared down at Mia where she slept beside me on the couch. Her lips were parted slightly, the milk-scented breath seeping from her tiny mouth. Watching her sleep filled me with so many emotions. A black anger at myself. A jagged red streak of love. The gleaming silver of guilt. The pink hope of possibility. All tinged by the yellow pallor of fear.

"Maybe we'll be okay," I whispered to her. If I moved too quickly, I was jarred by the pain in my arm or the heaviness of my head, a sharp-toothed reminder of just a few days earlier. But if I stayed very still, I could still see the pink edges, and it was this that I held on to. "Maybe Whit will stay with us."

I'd seen Franci's face when I told her Whit was coming over. It was pity and judgment all rolled into one, the same expression my sister wore during 90 percent of her interactions with me. *Give it up,* the expression said. *Let it go, Lottie.*

But how do I let go when he might be our only chance? How do you let go when you thought you were alone in the middle of the ocean and someone throws you a life preserver? Even if you jumped overboard yourself, even if you were trying to drown, how do you not breathe in the sweet taste of oxygen if you accidentally break the surface?

Franci

I was standing by my open suitcase, looking down at the browns and grays of my wardrobe, when Lottie shuffled into the bedroom. She peered into my bag. "Are you trying to find something for tonight?"

"I'll probably just wear what I have on." I was wearing jeans and a zip-up black sweater that was rumpled from napping.

"Let me dress you," Lottie said, a slow grin coming over her face.

I thought back to the night Whit came over and the white sundress of Lottie's that I'd worn. I shook my head quickly. "No, that's okay."

"Come on, I promise I won't pick anything outrageous. I'll make you look like the best version of yourself."

"Like you?" I asked, smiling in spite of myself.

"Exactly!" Lottie laughed. "Come on, sit down. I'll find something perfect for you. It's a swanky bar; you'll want to look nice." I let Lottie lead me to the bed before she hobbled over to her closet.

Fifteen minutes later I was wearing a simple black sheath dress with a red silk scarf draped around my neck. Lottie picked out a pair of chunky black heels that made my feet ache within a few minutes, but I kept them on anyway. I let her do my makeup, and she spent extra time lining my eyelids and putting on a mouthful of bright red lipstick.

When she was finished, she brought me over to the full-length mirror in her room.

"See? You look beautiful." We both stared at my reflection. In the outfit that Lottie had chosen for me, I looked confident and sure of myself. Lottie, in her flannel pajama pants and wraparound sweater, looked more like me. "You should dress like this more often."

"Where? To playdates and school drop-off?"

"Sure, why not?" Lottie sat down on the bed. Even as I laughed at the idea, I realized that there were other mothers who dressed up every day, even mothers like me who didn't have jobs to go to after the bell rang. I'd always silently mocked these women, as if not spending any time on my appearance made me superior to them. "There's nothing wrong with standing out," Lottie continued. "It's okay to dress in a way that makes people notice you."

"I'm just not comfortable like this."

"But why not?"

"I don't know. I feel like I'm trying too hard."

"But what's wrong with trying?" Lottie asked. She met my eyes in the mirror and looked truly puzzled. Trying meant that it might not work. Someone could whisper behind my back, someone else might stare, another could laugh. No one stared and laughed when you wore jeans and sneakers and sweaters every day. Besides, for as long as I could remember, Lottie had been the one who stood out, and I'd been the one who faded into the background. I couldn't imagine being any other way.

I sat on the bed beside Lottie, out of eyeshot of the mirror. "How are you feeling?" I asked instead of answering her question.

"Okay. My arm aches, but I just took some of the pain medication they gave me."

"Will you be okay with Mia tonight?"

"She's already down for the night. I'll be fine." Her voice was firm.

"When's Whit coming over?"

"Soon. He called to say he was on his way." She rubbed the plaster of her cast absently. "I kind of hoped Mia would still be awake so he could spend some time with her," she admitted.

"Lottie." My voice held an unspoken warning.

"What?" She caught my eye. "We have a history, Franci."

"I know you do. I just don't want you to get your hopes up." I paused, trying to choose my next words carefully. "He didn't want a baby with you, Lottie. Nothing's changed," I said gently.

She turned away from me and pushed herself off the bed. "A lot has changed. I almost died. Mia is here. He *met* her. That's different from just talking about some theoretical baby."

"I don't think it is for Whit." I stood up from the bed as well, and in the heels I was nearly two inches taller than Lottie.

"And what do you know about it, Franci? What do you know about Whit?" she asked, and there was a strange expression on her face.

"Nothing." I looked down at my feet in Lottie's shoes.

"Are you sure?" Her eyes were narrowed, and a malicious smile played at her lips. She knew. Whether Whit had told her or she'd discerned what had happened, she knew about the other night. "It seems like you really understand him. You guys must have gotten awful close over the years. All that time, trying to keep me from going crazy." Her words were daggers, laced with sarcasm and accusation.

"I don't. We're not," I insisted.

Lottie was silent for a moment as she held my gaze, and I wondered if she was going to ask me directly about what had happened. But when she spoke again, her tone had softened slightly. "In that case, don't pretend to know what he wants or doesn't want. It wasn't so long ago that he wanted me."

From the hallway we heard the sound of the doorbell ringing. "My date or yours?" Lottie asked, and her voice had gone light again. She began to make her way to the front door but then turned around. "Franci?"

"Yeah?"

"Now we're even." Her face was expressionless.

"What? What do you mean?" Even now, I was still feigning innocence.

"An eye for an eye," she said and raised her eyebrows at me.

It was what our mother used to say when we'd argue as kids except Lottie had left off the rest of the expression. *An eye for an eye leaves the whole world blind,* Mother would say as she smoothed back our hair and gathered us in her lap. Were we even now? An almost-night with your lover for the almost-life of my child? The exchange didn't seem equal. But I remembered Whit's fingers on my hips, across my belly, his mouth on mine, and my skin crawled with shame.

I nodded at Lottie without answering, and she stared at me for a moment longer before leaving the room. I stayed immobile on the bed. My heart was beating so fast, and I brought both of my hands up to my chest as if I could quell the angry drumbeat. Out in the hallway Lottie and Sally were talking, and I finally stood up and smoothed the skirt, staring back at my reflection.

If I didn't know better, I would have sworn I was looking at my sister.

Franci

When I'd finally left Lottie's bedroom, I enjoyed the click of the high heels against the wooden floor. Just the sound alone was enough to make me feel sexy. But it only lasted a moment. Sally stood in the hall in jeans and a black turtleneck sweater.

"Wow," Sally said. "You look great." She stared at me, taking in the outfit and the makeup, and I found myself unconsciously fingering my lips in an effort to wipe away some of the red lipstick.

"I dressed her up," Lottie said, flashing an insincere smile, as if I were a doll or a child in a Halloween costume, and I wondered if I'd been the butt of her joke all along.

A few minutes later, Sally and I slid into a plush red booth at a nearby bar. The waitresses carried trays piled high with delicate glasses in all sizes and colors. I reviewed the drink list that was filled with cocktails I'd never heard of and settled on something called a black-cherry fizz, only because I could identify all of the ingredients.

The waitress brought my drink in an oversized martini glass and Sally's mojito. It was sweet and tart and would be easy to drink too many. Now that we were here, I didn't know what to say. I felt awkward and old around Sally, but she seemed unfazed.

"Have you lived next door to Charlotte for a long time?" I asked.

"Just a year. But I knew her from school before that. I took a class with her my freshman year."

"Oh, really? Did you like it?"

"Well, it was a requirement." She shrugged sheepishly. "I'm not really much of an English student; I'm a nutrition major. But Charlotte is an amazing professor, and her classes always fill up fast. She gives a creative writing assignment for the final, which is kind of unorthodox."

I sipped at my drink, enjoying the sugary burst of sweetness. "What else is she like?"

"Charlotte? She's your sister. I'm sure you know her a lot better than I do." Sally shifted uncomfortably in her chair and looked around. She waved to someone across the room, a handsome guy at the bar. He tilted his head slightly to Sally, inviting her over. She shook her head, just a tiny shake indicating no.

"I'm too close to her. I'm not objective," I said.

"I don't know. She's great." Sally chewed on her straw, stalling.

"I just need to know what she's been like since Mia came along." Until I started talking, I hadn't realized I was going to bring this up with Sally, but now that I'd begun, I realized it was why I'd agreed to a drink in the first place. "I know you care about Charlotte and don't want to talk about her behind her back. I understand that, I just need to make sure Mia's safe with her."

"Safe?" Sally looked sharply at me. "What do you mean?"

I looked down into my drink and stabbed one of the black cherries with a straw. I hated this part. It wasn't right to share Lottie's business, but I didn't see how I could avoid it.

"She has bipolar disorder." Sally frowned and I continued. "She suffers from extreme depression and mania when she's not taking medication."

"Oh. I didn't know." She leaned back in her chair, absorbing the information.

I nodded. "She doesn't tell many people. I don't know what she's been like since Mia came along. I was just hoping you could fill me in a little."

Sally shrugged. "She's . . . intense. And fun. And moody. But that's who Charlotte is. I never realized she was . . . unwell."

"She's not, most of the time." I leaned forward in the seat. The backs of my legs stuck to the leather cushion of the booth, and I slipped my feet from the tight heels. "What do you mean, 'moody'?"

"She can be hot and cold. Some days I'll see her and she's friendly and warm, asking about school, talking about Mia. She'll be really interested. And then other times I see her and it's like we hardly know each other." Sally shrugged. "I don't take it personally. I just figured she's kind of moody."

The word was so weak and lukewarm for Lottie.

"What about with Mia? Does she seem like a good mother?"

Sally stirred her drink with the straw. She took a long time to answer. I could almost see her realizing that this drink with the neighbor's sister had been a bad idea. She looked longingly at the boy at the bar, most likely wishing desperately that he and I would switch places.

"I don't know. I guess. I've always thought so."

"Please. I need to know."

"Why?" She directed the question at the bottom of the drink, not at me.

"Because I need to know if my sister can take care of Mia. I need to know if I can leave Mia here with her."

"She's Charlotte's daughter; you can't just take her away," Sally said, and she suddenly seemed angry.

"I don't want to take her away. But I need to know if Lottie can take care of her. Can she?" I asked.

Sally sighed and looked up from her drink. "It's not easy. Anyone could tell that. I've seen her stressed out and tired. But why wouldn't she be? She's a single mom, trying the best she can." She'd begun to tear a cocktail napkin to pieces, white flecks of paper gathering on the table.

"Is she neglectful?" I asked, pressing.

"Neglectful?" Sally's eyebrows rose as she repeated the word. "No," she said firmly. "I mean, a few times I babysat and there wasn't a ton of food in the fridge, but Mia's only drinking milk anyway, and Charlotte always makes sure there's plenty of breast milk or formula for when I watch Mia. Lately . . ." She gestured vaguely with her hand. "I mean, you saw, the place had become a mess, but that was just in the past week or so. It doesn't usually look like that." She shrugged. "Charlotte's used to living alone. I think she's still figuring out how to adapt to having a kid in her life." She looked up from the table and locked eyes with me. "She *loves* Mia, more than anything. Neglectful? No."

Sally swept the shreds of paper into her palm and rolled them up in another napkin. She turned her body slightly away from me as she did this, just enough to signal that she didn't want to talk about it anymore.

"So earlier I mentioned helping out with Lottie over the next few weeks, while she's getting over her injuries. Are you up for that? Maybe in the mornings you could come over and help her and Mia get ready? We can work out the payment," I said.

"Of course." Sally looked grateful that the conversation appeared to be almost over. But I wasn't finished.

"And then later, once Lottie's injuries are healed—do you think you could check in with me every week or so just to let me know how she's doing? And that Mia is all right?" I hated to ask her. She looked like a child being asked to tattle on a parent. "It doesn't have to be a big deal. Just a quick phone call or an e-mail or text, even," I said.

"I don't know. That feels kind of weird, going behind Charlotte's back like that." There was a pained expression on her face.

"It doesn't have to be behind her back. I'll tell her." Lottie would hate it and would argue, but in the end she'd have no choice.

"Well, as long as Charlotte knows . . ." She chewed on her lower lip, considering the arrangement. "I guess that would be okay."

"Great. Thank you. It means a lot to me." The boy at the bar was looking at Sally again. He was nearly done with his drink. I finished mine in one quick swallow and stood up from the table. "I have to use the restroom; I'll be right back."

In the bathroom I looked at my reflection in the mirror. I didn't look at all like Lottie. She had applied the makeup with a much heavier hand than she used on her own face. My eyes were too dark, and the bright lipstick looked garish. I bent over the sink and washed the makeup away. I looked at my clear reflection in the mirror as the black and red remains of the clownish face slid down the silver pipes. I was myself again.

Sally's friend had joined her at the table. He was perched on the edge of the booth, close enough that his legs pressed against hers, and I noticed he'd brought over another mojito. When they saw me, Sally pulled back, turning to the young man.

"I'm going to head back," I said before she could introduce us. Relief and surprise rinsed Sally's face, but she quickly positioned her features into an expression of regret.

"Oh, are you sure?"

I nodded. "I should make sure Charlotte's okay." I stood up. The bar was hot and stuffy, and I was ready to leave.

"Are you okay walking home on your own?" Sally asked half-heartedly.

"I'm fine, fine," I mumbled, and then I was making my way through the crowded bar and pushing the heavy doors open, releasing myself into the cool evening air.

Though it was nearly nine, College Avenue was still busy with street vendors and performers. A man stood on the corner in front of a burrito place, singing opera. He was young, probably in his late teens or early twenties, yet his voice gave him the illusion of someone much older. I stopped for a moment to listen to the haunting words that the man sang in Italian. I wondered if he lived around here or if he slept on a nearby street, tucked into the alcove of a doorway. There were times when I missed living in the city. My own neighborhood bustled with baby strollers and dog walkers, not musicians. I didn't miss the panhandlers that lined the street, straggly-haired and desperate, holding cardboard signs that asked for help in black Sharpie letters. If I lived here, it would only be a matter of time before these people became invisible, blending into the scenery of restaurants and boutiques, as common to city life as traffic or pollution. Boston was no different, though at least here the winters were mild and people didn't freeze to death overnight. They would wake again tomorrow to the same uncaring world as today.

The musician's voice surged over the squeal of cars, and I recalled one of the first times Lottie and I walked this street during the first month of our freshman year at Berkeley. It was before Lottie's first episode, before our roles were irrevocably reversed. We'd bought our textbooks and a bunch of paperback novels, reluctantly shelling out several hundred dollars. Our backpacks were full, and we each carried an additional sturdy plastic bag. Though I'd balked at the cost, I felt a secret thrill buying the books, secure in the belief that all of the knowledge they held would be imparted to me by winter break.

As we walked back toward campus, we came upon a man in his midtwenties, though at the time he seemed old to us, gently strumming a guitar and singing Bob Dylan's "The Times They Are A-Changin'," and I cynically recognized the man as a cliché of Berkeley. I kept walking but Lottie stopped, resting her bag of books on the sidewalk beside her. She began to tap her foot lightly with the slow beat and sway side to side.

I watched as the singer noticed Lottie in the small crowd of only five or six people that had gathered around him. The corners of his lips turned up in a smile, and his voice grew a little stronger and surer as he sang. And then Lottie began to sing along.

She'd always had a good voice, and she was a confident singer after the many high school productions. Her voice was gentle but strong, and as she sang, she moved closer to the young man. We'd later find out that his name was Lloyd, and he had studied music at Berkeley for two years before dropping out. I'd learn through Lottie that Lloyd was twenty-four and worked as a busser in a four-star restaurant. But for this moment he was just a stranger singing on the street.

Their voices balanced well and, though I knew little about music, even I could tell that they were good together. Pretty soon a slightly larger crowd had pooled around them, and they moved seamlessly into a Joni Mitchell song. It was a song I'd heard before, enough times to recognize it, but I was surprised that Lottie knew all of the words. As they sang, I became aware of the smooth angles in Lloyd's face, his full pouting mouth, his delicate long eyelashes and startling green eyes. I noticed the thick knuckles and veins in his hands and the defined muscles of his forearms. None of these things had I noticed until Lottie began to sing with him.

My back ached with the books that I carried, and as the crowd started clapping and Lottie and Lloyd began to talk, I felt a sinking disappointment as I accurately predicted what the next few moments and then hours would hold.

Lottie and Lloyd would go somewhere—for coffee or lunch or a drink, and I would walk back to the dorm room, likely carrying Lottie's bag of books as well as my own. I'd spend the rest of the evening reading my textbooks alone, and while this had held a thrill just minutes earlier, it would now be tinged with defeat. I'd stay in the room all night, only leaving to eat dinner in the dining hall. Back in our room, I'd study some more, trying to stay awake as long as possible, even though I knew that Lottie wouldn't be home for hours. Eventually I'd fall asleep, waking in the middle of the night to turn off the reading lamp.

Lottie would come into the room as the purple light of dawn was creeping through the plastic blinds, and her keys would jingle as she entered. She'd bump her knee on the corner of the extra-long bed, and she'd smell of cigarettes and beer and the musky aroma of sex. I would want to sleep through all of it, but I'd wake anyway, ask Lottie about her night, about Lloyd, and she would tell me everything.

The evening lay before me in all its predictable emptiness. When Lottie came to ask if I minded going back to the dorm alone because Lloyd was going to show her the best falafel place in town, I didn't bat an eye, only offered to carry home my sister's books.

I thought of this now as I watched the opera singer. Briefly I wondered what had happened to Lloyd. I wondered if he still played music, if he still worked in a restaurant. I felt in the bottom of my purse, and my fingers closed around several sticky coins. But somehow, remembering Lloyd and those lonely weeks that he hung around Lottie like an over-powering perfume, I thought better of it and released the coins back into the bottom of my bag. I walked back to Lottie's house without stopping again.

Lottie

When Franci and Sally left, I went into Mia's room to watch her sleep. After she was born, it became one of the few things that could calm me when I felt my moods shifting. Today I was medicated, but too much so. Between the pain and the mood meds, I could barely connect with my feelings or thoughts. But I knew that without all of the drugs my mind would be stormy, bubbling hotly on the surface.

Even through the dull haze of numbness, I still felt anger at Franci and Whit, for whatever happened between them. He hadn't said anything and I'd never ask, but I could see the guilt written on Franci's face as clear as if she'd told me. There was no need to know the particulars, because who knew what dark and winding path the details would bring me. And if I was honest with myself, there was a certain relief that came with Franci's obvious guilt. At last, I was not the one guilty of hurting someone. At last, I wasn't the bad one. It was a dangerous card that I could keep tucked in my back pocket to withdraw whenever I needed it. Now Franci knew that I had it.

Whit's arrival back in my life filled me with hope. It was something I didn't want to admit, not to Franci and not even to myself. Because I knew that sitting right next to the tiny package labeled "Hope" was a much larger box labeled "Despair." To reach for the first, I had to be willing to reach past the other.

~

When Whit unlocked my front door, I was lying on the couch with a bag of pretzels and a glass of water, unable to prepare a more suitable dinner for myself. He let himself in with his key, the one I'd given him ten years earlier and never asked him to return. I sat up and wiped pretzel crumbs from my lips, wishing I'd been able to dress for him. But with only one working arm and leg, I was stuck in pajama pants.

"How are you doing?" he asked, taking a seat in the chair opposite the couch.

"You can sit here." I shifted, trying to make room. I wanted to feel the weight of his body against me.

"It's okay," Whit said, shaking his head. "You're comfortable. Nice boot." He leaned forward and rapped his knuckles lightly against the plastic of my foot. "How are you feeling?"

"I'm okay." I suddenly felt shy around him, this man who had seen me naked more times than I could count, who'd seen me in my darkest and most vulnerable moments. Though he'd come to visit me in the hospital, this felt different. Without the bustle of the hospital around us, there was nothing to concentrate on but each other. "It's good to see you."

"You too."

"How have you been?"

"Good." He sat with his hands splayed over his knees, a large man with a large presence, unsure what to do with his body in this overly familiar room. "Busy, but good."

"Me too." I smiled at him.

"Yeah, I'll bet." He looked around the room. "Where is she?"

"She's sleeping. Do you want to go see her? She's beautiful when she sleeps."

"That's okay. I got to see her in the hospital." As if once was all he needed. I reached for a pretzel to avoid his gaze. "How's it going with her?"

"What do you mean?" When I looked up, there was a stiff and pained expression on his face, and I could see how hard this was for him. Being here, talking about Mia, acting as if this were all normal.

"How's . . . motherhood?"

My eyes filled with tears at the question; it was a simple question with a complicated answer. For any woman, this would have been true. For me, it was true a hundredfold. "Great," I said simply.

"Good."

I went back to focusing on the bowl of pretzels. The conversation was unbearable.

"It means *mine*," I told him.

"What?"

"Mia's name. It means *mine*."

"Oh." He stood up from the chair and came to sit beside me on the couch. I shifted my good leg to the floor and rested the boot in his lap.

"I didn't want her to belong to anyone but me," I told him. "Partly because I was angry with you. But also because when she was born, she was all I had."

"And now?"

"Now? I don't know now." I closed my eyes and took a deep breath. "I'm afraid Franci will try to take her from me." We hadn't spoken about it since she arrived in California, but we both knew how carefully she was watching me, assessing what damage I was capable of.

"Should she?" His voice was even and without judgment, as always.

"*No.* She's my daughter. She belongs with me. I take care of her." His hand rested on the plaster cast, and I longed to feel the warmth of his fingers against my skin. I reached for his other hand and squeezed it. He let me, but he didn't squeeze back. "I've missed you."

"I've missed you too." I ignored the note of sadness in his voice, the echo that said it was too late.

"Are you seeing anyone?"

He shook his head.

"That's good."

"No, Charlotte, it's not," he said loudly. "It's not good at all."

I was silent, his hand limp in mine.

"Are you sure you don't want to see Mia?" I blinked back tears, hating the pleading tone in my voice.

He pulled his hand away, bringing it up to cover his eyes. "I can't do this, Charlotte."

"Why not?" I asked. "It's not too late, Whit. I know you still love me."

He took his hand from his eyes and turned to look at me. "You're right; I do." He looked tired, his eyes bloodshot, several days' worth of stubble on his face.

"We can do this together. She's only five months; we'll change her name. We'll use a baby-name dictionary and find one that means *ours*," I joked desperately.

"Charlotte, don't you get it? Don't you get it?" He was nearly yelling, and I looked anxiously toward the hallway leading to Mia's room, where she slept soundly. "I can't do this with you. I can't watch you hurt that child. I can't watch the damage you will inflict upon her."

I was crying silently, the tears making their way down my cheeks. "I won't," I promised. "This is different. I'll do whatever I have to. I'll do whatever you want." I reached for his hand, but he pulled away.

"I wanted *you*, Charlotte, just you, even with all of the complications that that meant. But I can't do this with you." Whit's eyes were bright with tears. "You make promises that you can't keep. It will happen, Charlotte; don't you get it? It *will* happen." He shook his head, in sadness, or resignation, or years' worth of disgust. "You'll hurt her over and over, and I'll come to despise you for it." He paused for a breath. "I think Franci may be right."

Something sharp snapped inside of me. "Get out," I ordered, struggling to sit up. "Get out of my house. You have no right," I shrieked at him. "Do you hear me, you have *no right!*" Tears ran down my face, but my heart was blazing with anger. "You stay away from my daughter,

Whit, and you stay away from my sister. Do you hear me? *Get out* of my house." Whit was already standing, shaking his head sadly at where I was huddled on the couch.

"I'm sorry, Charlotte. I wish it didn't have to be this way."

"Get out!" I yelled and reached for the glass of water on the table. I hurled it at him where he stood in the doorway. It missed him by over a foot, and he stood for another minute, looking at the shards of glass and water all over the hallway floor. I knew he was thinking about going into the kitchen closet and getting a broom to clean the mess up. And I hated him for it. "Stop taking care of me!" I screamed. He stood for one more minute before letting himself out the front door.

Down the hall Mia began to wail, but her cries were not as loud as my own.

When Franci arrived home, I was already in bed, depleted and wrung out from Whit's visit and getting Mia back to sleep. Franci tiptoed into the room, crawling in beside me. In the dark, I murmured a greeting, enough to signal that I was still awake.

"Did you have a nice time with Whit?" she asked.

"It was fine," I said after a moment. "Did you have fun with Sally?"

"It was okay." Outside I could hear cars passing, the honk of a horn, a car alarm going off—the sounds of the city at night. "I was thinking we could go visit Dad tomorrow," Franci said. "Have you been to see him recently?"

"Every Thursday."

"Does he recognize you when you visit?"

I shifted in bed beside her, unable to find a position that was comfortable with the cast on my arm. "Sort of. I mean, he recognizes me, but usually he doesn't know if I'm me or you or Mother. When I take Mia with me, he thinks she's one of us. He keeps asking where her sister is."

"It's good of you to visit him every week. I'm sure it's not easy."

"How could I not? He's the only family we have." Down the hall Mia let out a little cry, and we both went still, waiting to see if she would wake fully. There were no more sounds, and I felt Franci relax beside me.

"When are you going to go back to work?" I asked. It was partly to change the subject, but I'd wanted to talk to Franci about this for a long time.

"What do you mean?"

"I mean, the girls are, what, almost six now? Are you ever going to go back to work?"

"I don't know." Her voice was small in the darkness.

"What do you mean, you don't know?"

"I don't know. I don't know what I want to be when I grow up." She laughed, but her words were tinged with sadness.

"I thought you liked teaching."

"I did. And then I didn't." Her voice was suddenly thick with tears.

"What happened?" Beside me Franci shook her head on the pillow. "Franci? What happened?"

"There was a girl," she said finally. I waited for her to go on. "Her name was Caitlin. She killed herself."

"I'm sorry, Franci. That's awful."

"I should have been able to stop her," Franci continued. "She wrote something in my class. It showed she was depressed, that she was think-ing about suicide. I didn't read it until it was too late." I could tell she was crying quietly, and I reached out a hand to wipe the tears from her cheeks. Franci pressed closer to me. "I could have stopped her."

"Franci, you don't know that. It wasn't your fault."

"I should have reached out to her. I had a chance, and I didn't."

"You don't know that would have changed anything," I said.

"But it might have," she whispered. "I just don't see how I could go back into the classroom after that."

We were quiet again. We both lay on our backs and stared at the shadows on the ceiling as we spoke. Outside, Sally's porch light went on, the motion sensors indicating her arrival. Her keys jingled against the door, and I heard hushed voices before the door closed.

"So don't be a teacher," I said after a few minutes. "There are lots of things you could do."

"Like what?" I could tell that she really didn't know. My baby sister, still so unsure of herself at the bottom of it all.

"You could go back to your art. You were really good."

"I loved taking art classes in college. But it was the idea of being an artist that I liked more than anything."

"There are lots of jobs you can do with art skills, though," I persisted.

"Like what?"

"Graphic design or web design. Or portraits. You were so good at those. I bet lots of parents would pay to have portraits done of their kids."

"Mmm," she murmured noncommittally. "Maybe."

Down the hall, Mia let out another wail, and this time she kept going.

"I'll get her," Franci said, rising from the bed. I heard her in the kitchen making a bottle, and then in Mia's room, cooing softly as she lowered the side of the crib. A minute later, they were both back in my bed, Mia cradled in Franci's arms, sucking away on a bottle. Franci placed her between us, and I leaned down to kiss Mia's smooth cheek and inhale the smell of her skin.

"Are you going to take her away from me?" I asked.

"Should I?" she asked without answering.

"Franci, I love her."

"I know you do."

"I wanted her so much," I whispered. "I sacrificed everything for her."

"Do you regret it?"

"No. But I'm scared. Of how I'm going to fuck it up." I held Mia's tiny hand in mine. "Because we both know I will." We lay in the darkness and listened to the rhythmic sounds of Mia's sucking. When she was finished, Franci rose from the bed and carried my sleeping girl back to her crib.

In the morning we drove down to Palo Alto to see our father. He'd been in the nursing home for nearly three years. After he'd been diagnosed with Alzheimer's, Franci and I argued over whether he could continue to live on his own. I'd been stopping by his place every night, each time terrified by what I might find. I took his car keys away from him, though this was more frustrating for him than demeaning. He'd often spend minutes, maybe even hours, trying to find them, assuming he'd just misplaced them somewhere. I'd find jobs half-done—clothes and detergent in the open washing machine, eggs and orange juice still on the counter at six o'clock at night, the shower still running. One evening I arrived to find the burner on the kitchen stove lit; it was hard to tell how long it had been on, but the kitchen held the tangy scent of gas.

I visited him each week and he told me stories, reminding me of events I only half recalled. I was always amazed at how carefully these memories were preserved, as if they'd been canned and pickled, left in clear glass jars in the basement of his brain.

I knew he was deteriorating, but it wasn't until three years ago, on the night I couldn't find him, that we decided to put him in a home. On that particular Thursday, the front door was ajar and no one was home. I wandered through the condo calling for him, but it was empty. I returned to the hallway of the building, scanning the narrow corridor. When I rushed to the parking lot outside, I found his car parked in its usual spot, where it had been since I'd confiscated the keys months earlier.

He'd retired from Stanford nearly ten years earlier, but he lived only a few blocks from campus and would often stroll the grounds on his morning walk. It was getting dark, nearing eight o'clock, and it had started to rain. I quickly made the walk to campus.

I found him sitting on the front steps of the building of his former office. His short-sleeved polo shirt was drenched through, and he wore slippers on his feet. When I went to him, pulling gently on his arm, he looked at me with a blank expression for several minutes before his face took on any sort of recognition.

I guided him home, holding his hand as if he were a small child. I made dinner, turned the television on for him, and called Franci.

"Mark's found a nursing home in Belmont for Dad," she told me that night. "It specializes in Alzheimer's. We put him on the wait list a few months ago, but it's perfect timing—they have a bed that just opened."

"You mean someone just died," I said.

"What?"

"When a bed 'opens up' in a nursing home, it means someone just died." Franci didn't say anything. "I'm just saying." I shrugged, though she couldn't see the gesture. "Okay," I relented. "Belmont's pretty close to Palo Alto, so it won't be too hard to move him." In the other room the music of *Jeopardy!* was playing, and now and then my father would mumble an answer.

"Not Belmont, California." I felt the tension in her voice. "Belmont, Massachusetts." *Fuck you, Franci,* I thought to myself but managed not to speak the words aloud. "It's very close to us. We could visit a few times a week."

"*I* can't visit him a few times a week," I pointed out.

"I meant me and Mark. And the girls."

"Are you kidding me, Franci? Why not a place out here?" I asked. "Wouldn't that make a hell of a lot more sense? Rather than uprooting him and moving him all the way across the country? It's going to be a big enough adjustment for him as it is."

"I hardly see how it matters," Franci said. "He can barely keep track of where he is now. It's only going to get worse."

"Franci, why on earth would you want to move him all the way out there?" I asked.

"I'd like to be able to see him more often," she said in a small voice. For a moment I entertained the idea, but then she kept talking. "And Mark and I are going to be the ones paying for it."

"If that's what this is about, I'll figure out a way to pay half."

"You don't need to; that's not what I'm saying. I just . . . I think we should get some say in this."

But I wasn't going to back down that easily. Franci might have been paying for the nursing home, but our father wasn't a fancy car or an expensive toy.

"Eighteen seventy-three!" he yelled from the other room. "Charlotte, come in here. It's nearly time for Final Jeopardy!"

"I'll be there in a minute, Dad," I called back. "No," I said into the phone.

"What do you mean, 'no'?"

"I mean no. We are not moving him out there. I refuse. He's lived nearly his whole life in California. This is his home."

"You're being melodramatic. He can't even remember where his home is."

"Don't call me melodramatic," I said through clenched teeth. "You chose to leave here. He did not. I'm not moving him."

We were silent for a long minute on the line as Franci weighed my words. "Fine," she said. "Look into nursing homes out there. We'll see if we can find something else."

And so our father moved into the Pine Ridge Home in Palo Alto. He'd been there for over a year when I became pregnant with Mia. By then, his memory was truly failing. Each time I went to see him, my belly bigger than the week before, I'd have to remind him I was having a baby. I knew that Franci called him each week, and I secretly hoped our father would mention my pregnancy to her. But he never did, or if he did, not in a way that made any sense to her.

Franci

The Pine Ridge Home was a nice facility as far as nursing homes went. There were manicured green lawns with paved paths you could push a wheelchair down. There was a garden of bright flowers and an aviary that overlooked the grounds. The nurses were competent and relatively cheerful, and the rooms looked more like bedrooms than hospital rooms. But as we made our way toward our father's room, the hallway still carried the sour smells of urine, cafeteria food, and disinfectant. Many of the patients appeared nearly comatose, lying immobile in beds as they stared vacantly at television screens or sleeping away most of the afternoon.

I walked slowly, wanting to delay the arrival at our father's room. We'd gone during my last visit in April, and I'd brought the girls. The place had visibly scared them, and they'd cowered in the corner with a coloring book while my father tried to figure out who we all were. It was the part of every visit that I dreaded, and I hated myself for it.

When we arrived, I stood anxiously by the door with Mia, but Lottie hobbled inside.

"Hi, Dad," she said, and I followed her.

Our father lay on top of the covers, fully dressed with his shoes on. He read a medical magazine, holding the page close to his face, despite the fact that he was wearing his glasses. When we came into the room, it took him a moment to tear his eyes from the page. He looked older than when I'd last seen him, but it wasn't the aging that was jarring to see. It was the absence of expression on his face.

"Hello," he said, eyes moving from Lottie to me to Mia and then back to Lottie again. "Hello," he repeated.

"Dad, it's Charlotte and Franci. And your granddaughter Mia." Lottie took a seat on the edge of his bed.

"Hello. Hello." He didn't comment on Lottie's injuries.

"Hi, Dad," I said, stepping forward. I leaned in and gave him a kiss on the cheek, his untrimmed beard prickly against my lips. He grasped my hand, and I was surprised by how tight his grip was.

"Katherine," he said. Katherine was our mother.

"No, Dad, I'm Franci." I blinked back tears, having forgotten how difficult it always was to see him, each time worse than the last.

"Katherine?" His brows were drawn together in a look of permanent confusion.

"*Franci,*" I said, trying to smile at him. He released my hand and leaned back on the pillow, his interest in me gone as quickly as it had come.

"Franci, why don't you and Dad take a walk outside," Lottie suggested. "Mia and I will wait here."

"Oh, I don't know." I hated that my own father filled me with such discomfort, but I wasn't used to seeing him like this. Though I called every week, my phone calls were short and perfunctory, obligations that lasted less than five minutes and consisted of me talking without stopping until I finally signed off. On more than one occasion, one of the nurses got on to inform me that he was ready to rest, and I'd wonder how long I'd been talking to an empty phone line.

"Go on," Lottie urged. "He likes to be in the sun."

"Okay. Come on, Dad." I settled Mia on the edge of the bed with Lottie and then helped my father up. We found his coat hanging on the door, and once he was wearing it, he was surprisingly able, not needing me for support, able to walk easily on his own. Despite his failing mind, he was only seventy.

Outside the sun was bright and the air crisp. We walked along the stony path, past a man-made lake, and then paused to rest on a bench. My father had barely spoken since we'd come outside, but he turned to me now.

"Today is March eighteenth," he said solemnly. March 18 was the anniversary of Mother's death, a day that had been marked with silence during the last year that Lottie and I lived at home. Today's date was actually February 12, but I didn't correct him. "You left me so early, Kath." He shook his head, his wrinkled brow folding into creases. "You should have talked to me. You should have told me how unhappy you were." I felt a ripple go through me, as if I'd stumbled into my parents' bedroom in the middle of some intimate act.

"Dad," I said, but he waved his hand, commanding me to be quiet.

"The girls never got over it," he continued. "You should have talked to me. Maybe I could have helped."

"Daddy," I interrupted, tugging gently on his arm. I felt six years old. "Daddy, I'm Franci, not Mother. She's dead, remember? She died a long time ago." My throat was thick with unspent tears.

He looked at me in confusion, finally seeing me, taking in the curve of my face and the shape of my mouth, comparing these features with the memory of his wife. "Franci?" he asked.

"Yes, Daddy, Franci. You remember," I assured him.

"Your mother died," he said sadly.

"Yes. She died. But it was a long time ago." I let my hand rest on the thin cotton of his spring coat.

"I found her," he told me, leaning close as if this were some sort of secret. Our father had gone home for lunch that afternoon. He called the school after the ambulance came to take her away.

"Yes, Daddy, I know. You found her."

"I've never seen anything like that before," he whispered.

"I know, Dad. It must have been terrible."

"I don't know how she got up there." He shook his head in bewilderment.

"What? Up where?" I asked. "The stairs?"

"That part I never understood," he went on. "How did she get on that beam? It was so high up." He peered at me as if I might be able to tell him. Something shivered inside me, and I felt my breath catch in my throat. Puzzle pieces rearranged themselves, shapes swimming into some sort of order, though I still couldn't see the complete picture. My heart beat so quickly that I brought my palm to my chest, trying to still it.

"And the apple on the floor," he continued. "Was she eating before? Why would she eat before doing that?"

"Apple? Dad, what are you talking about?" I asked, trying to pull him back to the present. "Mother fell, remember? She was carrying laundry. She fell down the stairs. Remember how steep they were?"

"The stairs," he repeated, nodding vigorously now, the memory somehow reached. "Yes, the stairs. They were so steep. You're right, I remember." I nodded too, relieved to be back on familiar ground. "We mustn't tell the girls," he said, turning toward me again. His eyes were sad and full of emotion, the weight of Mother's memory and the millions of others glittering along the edges of his consciousness. "I'm tired, Katherine. Let's go back now, okay?"

"Come on, Dad," I said, grateful that my voice sounded normal. I led him toward the building where Lottie waited for us.

In the car on the way home, we were quiet. Mia slept in the backseat, and Lottie looked out the window.

"It must be a shock for you to see him," Lottie finally said, still staring out the window. "I'm used to seeing him like that, but I forget how hard it must be for you." I nodded, but didn't say anything. "Did he think you were Mother?" she asked.

"Yeah." I tightened my grip on the steering wheel.

"These days he usually thinks I'm her too."

"He thought it was March eighteenth," I told her.

She nodded, unsurprised. "Every day is March eighteenth."

"Do you remember it?" I asked, and my voice was almost a whisper.

"I remember everything about that day."

Mother had moods too. They weren't like Lottie's, at least not that I'd ever seen, but she went through bouts when she spent long hours in her bedroom with the shades drawn. "Mother's resting" would be the explanation from our father. What she needed to rest from, we were never quite sure. But during her resting periods, we were instructed not to bother her.

I remember coming home from school, standing outside the bedroom with Lottie and knocking softly on the door. Mother would be dressed, lying under a throw, her arms folded neatly across her lap, a cigarette burning in the overflowing ashtray beside her. Despite our father's tireless work on cancer research, our mother was a smoker her entire life, and in most of my memories of Mother, a thin cigarette burned in a nearby ashtray. A window would be partway open, and the room smelled of fog and smoke. Her bedroom would be cool even on the hottest days, a quiet, dark sanctuary, and Lottie and I would climb onto the bed. We'd lie on opposite sides of Mother, our heads pressed against her as we told her about our day. Mother would stroke our hair and foreheads, murmuring in response, asking a question here and there. Even though she didn't appear to be sick, we knew enough to treat her as if she were, using our best manners and quietest voices. We never quarreled when we were in the bedroom but were more united than ever, often clasping hands across the narrow frame of Mother's body. After an hour or so, it would be time to go.

"Okay, lambs. Mother needs her rest now," she'd say, closing her eyes. "You go fix yourself something to eat. I'll be down soon." We knew she wouldn't. Rarely during her resting periods did she emerge until our father came home. He'd cook dinner and then go into the bedroom, somehow finding a way to rouse her and bring her downstairs to sit with us at the table.

Mother's resting periods were not often, but they were not infrequent, either. They'd usually span a few weeks, two or three times a year, often around the end of fall and again in the bleakest months of February and March. I distinctly remember lying on Mother's bed and the patter of rain on the windows as her fingers spooled around the matted strands of my hair.

The rest of the year, these periods were hard to remember. Usually our mother rose early, before we were awake, and when we'd stagger sleepily down the stairs, she'd already be in the kitchen, a cup of black coffee and a cigarette in hand, a plate of toast with strawberry jam in the center of the table. When we were young, she walked us to school, holding tightly to our hands as we crossed the streets, prattling away about which assignments we'd completed and what books we were reading. As we got older, she kissed us goodbye at the door, double-checking that we'd remembered to bring the sandwich she packed or a pocketful of change for lunch.

In the weeks preceding her death, Mother had been in one of her resting periods. As Lottie and I got older, we no longer lay in bed with her. By then her moods had gotten tiresome and frustrating for us, and when we got home from school, we'd usually just knock on the door and yell, "We're home!" Only rarely did we bother to go inside.

On that morning, I thought she'd surfaced from her resting. When I came into the kitchen for breakfast, she was already there, leaning over a frying pan of scrambled eggs with a spatula in hand.

"Morning, hon," she said brightly, as if she'd done this every morning for the past two weeks. I sat down at the table and tried not to look surprised by the sight of her awake and dressed at this hour.

"Hi," I mumbled, reaching for a piece of toast. Whenever Mother retreated from her resting periods, I found myself acting cold and distant toward her for the first few days. Whether I was punishing her for the weeks she'd been away or protecting myself in case she retreated again, I wasn't sure.

"I'm making eggs," she said, giving the eggs a final stir in the pan.

"I'm not that hungry. Toast is fine." I slouched lower in the chair.

"Have a little. And sit up straight." She spooned the eggs onto my plate, and I sat up, rolling my eyes and sighing dramatically.

"Morning," Lottie said as she bounced into the kitchen.

"You look nice today," she said to Lottie.

"Thanks." She wore a yellow dress with white piping at the sleeves and brown cowboy boots. She'd picked the dress up at a thrift store, and it looked like a waitress's uniform from the 1950s, but somehow Lottie managed to carry it. I knew my mother hated the outfit, and her comment showed how hard she was trying. She put a steaming plate before Lottie.

"Yum. Thanks," Lottie said, and I felt guilty for my sulkiness.

We ate in silence, Mother perched on the edge of her chair, sipping her coffee and fingering an unlit cigarette. She didn't approve of smoking while people were eating, but as soon as we were done, she stacked our plates in the kitchen sink and lit up, taking a long drag off the cigarette as if she'd been waiting ages for it and not just the five minutes it took for us to eat the eggs.

"Do you have busy days?" she asked, as we gathered our bags by the front door.

"I have an in-class essay in English today," Lottie said.

"I have a French test." I hoisted my backpack onto both shoulders.

"Well, good luck to you both. I know you'll do wonderfully." She leaned in to kiss each of us, first on the cheek and then on the mouth, as she hadn't done since we were young. Pulling away, I noticed that her eyes were moist. I felt a wave of frustration and anger at her, certain that when we returned from school that afternoon, she would have retreated to the bedroom for another several weeks. The resting was not over. "I have every confidence that you will succeed in all that you do," she said, holding my chin in her hands.

"Thanks." I looked down at the ground so as not to let my disappointment show. I stared at my mother's white slippers, the furry cotton meeting her curved ankle.

As we let ourselves outside, the screen door banging behind us, I was aware of Mother standing in the doorway, watching us walk down the driveway. I didn't turn back to wave goodbye, though Lottie did.

"That was weird," I said softly when we'd turned down the road.

"I guess she's feeling better," Lottie said, the hope rising in her voice.

"No." I shook my head. "She's faking it. I can tell."

We talked of other things for the rest of the walk to school, how Marty had been ignoring Lottie, and if she should try out at the upcoming audition for *Pippin*. I listened, offering my thoughts when asked, but I was picturing Mother's feet, how sad and forlorn they looked in the graying slippers with their wilting pink bows. It was the last image I would have of her.

"Dad said something," I told Lottie now as I drove. It was the middle of the day, and the traffic on the highway was light. Lottie had put on a CD, something quiet and pretty, a haunting woman's voice melded with a guitar. "He said something about Mother."

"She's all he talks about," Lottie said.

"No, it wasn't just about her," I said. "He was talking about the day she died. When he found her." I swallowed the lump in my throat. "He said he didn't understand how she got on the beam. And something about an apple. Do you know what he meant?" Lottie was silent, still staring out the window, her head leaning against the pane of glass. When she didn't answer, I asked her again, this time more urgently. "What did he mean, Lottie?"

Finally, she took her gaze from the withered yellow fields along the highway and turned to me, and when she did, her expression was filled with such sorrow that I had to look away. "Do you really want to talk about this, Franci? We don't have to." Her voice was kind, protective, and it reminded me of when we were young. I frowned at the road. In some dark recess of my brain, I was already fairly certain where this conversation would lead.

"Tell me," I said.

Lottie sighed. "Okay, then. Pull over at the next rest stop," she ordered. "We can't talk about this while we're driving."

It was another five minutes before we came to a rest stop. Finally, we were parked off the highway by a public restroom and several picnic tables. A family of four was at the table nearest us, and I watched the mother dole out juice boxes to her husband and children. Lottie reached for my hand.

"What do you want to know?" she asked quietly. In the rearview mirror, Mia slept soundly, her flickering eyelids a pale lavender.

"Mother didn't really fall down the stairs, did she?" Lottie shook her head, holding me close in her gaze. "Then how did she die?" My throat was closing in, and tears fell from my eyes. "How did she die, Lottie?" I asked again.

"You already know, don't you? Don't make this worse than it already is."

"Say it," I commanded. "Say it."

Another moment of quiet passed before she spoke.

202

"She hung herself." Somehow Lottie's face was placid and calm as she told me this, the words having lost their power for her over the years. But I felt something inside me crumbling.

"Did you know?" My voice was a high-pitched whisper. "Did you know all along?"

She nodded. "I found her before Dad came home. I never told him. And I didn't want you to know." The weight of her words was like a bag of wet sand pressed into my chest. I thought of my father's words that afternoon, not the babbling of dementia, only memory. *How did she get on that beam? It was so high up. We mustn't tell the girls.*

Our parents' bedroom had a cathedral ceiling with wide wooden beams arching across the room. Mother was there suddenly in my mind's eye, hanging from the beam, attached with a belt, or a piece of rope, or a strip of sheet. Her neck hung at an unnatural angle; her tongue, poking from her mouth, swollen and bright; her feet dangling above the bed, the white slippers threatening to slide off. The image rose up before me so quickly and effortlessly that it was as if it had been there all along, just waiting for me to conjure it up.

I pictured our father arriving home to the scene. It was horrible to think of him standing on the bed to support her body, trying to get the homemade noose off her neck. Even while he worked, crying, sweaty, red-faced, he would have been thinking about the alternate version he'd tell his daughters and the rest of the world. There was a set of steep stairs, a load of laundry, a terrible fall.

I buried my face in Lottie's shoulder and cried.

Lottie

That day, March 18, I'd gone home during lunch. The high school had an open-campus policy for its students, and my friends and I would often walk to the deli on the corner for sandwiches and diet sodas. But on this day, I realized I'd left the notes for my English essay on the desk in our bedroom. I had a study hall after lunch, so I hurried home, eating the cheese and avocado sandwich Mother had packed for me that morning. As I walked the last three blocks, I wondered if she would be up or if she'd be back in bed as Franci had predicted.

The front door was unlocked, and I let myself in, calling out "Hello." Nobody answered, but that didn't mean anything. Our father often came home during lunch, and sometimes he took Mother to one of the restaurants in town. I hurried upstairs to the bedroom I shared with Franci. Both of the beds were made, though I didn't remember making mine that morning. The tight corners and smooth lines of the blanket suggested that my mother had been in here earlier, lining up shoes and throwing dirty tee shirts into a laundry basket. I felt a flash of annoyance at her for this small invasion of privacy, as well as a quivering relief that she'd been motivated enough to clean.

I found the page of notes right where I'd left them the night before, and I placed the page neatly into a folder in my backpack, pulling out an apple for the walk back to school. The door to my parents' room was closed, and I felt a sinking in my chest as I realized she was back in bed. I paused outside the room, debating whether to go in.

"Mother?" I knocked lightly on the door. "I just needed to get something for school. I'm going back now." There was still no answer. I reached for the doorknob, turning it and pushing the door slowly open. Inside it was dim, the lights off and the shades drawn. I didn't open the door all the way, just enough that I could poke my head inside. The air was thick with the familiar smell of menthol. "Mother?" I said again to the dark and silent room.

I didn't really see her. Not completely. At first all I noticed was a slight movement above the bed, a slow swaying, a dark shadow in the muted light, the soft gray of slippers, an overturned chair. I wasn't even certain I recognized the shape for what it was, my eyes taking on a distant, unfocused quality, not really seeing anything in front of me. The apple fell from my hand, hitting the floor with a dull thud, and I became aware that there was a strange sound filling the room, a breathy, high-pitched keening. It took me a moment to realize it was coming from me. I backed slowly out of the room, nearly falling on the landing at the top of the stairs. I left the bedroom door open but didn't look back.

Within seconds I was running down the street back toward the school. My heart banged in my chest with a force that frightened me. By the time I was three blocks from school, I'd begun to walk again, my breath coming in heavy rasps.

It was not real. The farther I walked, the more certain I became. I hadn't seen anything. It was a trick of the eye, bad lighting, a strange shadow thrown by my presence in the doorway. *It was not real. It was not real.* I repeated this to myself so many times over those three blocks that by the time I entered the iron gates of the school yard, I was certain I'd imagined it. I would go to English class, write my essay, and return home at the end of the day where we would find Mother drinking a cup of coffee or making a casserole for dinner. Franci and I would sit at the counter, eating strawberry yogurt, talking about school before going upstairs to do homework until dinner. I could picture the afternoon so clearly, all of the mundane details unfolding, that I couldn't imagine anything else. *It was not real. It was not real.*

I proceeded to study hall, where I miraculously managed to outline my essay, the few moments in the bedroom pushed back into some far corner of my mind, some dark crevice that I would try to never peer in again, though I'd always know that it existed. It would never leave me.

I had just sat down in English class ready to write my essay, the neat page of notes on the desk in front of me, a sharpened number two pencil in hand, when I heard my name over the loudspeaker calling me to Mr. Lombeck's office.

While I waited for Franci, I didn't think about it. The moment had already been sealed up and shut away. But even though I couldn't look at the memory directly, a tiny voice whispered in my ear that Franci must never know. It was my mother's voice, and she spoke to me across a deep abyss. *Don't tell Franci,* she whispered. *She's not strong enough. It is your job to protect her.*

Maybe it wasn't Mother's voice after all. Maybe it was my own desire to protect Franci from the truth. Our whole lives, all I ever wanted was to protect her, since we were placed in the same incubator, two underdeveloped babies breathing as one.

When our father came to tell us Mother fell, I didn't contradict him. I didn't say a word, only nodded numbly beside Franci. I'd seen nothing. Nothing at all. Our mother had fallen down the stairs with a basket of laundry and broke her neck. It was a terrible accident, a freak accident, and I would never disagree. I had not seen a thing.

Franci

"Did she have what you have?" I asked when I was empty of tears. I had often thought about my mother's resting periods, comparing them to Lottie's. I remembered the hush that descended over the house during those times, yet when she was better, the darkness of those days seemed so far away, it was hard to remember them. When she was well, it was easy to believe it would never happen again. Our mother held her sadness close, never letting us see its ugliness, as I had seen Lottie's. While I understood their pain was similar, I hadn't realized how deep my mother's was, how all-consuming it must have been for her to leave us behind.

"I don't know. I don't think so," Lottie answered. "I never saw her manic. I think hers was clinical depression without the mania."

The family at the picnic table was packing up, the mother gathering wrappers and throwing everything in the trash bin. I clutched the leather of the steering wheel tightly in my fists, enjoying the ache in my knuckles.

"We should have helped her," I said. "Dad should have gotten her help. Or we should have. But nobody did anything. We just let her hole up in her bedroom for weeks at a time. How could we do that?" I was nearly shouting, and Mia stirred in the backseat. "Why didn't anyone do anything?" I asked more quietly.

Lottie let a moment pass before she spoke, but when she did, I could tell that she'd thought about the question for a long time herself, for years before I actually asked it out loud.

"It was a different time, Franci. We were just kids; we didn't know what was going on. Mother 'resting' was normal. We didn't even know to question it." Lottie ran her thumb along the plaster of her cast, a new habit she'd acquired in the past few days. "Medication wasn't nearly as common as it is now. And you know Mother," she said with a shake of her head. "I don't think she would have agreed to therapy. And Dad." She gave a sad smile. "He didn't know how to deal with it, and he's blamed himself since she died. Then when I started having . . . problems . . ." Lottie trailed off and sighed. "It was too much, so I've always kept it from him."

"But it's different. She had *children* to care for. How could she have been so selfish?" I asked bitterly.

"I understand why you're so angry with her, Franci. I was too, for a long time," Lottie said patiently. "You can't understand if you've never suffered through it. And then I found myself there. Not wanting to live." She shook her head. "It's not something you come out of through willpower or love. It takes all that away. It's stronger than anything you can imagine." I saw the pain in her eyes as she spoke.

I unclenched my hands from the wheel and flexed my fingers. "Have you thought about it?" I asked, not sure if I really wanted to hear her answer.

"Many times." She let her head rest on her window. "Many, many times." We were silent, both of us staring straight ahead at the squat brick building of the restroom. "I once heard a program on the radio about suicide being contagious," Lottie said after several minutes.

I turned to look at her. Though she wasn't crying, her skin had gone blotchy with emotion, her eyes rimmed pink. I knew if I were to look at my own reflection in the mirror, I would see the same pink-and-white complexion, the same bloodshot eyes. Mirror images.

"What do you mean, 'contagious'?"

Lottie wouldn't look at me, but she kept talking. "Not contagious like the flu, but in the sense that once you know someone who's committed suicide, you may be more likely to do it yourself."

"That's horrible. Why?"

Lottie rubbed the cast with her thumb again. "It's like opening a door. The idea of suicide is so . . . taboo, so awful. But when you've been exposed to it, it loses some of that forbidden quality. It's more likely to feel like an option." She took a deep breath and met my eyes. "At least, that's according to the program I heard. It could be a load of bull, for all I know," she said, trying to take the weight out of what she had just said.

"Is it, for you?" I asked.

"Is what for me?"

"Is it an option?"

Lottie turned to look at me, holding my gaze steady in hers. "You want me to say no. You want me to tell you that I could never do what she did, that I hate her for it, that I would never do that to Mia. And I really want to tell you that, because I want it to be true." She looked away, unable to face me as she continued. "But you're my twin, Franci, my other half. And you would know that I was lying." She closed her eyes and leaned back in her seat. I watched her, my heart filled with so many emotions, past and present—anger and love and pity and fear and a deep, deep sadness that had always been there but was sharper and clearer now too. Lottie didn't open her eyes or shift in her seat.

"Can we go home now, please?" she said finally in a small voice. "Can we please just go home?"

I started up the car and squeezed the wheel, trying to calm myself. I shifted the car into drive, and we headed back.

Lottie didn't speak, and I didn't ask any more questions. As I drove, trying to pay attention to the traffic and road ahead of me, my mind was a thousand miles away. The magnitude of what Lottie had seen was slowly sinking in. I imagined the trauma of that day in our parents' bedroom. I could imagine, but it wasn't real. What Lottie had seen was burned into her memory, the last image she'd have of our mother.

I shifted lanes, catching a glimpse of Lottie in the passenger seat, slumped and silent, possibly sleeping. I knew enough about bipolar disorder to know that a traumatic event could trigger the onset of one's first episode. Stress was another contributing factor. What kind of stress did keeping that secret cause? Had that been the start of everything?

Those six minutes that made her older might not have been much, but they were the foundation of our whole relationship for the first nineteen years of our life. Had I been weak because Lottie was strong? Was I stronger than her now, or was she still the strong one at the end of it all? I remembered what Whit had said, the terrible accusation that Lottie fell apart to please me, and his claim that I equated sickness with weakness. At the heart of it, I knew he was right, and while I would have given anything to have my sister healthy and well all of the time, a tiny, unconscious part of me felt slightly superior every time she did fall apart, a little smug that my powerful and magnetic sister wasn't so invincible after all.

Part of me was angry at her—all this time she'd kept the truth from me, so certain that I wouldn't be able to handle it. Then I thought about how I would have responded at sixteen, knowing our mother took her own life, and I knew that Lottie had been right. As agonizing as my mother's death was, that pain was nothing compared to the knowledge that it was intentional. Even as an adult, I couldn't grasp it. As a child, I would have been destroyed. Lottie had shielded me not to prove that she was stronger than me—she had never felt a need to prove this. Lottie had hidden Mother's suicide only for selfless reasons, despite what it may have cost her.

I reached out a hand and caught Lottie's fingers where they lay in her lap, squeezing them quickly before bringing my hand back to the steering wheel. She kept her eyes closed, but I knew she was awake by the way she stirred in her seat.

"Thank you," I said softly, keeping my eyes on the road.

Lottie didn't answer or open her eyes, but her lips rose in the tiniest and saddest of smiles.

Lottie

When we arrived at my house, Mark was sitting on the front steps with Ana and Autumn. Behind them was a black suitcase and two smaller purple suitcases. My head had begun to pound lightly on the drive back from Palo Alto, and the headache's pressure increased at the sight of them. Franci let out a little "Oh" and double-parked, nearly running from the car to her family. The girls' faces lit up when they saw her, and Franci dropped to her knees to embrace them. I saw the relief that filled her body when she stood up and leaned into Mark's chest. So many gifts my lucky sister had been given.

Always the gentleman, Mark came to help me from the car. "Hello, Charlotte," he said formally, as he leaned down to kiss my cheek.

"Hi, Mark." I accepted the hand he extended and allowed myself to be pulled gently from the car. The girls stood on the porch, Franci's arms draped over each of their shoulders.

"Hi, Aunt Lottie," they said shyly.

"Hi, girls." Once out of the car, I shrugged off Mark's help and stood by Mia's window. She was awake and rubbed at her eyes with a fist. "Want to come meet your new cousin?"

Mark looked in the backseat in surprise, as if he'd forgotten there was going to be a baby somewhere. Ana and Autumn came to the window and pressed their cheeks to the glass, hands splayed by their faces as they peered at Mia.

"She's so cute," crooned Ana. Though they were identical, I had always been able to tell them apart.

"She's sleeping. Should we get her inside?" I turned to Franci, who stood beside Mark, leaning her weight into his. "Franci, can you help?" I asked, barely trying to keep the encroaching irritation out of my voice.

Once we were all inside, Franci made tea while the rest of us sat in my living room and watched Mia. I held her carefully on my knee. She had woken and was working her mouth in the way that indicated she was hungry. Each of the girls leaned in close to run their hands along Mia's soft cheeks, to stroke her hair, to feel the silkiness of her tiny ears. Mark watched them carefully. Franci came back from the kitchen with cups of tea for the grown-ups, plastic cups of apple cider for the girls, a bottle for Mia, and a small plate of gingersnaps.

"Just two apiece," she told the girls as they eagerly reached for the plate.

"So, you guys just dropped in for a surprise visit?" I asked, not sure to whom I was directing the question.

"The girls missed Franci," Mark said. "Since she wasn't sure when she would be coming back home . . ." He glanced at Franci, and something unspoken passed between them. "We decided that we'd come to her. And the girls were so excited to meet Mia." He pronounced it *My-ah*.

"Mia," Franci and I both corrected at the same time.

"Sorry, right, Mia." Mark looked at me. "Don't worry, we won't be staying here; we've got a room at the Marriott. We just wanted to come here first." We fell into an awkward quiet as the girls crunched their cookies. "So, Lottie," Mark said after a moment. "How are you feeling?"

"I'm okay. A little banged up, but fine." I smiled tightly at him. I wondered if Franci would tell him about whatever had happened with Whit.

"You seem to be getting around okay," he said.

"I'm managing. Franci's been a huge help. I don't know what we would have done without her." I pulled Mia to my chest, resting my chin against her warm scalp.

"She's beautiful," he said, his voice softer now. "She looks just like you and Franci."

"Can I hold her, Aunt Lottie?" Autumn asked.

Like me, Autumn was the older twin. Those extra three and a half minutes had already given her the assertiveness that Ana hadn't yet acquired. "Of course, sweetheart. You can feed her." With Franci's help, we positioned Mia in Autumn's arms and showed her how to hold the bottle. They stared at each other, Mia grasping a fistful of Autumn's long blond hair and Autumn giggling.

"You look tired," Franci said to me. "You should go lie down."

"I'm okay," I said.

"No, really, we'll take care of Mia. The girls are dying to play with her anyway; you might as well get a rest." Ana had come to sit with her sister, and the two of them were singing "Rock-a-Bye Baby" to Mia.

"We won't stay long," Mark said. "I rented a car for the week, and we'll check in to the hotel pretty soon. These two are going to crash in the next hour." He gestured with his head to his daughters.

I clutched Mia's foot, wanting to physically have some part of her touching me, not ready to relinquish her. But the headache was a dull pain over my eyes. The room was too bright, and I longed to close my eyes against all of this. I released her foot and struggled to rise.

"Okay, I guess I will lie down for a few minutes." Mark got me by the elbow and helped me up. He walked me down to my room, and this time I didn't pull away.

"It was good of you to come. I know Franci is glad you're here," I said to Mark.

"We missed her," he said. He looked at me closely, his face gentler than I remembered it. "Charlotte, we're not here to . . . take over. I just wanted to help Franci." I nodded, swallowing a lump in my throat. "We'll be gone by the time you get up," he said, stepping back into the hall. I stood in the doorway, listening to the sounds coming from the other room. Ana and Autumn's chatter, Mia's squeals and gurgles, the quiet hum of Franci and Mark's voices.

They sounded like a family.

Franci

When I saw Mark sitting with the girls on Lottie's front steps, I was surprised by how much my heart lifted. I hadn't wanted him to come, had convinced him several times on the phone that he didn't need to come, but when I saw him sitting there it was as if the world clicked into place just a little. After the afternoon's terrible revelation, I needed "normal" more than anything; I needed my husband and children to ground me and remind me who I was now that the floor of my childhood had collapsed. I breathed in his smell, my face fitting perfectly in the soft groove of his neck.

"You're here," I said to him in disbelief.

"We missed you," he said, planting a kiss on my mouth, and I thought to myself, *How could I have almost forgotten how good this is?*

Now, in Lottie's living room, the girls fawned over Mia, and Mark and I shared a chair. The days apart had left us affectionate and loving in a way we rarely were lately. Ana and Autumn were kneeling by the coffee table in front of Mia's infant seat. They cooed at her, sang her songs, and reached out their fingers for her to grasp. Mark and I watched them.

"Thank you for coming," I said to him. "How long are you here for?"

"Till Saturday. Are you going to come back with us?" Today was Tuesday.

I adjusted in his lap, leaning back against him. "I don't know."

"She seems like she's doing all right." He gestured with his chin toward the hallway that led to Lottie's room. "She's up and walking around."

"But she can hardly do anything for the baby," I said, trying not to get annoyed.

"I thought you said you'd talked to her neighbor about helping out."

"I did, but I don't know how available she is."

"Well, is there anyone else who might be able to help? What about Whit?"

I blushed unconsciously, the fever creeping into my cheeks. I'd almost let myself forget about what had happened, what had *almost* happened, the other night. Somehow, seeing Mark, feeling such joy and relief at his appearance, I'd allowed the shame of the other evening to slip away. But it was suddenly back, pricking at my skin with its sharp needles. I fussed in the diaper bag for a wipe to clean Mia's hands so that my hair fell forward to mask the pinkness of my face. When I turned back to him, I hoped my color was a little more normal.

"They're not together anymore. I don't know how much he's going to be around. I don't think he can be counted on to help," I said.

He was watching me closely. "Well, is there anyone else?"

"No, Mark, there's not," I said, unable to control the snippiness in my voice. "There's just me." I stood up and moved to the couch.

Mark shifted in the chair. "Well, you need to talk to Sally about her schedule and how much Charlotte normally pays her. Also, doesn't Charlotte have Mia in daycare?"

"Yeah, I don't know if it's every day, though." We looked at the three girls. Mia was blowing bubbles, and Ana and Autumn were giggling, each holding a pudgy hand.

"We need to find out the daycare's hours. Do you know when her cast and that boot are coming off?" I shook my head. "Well, that's also important to find out. Does she have a follow-up appointment with the doctor?"

"I don't know," I said, feeling somehow foolish for not knowing the answers to any of these questions. "I've been busy taking care of an infant and an invalid," I snapped, reaching for my tea so I didn't have to meet his eyes. It had gone lukewarm.

"Well, we need to find out," Mark said, ignoring the annoyance in my tone. "We need to have all of the information to be able to go from here. We need all the facts."

The facts. Mark was big on facts. I supposed in his job, they were important. Facts, not feelings or emotions, were the things that decisions were based upon. Sometimes I thought about how easy it was to be a man like Mark. To him numbers and statistics, truths and untruths, were the real stuff of life. He saw the world in clear terms, and I was often envious of this. You loved someone or you did not. If you loved them, you made sacrifices. If you did not, you were bound by no such obligations. I suspected that Mark didn't know what it was like to love someone so much that you were consumed by them, when your love for them was so powerful and red and raw that you sometimes wondered if it was closer to hate. In Mark's world, if you had the trappings of a good life—healthy children, a loving spouse, enough money, a beautiful home—then you should be happy. He understood little about a sadness that was like a festering sore, tender and open, and not a sharp, stabbing hurt, just a general ache that never fully went away.

Sometimes I wondered if he wished he'd married a different sort of woman, one who could simply be happy, without guilt or rage or malaise, a hearty woman who could weather the storms of life without cracking.

"Okay," I said to him now. "We'll get the facts."

"Is there some other reason you don't want to go home?" he asked, leaning closer so that the girls couldn't hear.

There was so much to tell him. Whit, my mother, Caitlin, my own confusion and aimlessness, all of the things that had remained unspoken between us for too long. It was easier to focus on Mia and Lottie.

"I'm afraid to leave her here," I said, my voice low.

"Who? Your sister?"

"Yes." I nodded. "But also Mia."

"Why?" he asked carefully.

"Because I'm afraid of what Lottie might do."

Mark was quiet for a moment. "Is she abusive?"

"No," I said quickly.

"Neglectful?"

"No . . ."

"Then what?" he asked.

"It's not what she is now. It's what she might become. It's what she might be capable of doing later," I tried to explain. Mark reached for my hand and held it a moment before he spoke.

"Franci, there's not really anything we can do about that right now."

The reality of his words was both a shock and a relief. Of course he was right. I couldn't take Mia from Lottie. I couldn't go to social services. Even if there was something that they could do, which I doubted at this point, I'd never be able to bring myself to take Lottie's baby from her. After what she had done for me, the secret she'd carried like a hot coal in her pocket, how could I take anything from her?

Yet even while I knew this, I wondered if Mia would hate me for this moment years from now, or if I would hate myself for what I couldn't do to Lottie.

Lottie

Since Mark arrived with the girls that afternoon, I'd found it difficult to leave the bedroom. Seeing Franci's family with the only member of my tiny and truncated family made me aware of all that I didn't have, that I couldn't have. It made me want to hide.

I'd been watching old movies in bed, high school romances from the '80s—*Sixteen Candles* and *Some Kind of Wonderful*—wishing my own life were so simple that my only worry was if the boy I liked would ask me to prom. Franci came in during the opening credits of *Pretty in Pink*.

"Hey." She hovered in the doorway anxiously.

"Hey." I returned my eyes to the television screen. Molly Ringwald was applying pink lip gloss and putting on stockings to the music of the Psychedelic Furs.

"God, I haven't seen this in ages," she said, coming to sit beside me on the bed.

"I own it. I watch it at least once a year. I love this movie." I sighed. Back then I'd wanted to be Molly Ringwald. The movie was a staple at sleepovers, and I'd started making my own clothing after seeing it for the first time, developing an affinity for weird, floppy hats. Franci lay down beside me on the bed. "Where is everyone?" I asked after a while.

"Mia's taking a nap. Mark and the girls are back at the hotel. They're going to come back for dinner around six." The day had seemed impossibly long. It was hard to believe that just this morning we'd visited our father.

And life went on. I felt sick with the knowledge that Franci now knew the truth about Mother. All that time I'd kept it from her, all the time I'd carried the weight of it alone, to tell her now. What a waste.

"Do you want them to leave? Mark and the girls?" Franci asked after a moment.

"It's fine," I lied.

"He should have told me before he came. He should have let me know so I could ask you first." Franci wrinkled her brow and flopped back against the pillow. "But I haven't been very good at communicating with him lately. I think he was getting worried."

"It's fine, Franci. He cares about you." We were quiet for a moment, watching the screen, though I doubted that either of us was paying much attention to the plot.

"We're going to have to start talking about what happens next," Franci finally said. I didn't answer, pretending to be absorbed in the unfolding high school drama. "Mark talked with Sally before he left. They've figured out a schedule so that she can drop Mia off and pick her up at daycare every day."

"He doesn't waste any time, does he?" I asked.

"He's just trying to help," Franci said. "That just leaves the nights to figure out. Is there anyone else who might be able to help you out? Any coworkers or friends?"

I shook my head. "No one that I could ask to do this."

"I can stay for another week, maybe two. But that's about it."

"Why?" I asked selfishly. Even now, nearly six years after Franci's beautiful daughters had come along, I couldn't gracefully accept no longer being first in her life.

"Because I have to go home, Lottie. I need to take care of my family."

"Why can't Mark?"

"Because he can't," she said in exasperation. "Not alone. He works long hours, and he's not able to pick the girls up at school. He's got his mom doing as much as she can, but she's in her seventies." Franci paused. "And I miss them, Lottie. I want to go home to be with them."

I swallowed the lump that was forming in my throat. "We'll be fine," I told her, forcing myself to smile. "Two weeks from now? I'm sure I'll be walking almost normally. And I only need one arm to hold Mia, right?" I was half-joking, half-serious.

Franci shook her head. "Lottie, you're going to need some help. If it were just you, that'd be one thing. But how are you going to take care of a baby with only one arm? It's not safe."

"Well, I guess I'm just going to have to, aren't I?" I snapped. "I'll figure it out."

"There's one other possibility." There was something tentative in the way she spoke.

"What's that?"

"You and Mia could come home with us. I can help take care of her until you're better." She looked so hopeful, her eyes pleading with me not to make this any harder than it had to be. "Just for a few weeks. A month or two tops."

"Come on, Franci, Mia and I can't go home with you," I said. "What about my job?"

"You'll take a leave of absence. You're injured, Lottie; it's not as if you'll be going in next week anyway."

"What about Dad? I visit him each week."

Franci's face clouded over, and I knew she was remembering our visit. "He doesn't even know who you are. I'm sorry, but he's not going to notice if you don't come for a few weeks." She reached up to brush the hair from my face and let her hand rest on my cheek. "Please, Lottie, it's the only thing that makes any sense."

"Have you talked with Mark about this?" I asked.

She dropped her hand and looked away. "No, but it will be fine. He wants me to come home, so this is the only way that I'll be able to."

Somehow I doubted it would be this simple, but Franci looked so desperate that I couldn't say no. "I'll think about it."

"Okay," she said, satisfied for the moment. She pulled the comforter up over us, and we watched the film.

Franci

Mark made spaghetti Bolognese for dinner. It was an awkward meal without a dining room or dining room table, and Mark, the girls, and I sat on the floor around the coffee table. Lottie, on the couch, unsteadily balanced the plate on her lap, and Mia sat in her infant seat on the floor. We were a precarious, botched-together family, but we didn't talk about anything too serious and managed to get through the meal.

After dinner Mark and I cleaned up the kitchen while the girls watched a movie, and Lottie took Mia into her room to nurse. She'd grown surprisingly adept at carrying the baby with only one working arm, and before dinner I watched her change Mia's diaper with only one hand. I knew this was the beginning of her campaign for me to leave the two of them here alone, but I couldn't yet steel myself for that fight.

"Let's go sit outside for a few minutes," I said to Mark as I put the last pot away. I opened the door that led to Lottie's patio. It was a small city backyard, unlike our own spacious yard in Brookline, but the plants that grew were exotic by New England standards. There was a fairy duster shrub with red flowers that looked like paintbrushes. Near the house, white and green calla lilies sprouted, and in the corner of the yard a palm tree grew. Lottie had wound a string of Christmas lights around the thick trunk of the tree, and when I plugged them in, the yard was cast in a pale golden glow. We sat down in plastic lawn chairs. The air smelled like eucalyptus leaves.

"How are you holding up?" Mark asked.

I sighed and breathed in the pungent air. "My mother killed herself." I hadn't planned to tell him like this, but the words came out anyway. The revelation had hovered around the edge of everything else all day, my mother's choice brushing up against Lottie's determination to shield me from it. How alone she must have felt, intent on protecting me and our father yet forced to face the brutal possibility of her own future.

"What?" Mark sat forward in his chair. "What do you mean?"

"I found out today, when we went to visit my father. He said something, and I asked Lottie about it. She's known all along but didn't tell me. To protect me." I thought of every secret and confidence I'd shared with Lottie over the years, my whole life laid bare before her. I wondered if I'd ever known my sister at all. What other hidden pockets of darkness had she kept from me? A tear rolled down my face, but I didn't wipe it away. "She hung herself, and Lottie found her. She never told anyone—not me, not our father. She kept it a secret." I imagined the secret like a stain that spread until it could not be contained.

"Jesus," Mark whispered. "You told me she'd been depressed, but I didn't realize."

"Me, either. I didn't understand how bad it really was. After she died, I didn't want to think about it. She used to disappear into her bedroom for weeks on end. Like Lottie, but different."

"You hardly ever talk about her."

It was true, yet I thought about her all the time. "It's hard to talk about her. After she died, I tried not to think about those times. I wanted to believe she was happy."

I got up from my own chair and sat down on his lap, leaning into his chest. My cheek scratched against a day's worth of stubble on his chin, and I thought about Whit, the kiss we'd shared, the feeling of his hands on my body. My eyes filled again, with regret.

I imagined telling him now. How would the sentence begin? *I betrayed you. I may have destroyed everything. I'm so sorry.* Such flimsy words.

We built our lives around people and dreams. We lived inside of them as if they were houses, strong buildings of brick and mortar, wood and nails; as if they were solid and unbreakable. We believed these houses could weather all sorts of storms, and so we neglected them. We waited to reshingle. We forgot to clean the gutters. We let the roof go too long. But really, I suddenly understood, our lives were not houses. These fragile shelters were more like teepees: potentially temporary and capable of crashing down on the occupants if one stick snapped or if one branch fell out of place. What arrogance to treat them as if they were incapable of destruction.

If I told him, our life together might very well be over. He might leave me. He might leave the girls. Or he might try to take them with him. Already I could feel the absence of my family and our life together as a hollow pain inside of me. I was ashamed that I'd needed to come this close to realize how desperately I wanted everything inside this fragile shelter that we'd created together.

So I didn't say anything. I swallowed my words back down and felt his arms around me. But when he spoke next, I knew he'd been thinking about our relationship too.

"Do you love me?" he asked.

"Yes. So much." I reached around to hold his face in my hands.

"Then that's what's important." He reached up and took my hands in his. "Right here, you and I, this is what's important." He gestured with his chin toward Lottie's house. "Inside that house, all of those people that we love, that's what's important."

"I know," I whispered.

"We need to find our way back to that, Franci."

"I know," I said, chastened.

"What's happened with you and your sister this past year has been hard on you," he continued. I looked down at my lap. "I'm sorry that it's been so hard. And I'm sorry that I made it harder." I was silent. It still hurt, all of those times he'd convinced me not to call her back, the times he gently yet firmly said he didn't want the girls having anything to do with her, all the times I'd reached for the phone to call her only to think about what Mark would say. "The girls come first," Mark said to me now. "I know you know that. I know you understand that, Franci."

"Of course I do," I said, feeling a rush of anger. I'd known that the moment I walked into the bathroom and saw blood all over Ana's face. I'd known it the moment they were born and I held them in my arms for the first time. I didn't need him to remind me. "But she's my sister, Mark, my twin. I don't know how to live without her."

He nodded. "And I won't ask you to again. But they need to come before her. Always."

"I know," I whispered. "I know."

The lights from the palm tree illuminated his face, and I saw the small lines around his mouth and eyes. My husband would be forty this year.

"Franci," he said, and his voice was stern. "No matter what happens with your sister, here or in Boston . . ." He seemed to struggle to find the words. "You can't blame me for it."

"I won't." But I did. All this time Lottie and I hadn't spoken, it was easier to hold it against Mark than to accept that I'd cut her out of my life because I needed to.

"No, Franci, I'm serious." He pulled me up so that again I was looking into his eyes. "Whatever happens over the next few months or years with your sister, it's not my fault. You can't blame me for it. If you do, we'll never survive it." He didn't tell me what he foresaw. A quiet phone call to social services, a custody battle, my sister's rage and manipulation raining down on all of us. Or something smaller, less significant, the distance between me and Lottie growing wider until it was an unpassable gulf. He was quiet, waiting to make sure I understood.

I was sickened by how close I'd come to losing him this past year, and then, more pointedly, just the other night. My breath caught in my throat as I swallowed back tears, nodding. "I won't. I won't blame you, Mark. I promise I won't."

He pulled me to him, and I let myself relax for what felt like the first time in months. Inside I heard Mia crying and realized that she'd been at it for a while. In a moment I'd have to get up and help Lottie. I heard her calling me, but I couldn't bring myself to rise just yet. I leaned into Mark, inhaling my husband's warm, familiar smell. He held me steady in his arms, and we stared at the palm tree covered in Christmas lights in February in my crazy sister's tiny backyard. Inside the house all of the drama of our family waited, but for a few moments, we had found a tentative peace.

Lottie

The cry of an infant has the power to drive a person insane. This was one of the first things I learned after becoming a mother.

Mia had many different cries, each one subtly unique. One was reserved for hunger. It was insistent and immediate and could be quickly silenced. Another was a cry for comfort. This one started off as a whimper and then built into jagged sobs if I didn't get to her fast enough. And then there was the one I had come to call the Cry of Insanity. It was not a cry with any purpose, as far as I could tell. Rarely was hunger or discomfort involved. Instead, it was an endless cry that had no purpose and no destination. It left me feeling useless and inept and on the verge of tears myself. It would end as suddenly as it began, and in its place I would find my cheerful baby girl, while I was left depleted and exhausted.

After dinner I brought Mia into the bedroom to nurse and get ready for bed. My milk was slowly drying up. While in the hospital my breasts were sore and leaked the first day, but by the time I came home, my milk was slowing down, not coming as fast and not lasting as long. The doctor had said that if I kept nursing, it would return to its regular amount, but it was so hard to nurse with the cast, so uncomfortable and awkward that I'd been letting Franci prepare bottles.

But when Franci's family descended upon us, I wanted Mia back, all to myself. *Mine, mine, mine.* I brought Mia into the bedroom with the intention of nursing, but she'd quickly grown frustrated. With the frustration descended the Cry of Insanity, a shrill and breathless sob that turned her tiny face red, her mouth stretched wide as she expelled her misery. I tried to comfort her, singing, rocking her, and cooing in her ear. Nothing worked. I hobbled around the bedroom, holding her to my body with my one good arm while trying to sway side to side. Mia continued to howl, and I felt the panic rising up, the dread that always came with this cry.

"Franci," I finally called out of desperation. My sister had been so attentive over the past few days that I was surprised she hadn't come at the first sounds of Mia crying, but she didn't come even now. "Franci? Mark?" I called again. I thumped down the hallway and into the living room. Ana and Autumn were on the couch in the dark, the blue light of the television flickering on their faces. At the sound of Mia's crying, they looked up.

"Where are your parents?" I asked. My arm ached with fatigue, but there was nothing I could do about it. Mia continued to squall against my chest.

"I don't know. What's wrong with Mia?" Autumn asked.

"Sometimes babies just cry. You don't know where your mom is?" They shook their heads, returning to the television screen.

I hobbled into the kitchen, which was all clean and organized, thanks to Franci. I'd make Mia a bottle, and that would calm her, I decided. But I hadn't fully thought about how I could do this with only one arm. I had only the use of the fingers of my right hand and the can of formula was on the top shelf, along with the bottles. I'd have to put Mia down in order to make the bottle.

I returned to her bedroom and awkwardly plunked her into her bed. Her cries grew louder and more desperate.

"I'll be right back, sweetie," I said, though Mia just looked up at me through wet lashes and shining eyes, as if I'd betrayed her yet again.

Back in the kitchen I pulled down the bottle and formula, mixing everything together quickly, shaking the bottle, cursing under my breath. By the time I got back to Mia's bedroom, her face was the deep red of a cooked lobster. My back and neck and arm muscles all screamed out at me as I bent into the crib and scooped Mia up with only one arm, her head flopping awkwardly. It wasn't until I'd stood up with her that I realized I'd left the bottle on the kitchen counter.

"Shit," I hissed. Where the hell was Franci? I could put Mia back in the bed, but then I'd have to maneuver to pick her up again, and I didn't think my arm could stand another jostling. "Ana? Autumn?" I called. Neither girl answered, too drugged out by the lure of Disney to come to my rescue. "Goddamnit, Franci," I cursed, because somehow it was easier to direct my anger at Franci than at myself or this untenable situation.

I began the long walk back into the kitchen, Mia draped against my chest. She continued to howl—earsplitting, mind-numbing, hair-tearing cries—and I felt the rage and fear and frustration all boiling up inside of me. "Calm down, Mia, just calm down," I snapped. Mia began sliding down my body, and I struggled to redistribute her weight, hoisting her back up clumsily.

While the kitchen was neat and tidy, the rest of the house was not, having already been monopolized by Ana and Autumn's toys. With my eyes on Mia's slipping frame, I took my attention away from what was in front of me, and my socked foot slipped on a stuffed penguin. Before I knew it, I was falling, though I had enough time to clutch Mia even tighter. Even so, we both let out a cry when we landed with a thump. My good shoulder bounced off the hardwood floor, just inches from Mia's head. Pain shot through every corner of my body, ricocheting through my arm, foot, and head with a force that made me cry out. The back door that led to the patio slammed shut. When I looked up from the floor, both Franci and Mark stood over me, Ana and Autumn hovering a few feet behind.

"Oh my god, Lottie, are you okay? Is Mia okay? What just happened?" Franci crouched beside me.

"Where the hell were you?" I yelled at her, tears suddenly appearing now that my sister was here. "I called you. I needed help getting Mia's bottle."

"We were outside. I'm sorry, I didn't hear you." She reached toward Mia, who continued to cry. "Is she okay? Did she hit the floor?" Though my whole body was screaming with pain and fatigue, I didn't want to let go of Mia.

"No, I held on to her. She was already crying. She just won't stop. Her bottle's in the kitchen." I wanted to close my eyes and press my cheek against the cool hardwood floor, but I held Mia instead, struggling to keep my body upright.

"Lottie, let me take her. Let me help you," Franci said, reaching for Mia again.

"No!" I shrieked, holding Mia tighter. "You can't take her. *You can't take her.*"

Franci cringed and leaned back, loosening her grip on Mia. "Okay. It's okay, sweetie. No one's going to take her." She turned to where the rest of her family stood watching me unravel. Ana and Autumn were looking at me with fear, the same way they had looked at me that night in the bathroom. Mark stood frozen in place, observing me with a calculating wariness. In that moment, I hated them all even more than I hated myself. Only Franci sat beside me on the floor, trying to share the weight of Mia without taking her out of my arms.

"Mark, go get the bottle," Franci calmly instructed. It took him a moment to process the direction, but then he went into the kitchen. He returned with the bottle, his arm extended to Franci, as if I were contagious and he'd risk catching whatever strain of crazy I had if he came in physical contact with me.

Franci brought the bottle to Mia's lips, and she began to suck away hungrily. With the sucking, the crying stopped, and the apartment was filled with a blissful silence. I let out a deep breath and let my head rest against Franci's shoulder.

"Mark, it's late. You should get back to the hotel, okay? Girls, go get your things together," Franci said. I watched a look pass between Franci and her husband. There was so much in that look. It said, *Trust me*. It said, *I can't talk now, but I'll call you later*. It said, *I told you, this is a bigger mess than you realized*.

I turned away from them so I wouldn't have to see what else they were saying about me without even uttering a word. I looked down at Mia instead. Her eyes had drifted closed, and her lids were pale petals. She drank milk that came from a can instead of my breast, brought to her by her aunt instead of me. Yet she was finally content.

Franci

"What are we going to do, Mark?" I said into the phone. Though I was sitting on the front steps of Lottie's building, I was still whispering. Mark had taken the girls back to the hotel. Inside, Lottie was getting ready for bed while Mia had fallen into a heavy sleep after the drama in the hallway.

"Mia needs to come home with us until your sister can take care of her," he said, matter-of-factly, as if taking my sister's daughter away from her was the simplest thing in the world.

"And how exactly do we do that?" I asked, the exasperation already creeping into my voice. "Did you see what happened tonight when I tried to take Mia away from her for a minute, just to feed her a bottle? How am I supposed to take her across the country?" I brought the heel of my hand up to my eyes, rubbing the tears and exhaustion from them. I focused on the step in front of me where raindrops had begun to fall. From the glow of the streetlight, I watched the white cement of the step as it became speckled with dark spots.

"Lottie will come too." His voice was calm and firm. "But there's no debate about whether your sister is capable of caring for Mia at the moment. I think that was pretty clear tonight, don't you?" I was silent. "Franci. We don't have a choice."

"It's not our place to decide if she's a good mother," I said weakly.

"Franci." He sounded sad, disappointed. "Of course it is. Mia's our niece." On the other end of the phone I heard the sound of the television, and I wondered if the girls were still awake. It was well past their bedtime. "I'll tell her. That way she'll blame me, not you. Right now we're only talking about taking her while Lottie recovers from her physical injuries. But with or without Lottie, that baby is coming home with us."

Mark's words hung between us as I clutched the phone to my ear. The step filled with more dark spots, the rain coming faster now. The cool drops landed on the back of my neck, in my hair, on my hands. I tilted my head back, letting the rain lightly tap my face. *The calm before the storm,* I thought to myself.

Lottie

It rained all night, the noise of the storm broken by flashes of lightning that brightened the sky with a silent yet ominous force only to be followed by a clap of thunder. Miraculously, Mia slept through it all, though both Franci and I tossed all night. Though we'd shared crowded spaces many times before, neither of us could get comfortable.

When Mia woke in the early hours of the morning, the storm had ended, and Franci brought her into the bed. Mia drifted off to sleep with the bottle in her mouth, cocooned between us. She slept deeply, hardly stirring at all, and we both curled up close, flanking her like sentries.

With her eyes closed, Franci looked like a child, a grown-up version of my own daughter. I imagined a life where it was just the three of us, Franci and me raising Mia together. We would offer the best of our own mother without the pain. We'd create our own Mirabella and Louisa Strout stories, but they wouldn't be dark. We'd fill them with fairies and flowers, magic and pixie dust, all of the things that our mother had left out.

"Once . . . in a place that is not here and now, but is very close, once . . . there lived two girls," I whispered into Mia's ear. Though I'd thought Franci was asleep, I suddenly sensed her waiting for me to tell the story. And though moments earlier I'd thought of sprites and rainbows, I couldn't continue. Any story I told would have feral cats and homeless strangers, beady-eyed rats and frigid winter nights. The darkness was always there, like it or not.

I turned my head away and waited for morning.

Franci

Mark arrived before nine, bearing breakfast. I was still in my pajamas and carried Mia in the sling, and when I answered the door, Mark and the girls were standing on the landing. Ana held a paper bag, and Autumn was carefully balancing a cardboard drink caddy with paper cups.

"Good morning," I said, patting each of my daughters and opening the door for them to come inside.

"We brought breakfast. Bagels and cream cheese. And hot chocolate!" Ana said.

"And coffee for the grown-ups," Mark added. He came to stand beside me and peered down at Mia. She blinked back up at him.

"Bring the food into the kitchen," I told Ana and Autumn. Turning to Mark, I said, "I wasn't expecting you so early."

"Well, we have to talk to Lottie."

"Now? So soon?"

"It's not going to be any easier if we wait." He looked down at Mia again. "How's she doing?"

"She's fine." He reached his hand into the sling. Mia grabbed his finger and held on tight.

"Could you love her?" I spoke quietly, so Lottie wouldn't hear. He met my eyes, though Mia still clutched his finger. "If you had to. If she ended up staying for longer? If for some reason we ended up raising her?" The various permutations of the "some reason" sickened me, and I couldn't dwell on any of them, but I needed to hear the answer.

"Yes," Mark said. "Without a doubt, yes." I wished his answer brought more comfort, but I knew it was the most I could hope for. From the other room Ana let out a yell when she burned her tongue on the hot chocolate, and Lottie comforted her, urging her to take the lid off and let it cool down. "Come have some breakfast," Mark said, and we joined the rest of the family on pillows on the floor.

Lottie

Assaults come in different colors and different shades. I was armed and ready for Franci. What I didn't expect was Mark.

We'd finished breakfast, and the plates were empty on the coffee table except for a few smears of cream cheese and sprinkles of poppy seeds. It was a choreographed attack in its delivery, Franci and the girls suddenly busy stacking plates and washing dishes in the kitchen, leaving just Mark and me together. We'd never spent much time alone, whether out of mutual avoidance or because of Franci's careful planning, I wasn't quite sure.

"I'd like to discuss something with you, Charlotte," Mark said. He was a businessman through and through, direct and calculating, a careful weigher of pros and cons. Though I wore pajamas and lay on a velour couch in the comfort of my own living room, my body tensed immediately. I sat up, not wanting to lie down for whatever this conversation would bring.

"Go ahead." I picked up my lukewarm coffee cup from the table only to have something to do with my good hand.

"I know it's going to be a little bit of time before you recover from this accident. Franci and I would like to help." He leaned forward in his chair, elbows on his knees, his hands clasped together.

"Mia and I are fine," I told him. He was a good-looking man, I noticed, not for the first time. His dark hair was becoming lightly flecked with gray, but he would become distinguished looking as he got older. He was trim and in good shape, and I wondered if he worked out every night before coming home to Franci and the girls. Or maybe he was the type who packed a gym bag and exercised during his lunch hour.

"Last night you seemed pretty rattled. Taking care of a baby on your own is hard even when you've got full use of both legs and arms." *And a clean and working mind* was certainly what he wanted to add, but didn't.

"I think I'm just a little overwhelmed with so many people around," I told him. "I'm used to it just being me and Mia. This is a small apartment." I smiled sweetly at Mark, determined not to let him get under my skin. "It might take us a few days, but I'll figure out how to do it. Mia and I are just fine."

"You're not, Charlotte. Clearly, you're not." He held my gaze to show me that he wasn't backing down.

"Where are you going with this, Mark?" I asked, dropping the niceties.

"Franci and I would like you and Mia to come back to Boston with us. We've got plenty of room. Mia can sleep with you, or she can have her own room. We can help take care of her until you get better."

"But I'm never going to get better," I said bitterly.

"Franci said that you'll have full use of your leg within the next six weeks," Mark said. "Six weeks is not that long a time to come and stay with us. You might enjoy yourself."

"I'm talking about my mental health, Mark. And I know you and Franci are too. So let's drop the bullshit. You're not asking me if I'd like to come for a little visit. You're telling me you're going to take my child whether I want to come or not. Am I right?" I was sweating slightly, and my nerves jangled inside my skin.

"You're right." He let out a sigh. "Franci might want to cross her fingers and hope that you and Mia are just fine, but I can't. I can't put that child in jeopardy because I don't want to hurt your feelings."

"But you're not really talking about six weeks, are you?" I asked. "You're talking about permanently. You don't think I can be a good mother."

"Jesus, Charlotte, this isn't about that," Mark said, standing up and walking to the window. He stood with his back to me and stared through the sheer white curtains, running a hand through his hair. "Maybe it is for Franci, but it's not for me." He turned to face me, his arms crossed against his chest. "What I'm talking about right now is leaving that baby with you when you can't even make a goddamn bottle by yourself. And maybe you've convinced Franci, and even yourself, that you'll be able to get by, but I'd have to be pretty callous to stand by and let myself be convinced of it too."

He came back to the chair and sat down again. I was clutching the cup so tightly that the paper had started to collapse on itself. "So here's the deal," he continued. "I've booked tickets for this weekend. One of them will have your name on it. You can think about it, but either way, Mia is coming home with us. There doesn't seem to be any other realistic options."

I hated him in that moment, so smug and certain of himself. How easy for him to judge me when he was married to Franci. She might have been scared of her own shadow, but everything looked perfect from the outside, and that was all that mattered to Mark. *It could just as easily have been Franci,* I wanted to tell him. It was only luck that allowed Franci to care for her daughters without worrying that her mind might deceive her. *It's only luck that you married the right twin.*

The kitchen had gone silent. The girls were in Mia's bedroom with Franci. They were singing a song about the moon and a meatball.

"What am I supposed to do about work?" I asked.

"Take a leave of absence. I'm sure you're covered by disability for the next six weeks."

"And after the six weeks?" I asked.

"You and Mia come home."

"I don't believe you." My eyes filled, and I pursed my lips to keep the tears from falling. "You'll try to take Mia from me."

Mark shook his head. "I'm not trying to take her from you. This is the only practical solution." He lifted his empty hands. "Franci needs to come home. We need her. But you still need help."

I tried to imagine the next six weeks. I'd only been to Franci's house once before, but I knew that it was large and beautiful, tastefully decorated like something from a magazine. There were two extra bedrooms connected by a bathroom, and there was a large yard with a swing set outside, though in February it would be covered in snow. With the girls at school and Mark at work, it would be just me and Franci and Mia. How long would it be before we started to drive each other crazy? How long before Franci started counting the pills in my toilet kit? How long before she started scrutinizing all of my interactions with Mia?

But what were my options? To not go meant to lose Mia for certain. To fight Franci and Mark also meant losing. And a tiny and resentful part of me knew that the two of us had been hanging on by a thread before the accident. What would become of us now?

The flight wouldn't be till the weekend. That gave me several days to figure out a plan. If I couldn't come up with one, I'd get on the plane with them.

"Okay," I told Mark.

"Okay?"

"Okay, we'll come with you."

Mark nodded, clearly surprised that I had acquiesced so easily. "Great. That's great. We can tell Franci."

I nodded. "When do we leave?"

"Saturday."

"Today's Wednesday?"

Mark nodded. "I figured while we were here, we could do a little sightseeing. I've only been to California once before," he said sheepishly. "I've always wanted to walk across the Golden Gate Bridge."

I forced myself to smile at him. "It's beautiful. You should visit more often."

"We should," Mark said with a chuckle. He pushed himself up. "I'm glad you're coming, Charlotte," he said, extending his hand to me. I reached out tentatively, and he squeezed it gently. "It will be okay." I nodded, letting my hand fall to my lap as he went to tell Franci.

I lay back down on the couch, under an orange blanket. I pulled it up and over my eyes, inhaling the musty smell of the wool. Under the blanket, all I could see was the dark glow of the world outside.

Franci

Ana and Autumn hovered beside me while I prepared to change Mia's diaper.

"Look at her little toes!" Ana said, catching the baby's foot.

Autumn stood on tiptoes beside me. "Can I put the diaper on?"

"You can help," I told her.

"Me too!" Ana squealed.

They helped pick out an outfit for Mia, and the girls were tugging on a pair of yellow socks when Mark came into the bedroom.

"The girls are helping me change Mia."

"I see that. Nice work."

"Did you talk to her?" I asked, lowering my voice slightly.

He nodded. "They're going to come."

I raised my eyebrows in surprise. "Just like that?"

Mark shrugged. "What can I say? I must be pretty persuasive."

I lifted Mia from the table and brought her to the rug on the floor, laying her down on her back. "Can you guys play with her down here for a minute? I need to talk to Daddy." I brought a collection of toys to the rug and went to stand beside Mark in the doorway. "She just agreed to come? What did you say to her?"

"I don't know," he said vaguely. "I just told her we'd help her."

Things were never this simple with Lottie. She would trap me later and try to convince me to help change Mark's mind; she'd throw a teary tantrum in the airport; she'd disappear with Mia the morning of the flight.

"Hold on, Mark, tell me exactly what you said to her."

"Franci, what does it matter? She said she would come with Mia. She asked when we were leaving."

"I don't buy it," I said, shaking my head.

"It's going to be okay," Mark said, slipping his arm around my waist. "I told her that you needed to come home, but that we knew she needed help while she was recovering. I don't know what else to say." He shrugged. "She seemed to get it."

I frowned, still skeptical. "Is she mad?"

"I don't think so. She really seemed okay with it."

I nodded, and we watched the three girls together on the floor. "God, you guys are going to be at each other's throats within a week," I said after a moment.

"Hey, you never know," Mark said with a smile. "I'm not positive, but I think your sister and I might have just come to a little truce."

"Humph," I said. "Now if only we could."

He kissed me lightly on the cheek. "I was thinking we could play tourist for the next few days. See the sights? Pretend we're on a regular vacation?"

"A vacation? This is hardly a vacation," I said.

"I know, but we're here. We might as well make the most of it."

"What do you want to do?" I asked.

"Get in the car and drive. I want to see the Golden Gate Bridge." He brought my fingers to his mouth, kissed my forefinger lightly. "I'd like to be shown around by a native."

"What about Mia?" I asked.

"She could come. Or we could see if Sally is free to babysit for a few hours."

"Yeah, I guess we could," I said reluctantly.

"We can give your sister a little break from us all. Besides, we're going to have a full house for a while," Mark said. "We should try to enjoy a little time, just the four of us."

"Why are we going to have a full house?" Autumn asked. From the way she had pushed herself up onto her knees, I could tell she'd been listening to us for the past few minutes.

Mark looked at me. "Because your aunt Lottie and Mia are going to come stay with us in Boston for a few weeks. Does that sound like fun?"

"Yeah!" both girls cheered in unison.

"Mia will be like our little sister," Ana said.

"Well, she's your cousin, honey," I said.

"But we can pretend. Right?" Ana asked.

"I suppose so, yeah," I said uneasily.

"Come here, little sister," Autumn crooned into Mia's ear, flopping down on the rug beside the baby.

I felt my skin go cold and turned away from them. "I'm going to go take a shower. Will you guys be okay in here?"

"Sure," Mark said.

In the bathroom I stripped off my pajamas and stood under the scalding water. My heart was beating fast, but the quiet of the steamy bathroom began to calm me. I took my time washing my hair. I shaved my legs with Lottie's razor and used her expensive bath scrub. I washed and conditioned my hair a second time because I wasn't ready to get out of the shower, wasn't ready to face whatever lay outside these warm walls. Mark and the girls had already opened their hearts to Mia, and while that should have made me happy, it scared me. The stronger their love, the harder it would be to hand Mia over to Lottie once she was better. The more we loved her, the more Lottie would retreat. All of us boarding a plane together in a few days and playing happy family? It couldn't be this simple. Nothing with Lottie ever was. I lay down in the large claw-foot tub with the water from the shower still running. I closed my eyes, letting the pinpricks of water cover me from head to toe.

Lottie

The house was silent. Franci and Mark had taken the girls into San Francisco for the day. Sally had brought Mia to her daycare, armed with a large box of diapers and a new can of formula. I'd promised Franci that I'd call the head of the English department to negotiate a leave of absence. Before she left, Franci helped get me settled on the couch, and I was surrounded by magazines, books, snacks, my laptop, my cell phone, and the remote control, all at easy access.

I tried to read. I tried to watch television. I checked my e-mail. But I couldn't stifle the anxiety that clutched me by the neck. If I had full use of my body, I would have gone for a walk or a bike ride. But, instead, I was stuck in a body that felt as if it were moving through mud, every step an effort, every movement slow and painful.

I looked around the living room. It was my favorite room in the apartment, light and airy with a working fireplace. Though I'd lived in the apartment since graduating college, I had decorated the living room only a few years earlier, throwing out much of the cheap secondhand furniture and replacing it with what I considered "grown-up" furniture. The year I was decorating the room, I scavenged flea markets and small boutiques for artwork and handmade crafts. I was happy with the result. It looked like it belonged to me.

There were only two photographs in the room, on the end table beside the couch. One of me and Franci, and one of our mother. I'd seen Franci examine the picture of our mother just the day before, running her thumb along the smooth glass.

It was a photo taken in the sunlit study of our house in Palo Alto. Mother looked to be in her early thirties, which would have meant that Franci and I were only toddlers. She sat cross-legged on a wooden bench, barefoot in black leggings and a pale pink leotard, her hair pulled into a loose bun. She had stopped dancing when Franci and I were born, but she continued to do her "exercises" every day, stretching and bending and plié-ing in the study. The gentle tapping of her feet against the wood floor could be heard many weekend afternoons.

It was nearly unfathomable to me that she had died twenty years ago. Though I'd grown used to her absence, I still felt it every day. I wondered how things might have been different if she had never died. She would have been here for Mia's birth. She'd be the one taking care of us now. She'd be a doting grandmother to all three of her grand-daughters. Franci might even still be living in California.

We could have talked. Though I didn't think that Mother had experienced the highs of the White, she certainly was familiar with the Black, and I wondered if it was similar to my own dark room of pain.

But, instead, it was just me and Franci, motherless mothers trying to survive, trying to save each other over and over.

Franci was trying to save me again now. She wanted me under her careful eye so she could monitor me, mother me, patronize me. But if I'd learned anything about my sister, anything about motherhood, it was that Mia would come first. Franci's instinct to protect her own children, and by extension my child, would ultimately trump her love for me.

I was also a mother now. Mia was mine, and I loved her more than the world.

But I was hazy. The medication, the goddamned medication, left me in a fog. It disconnected me from everything—love, anger, pain, strength. Right now my love for Mia was in my head. I understood it,

I felt it, and I abided by it, but it wasn't the bone-deep love that I knew was there just below the surface, beneath the cloudy layer of drugs.

Without that closeness, without that raw and naked love, I couldn't protect Mia. The drugs made me docile, and I couldn't afford to be docile if I was going to keep my child.

I didn't need to go off them completely. Just miss a day or two. Just skip enough that I felt the burning love for Mia right below the surface of my skin where I knew it pulsed. I just needed to feel the throb of that love enough to fight for her, enough to stand up to Franci and Mark, to be the mother I knew I could be.

It was my only choice.

Franci

The cars on the bridge flew past us with a speed that was disconcerting. Though a thick metal rail separated the footpath from the traffic, I couldn't help but clutch Ana and Autumn's hands. Below us the blue-black water of the Pacific frothed in icy waves, tiny surfers bobbing toward shore. Up here, atop the sunset-colored bridge, the wind was fierce and loud.

Mark was several steps ahead, and he turned back periodically to grin at us or to shout something that was quickly eaten up by the wind. I hadn't walked the bridge in many years, though each time I remembered how dramatic an experience it was. It was cold, loud, breathtaking. The girls skipped ahead cheerfully, their hair blowing behind them in sheets, and Mark looked more relaxed than I'd seen him in a long time. Because it was too loud to talk, we just walked. Eventually Ana joined her father, and Autumn and I followed behind.

It was a beautiful view; there was no doubt about that. From up here we could see the Marin Headlands ahead of us. To our left the open ocean extended as far as I could see. To our right was San Francisco Bay and the city laid out at its feet. Even farther to our right extended the Bay Bridge, which led back to Berkeley and to Lottie. So different from the Golden Gate Bridge, the Bay Bridge gleamed silver and was built solely for functionality. But the Golden Gate Bridge was built for beauty.

Even while I saw its splendor, I couldn't help but notice the telephones posted along the bridge that connected directly to counselors standing by to dissuade people from jumping. I remembered the chilling article I'd read years earlier that called the bridge a suicide magnet and revealed it had had more suicides than any other bridge in the world. There had been nearly thirty that year, possibly more if you factored in the bodies that were never found.

I forced myself to pull away from these grim and morbid thoughts. I looked instead at the sun gleaming in my daughters' hair; at my proud and patient husband; and at the undeniable glimmer of possibility that seemed to sparkle from this bridge overlooking so much magnificence. I would focus on that. I would choose to see that.

Lottie

Franci arrived home a little after four. She looked windswept and flushed, her hair a wild mane around her face, her nose and forehead tinged pink from the sun. She flopped down on the couch beside me, moving aside the stack of books and magazines. She glanced around the room; it looked as it had when she'd left that morning. "Where's Mia?" she asked.

"Sally just went to get her. They should be back soon," I said. "What did you guys do today?"

Franci looked tired but happy. "Oh, we walked along the Golden Gate Bridge. And then we drove through Golden Gate Park and the Presidio. God, I'd forgotten how beautiful it all is. Mark wants to take the girls back to the park to go to the Japanese Tea Garden. He bought them San Francisco sweatshirts, which I'm sure they'll be wearing till we get home."

"Did you have fun?"

"Yeah, I did," she said, wrinkling her nose as if this surprised her. "They went back to the hotel. I think he's going to take them to a movie tonight. What about you? What did you do today?"

"Not much," I said.

"Did you call about work?"

I nodded. I'd had a short conversation with the head of the English department, telling her that I would be with my sister in Boston while

I recovered from the accident. My TAs would take over my classes for the next six weeks, and I'd resume teaching after I returned. She directed me to the Human Resources department to figure out disability for the time I was away.

"And everything's okay?" Franci asked.

"Yup."

Franci nodded, reluctantly relaxing on the couch. "I'm glad you decided to come home with us," she said after a moment.

"Yeah." I picked at a stray piece of thread on the couch.

"Are you sure you're okay with it? I was surprised when Mark said you'd agreed." She watched me intently, scanning my face for signs of lies or omission.

"Well, I can't say I'm thrilled about it, but it looks like the only option."

"The girls are so excited to have you guys coming home with us. It will be like when we were roommates."

I stared at her for a moment, trying to gauge if there was any sense of sarcasm in what she said. The last time we were roommates, Franci had force-fed me drugs. The last time we were roommates, Franci had counted the pills in the medicine cabinet and manipulated Whit into being part of her martyrdom. Could she seriously romanticize those days?

"If I remember correctly, we didn't have the easiest time being roommates," I said carefully.

"I know. But that wasn't all there was," Franci said. "Remember Monday movie night? And the months when you were obsessed with Indian cooking? You made those elaborate feasts for us every night. I think we both started to smell like curry."

I smiled, nodding.

"And the time when you wanted me to ask out that guy from the coffee shop?" Franci continued.

"Yeah, I remember. You were too scared to ask him yourself. So I dressed up like you and did it for you."

It had felt odd to pretend to be Franci. I felt naked—without the armor of clothes or makeup, there was so little to hide behind. I'd even had to adjust my smile—from my own loud and overenthusiastic grin to Franci's softer, more reserved smile.

"I'm just saying we *do* have fun together. We can still have fun together." She reached out for my hand on the couch. I let her hold it loosely in her lap.

"If you say so," I said noncommittally, but I didn't pull away.

Franci

On Thursday I helped Lottie pack. When I brought Mia to daycare that morning, I told the teachers that she wouldn't be coming for the next six weeks.

"I can't hold her spot for six weeks," the lead teacher said. "We have a waiting list. I most likely won't have room for Mia when Charlotte gets back."

"But what is she supposed to do?" I asked her.

The teacher made a face in sympathy. "The only way I can guarantee the spot is if Charlotte continues to pay for the next six weeks. I'm sorry."

"How much is it?" I asked, struggling in my purse for my checkbook. I wrote out a check for an exorbitant amount of money and handed it to the woman. "She'll be back in six weeks. Please don't give Mia's spot up without talking to me first." I wrote my phone number down on a piece of paper and gave that to the woman as well.

In the car on the way back to Lottie's, I made a mental list of the things we would need to do to get ready. Ana and Autumn's cribs were somewhere in the attic. We could pull one of them out and set it up in the study upstairs. There were the girls' old baby clothes up there too, if they ended up staying longer, but I didn't want to think about that yet.

It would be hard to let Mia go after six weeks. I could see that already. In the week that I'd been here, I had fallen in love with her a little bit, surprised by how easily I remembered how to care for an infant. When Ana and Autumn were Mia's age, I'd been so overwhelmed with what was required to take care of the two of them together. Mark returned to work after only two weeks, and I was left on my own with the girls. It didn't take much to conjure up the exhaustion and fear of that first year of motherhood.

But somehow with Mia it was different. It was just her, which obviously made it easier. But it was more than that. *I* was different, more confident, more at ease, calmer. I wondered if that was because she was not my child, or because I had changed somehow.

Back at Lottie's house, I pulled out the large suitcase from under her bed and we began to make piles. It quickly became clear that we would need another suitcase, and I pulled out a second one.

"Babies sure do need a lot of stuff," Lottie said once we'd filled the second case.

"She'll need a diaper bag for the plane too," I said. Lottie nodded, sitting on the bed. She was perspiring lightly, her face flushed. "Are you feeling okay?"

"I'm fine. Just a little tired." She rubbed her hand against her eyes.

"Do you want anything? Something to eat or drink?"

"I'm not hungry." She stared into the suitcase at the brightly colored stacks of Mia's clothing that I'd neatly packed. Though she was looking at the clothes, her eyes seemed unfocused, as if she didn't actually see them.

"Do you want me to get you one of the pain pills?" I asked.

She shook her head without looking up. "No, that's okay."

"Lottie? Are you all right?" I swallowed, unable to push the rest of the sentence back down. "You're still taking your other medication, right?"

"Franci," she said sharply, holding a hand up like a traffic guard.

"I'm sorry, I'm just making sure you're okay."

"I'm fine. I'm just tired," she snapped.

"Okay." I returned to the packing.

Lottie stayed where she was, her shoulders turned slightly away from me, though she began to help fold the clothes as best she could with only one arm.

"Are you going to tell Whit you're leaving?" I asked after a few minutes.

She shook her head. "It's over. For good this time." Her face was hard, her mouth a straight line.

"I'm sorry. I know you were hoping he'd come around."

"Deep down I think I knew he wouldn't change his mind." She let out a harsh laugh. "He's like me that way. Stubborn." I was quiet, and she continued. "It's funny. There's really no one to tell that I'll be gone." She looked a little dazed and surprised by this.

"But you've always had tons of friends. I'm sure there are people for you to tell."

"Oh, I have friends. I have people I go out for dinner with and people to go to the movies with and out for drinks." She gestured vaguely with her hand. "They're fun to talk to and go out with. But they're not . . ." She grasped for the word. *"Confidantes."* She grimaced at the term. "I'm not really close to any of them. Just you and Whit."

"Would you ever think about staying? In Boston?" It wasn't what I wanted. Was it? The idea of having Lottie close by again was both terrifying and thrilling.

"Oh, Franci. I don't know," she said, shaking her head. "My life is here. My work is here." She gave a small smile that looked like it took effort. "But never say never, right?"

We turned back to the suitcases, both of them fully packed now. I lifted them from the bed and placed them on the floor by the closet, still open in case we needed to add anything later.

"I'm going to take a nap," Lottie said, hoisting her leg up onto the bed. She pulled back the covers and lay back down, her features suddenly overcome by exhaustion.

"Are you sure you're okay?" I asked again, hovering in the doorway. I realized that she hadn't actually answered my question about the medication, only insisted that she was fine.

Lottie had already closed her eyes, and she didn't open them when she answered. "Franci, just try to relax. Really, you don't have to worry so much."

But I do, I thought to myself. I closed the door lightly behind me.

Lottie

It had only been a day and my mind was heavy, my head swirling with a milky black mud that seeped into my nose and eyes and ears. It was the middle of the night, and I couldn't sleep, though I'd wanted nothing more than sleep for most of the day, scaring Franci, scaring myself.

Already? I thought. *Are we here again so fast?*

I stood in the bathroom that night, the magic bottle of pills in my hand. *Just take one and you'll begin to feel better,* I instructed myself in the same voice I knew Franci would have used. I had a foggy memory from years earlier of Franci and Whit wrestling me to the bed, pinning my arms and legs down, shoving the medicine into my mouth. Franci pinching my nose, cutting off my air supply, until I had no choice but to swallow. If I closed my eyes, I could still feel the lump in the back of my throat from the pill going down. That was the night that Franci and Whit entered into a twisted pact that I knew, *I knew,* ultimately had my best interest at heart.

But what was the price of better?

I tucked the bottle into the pocket of my plaid pajama pants and made my way slowly into Mia's bedroom, trying to walk as quietly as possible in the heavy plastic boot. The bottle clicked against my thigh, a reminder. As soon as I entered Mia's bedroom, I was overcome by the smells I'd come to associate with her—lotion, powder, milk, something sweet. A calmness in the terror of the night.

She'd learned how to roll over just a few weeks earlier, and she slept more soundly now on her tummy, her small back rising and falling, her head a mess of black curls against the pink sheets. I settled myself into the rocking chair and leaned forward to watch her through the slats of the crib. Until the accident, she had slept with me at night, using her crib only for naps. Yet she seemed to sleep more soundly in her own room, her own bed, alone.

I slipped my hand into my pocket, rubbed my thumb against the smooth plastic of the bottle. I was sliding. I felt the Black working to get its slippery claws on my mind, its liquid presence ready to fill my limbs and head and mouth with its mud.

But here and now, with Mia, I also felt the heat of my love for her, the pain of it, more fiercely than I had just the day before. Wasn't this truly who I was, when stripped of everything else? Without the drugs running through my blood, my heart was tender in a way it couldn't be while medicated. It was open and strong and fierce.

And, yes, raw too.

So often I wondered if I'd passed this sleeping beast down to Mia. Would her mind turn in on itself someday? Would I be here to see it?

It didn't make sense that just a few hundred milligrams of some chemical mixed in a lab should hold the key to my undoing. I was more than that. I was more than an illness, a label, a list of symptoms. I was more than a problem to be managed.

In a few days I'd rise up above the Black, and I would hold the power of the White in the palm of my hand. I'd have the strength that people dream of, that people read self-help books to discover and run on treadmills to develop. I would soar above the pain that ran, squalid, on the earth, and I'd hold Mia close to my heart.

I was stronger than the disease; I knew that now. I just needed to convince Franci.

I rose from the rocking chair, my fingers lingering on Mia's warm scalp.

"Good night, sweet girl," I whispered. I placed the bottle of pills in the diaper pail on my way out.

Franci

I awoke early Friday morning. I lay in bed and stared at the cracks and watermarks on Lottie's ceiling, remembering the story of the character who believed a woman was trapped in her walls. Lottie had been so confident in her understanding of the story, so certain of its outcome. I was the one who wanted to believe in another ending.

Lottie lay beside me, sleeping heavily in the early morning light. She'd slept restlessly, tossing and turning, struggling to get comfortable. I'd heard her in the bathroom and then checking on Mia. When I asked her if she was okay, she murmured that she'd slept too much during the afternoon and then rolled away from me.

But she slept now, peacefully, deeply, her mouth parted slightly, eyes flickering rapidly beneath the lids. I forced myself to lie in bed beside her until I heard Mia call, and then I rose quietly and went to change and feed her.

When Lottie finally emerged from the bedroom, it was after nine.

"Morning," Lottie murmured, scratching her hair absently.

"There's coffee in the kitchen," I told her. "I was going to take Mia to daycare in a few minutes."

"Okay." Her face was slightly puffy, her skin pale. She fixed herself a cup of coffee and came to sit beside us, leaning over to give Mia a light kiss on the cheek. "What are you doing today?"

"Mark wants to take the girls back to Golden Gate Park." I hesitated. "Unless you want me to stay here?"

She sipped the coffee. "No, I'll be fine."

I waited just a beat before I offered. "You can come with us if you want."

Lottie shook her head, making a face. "Nah. I've been tons of times. I'll just hang out here."

"Are you sure?" I asked, generous now that she'd declined.

"I'm sure." She scooted closer to us on the couch, rested her coffee cup on the table. "Can I feed her?"

"Of course." I helped place pillows both underneath and on top of her arm in the cast, and we rested Mia on her carefully. Lottie looked serene, her face washed in a kind of peace that hadn't been there in previous days. I felt a hopeful lightening of my chest as I watched them together. I forced myself to stay quiet, to not ask questions, to not make conversation, to just sit silently beside them.

The moment was interrupted by the doorbell, and suddenly Mark and the girls were upon us, filling the room with noise and laughter and chattering. Lottie looked a little stunned at the arrival of my family in her house, both filling it up and emptying it at the same time.

"Are you ready to go?" Mark asked me.

"In a minute," I said. "I need to pack some things for Mia for daycare."

"I thought we could take her with us," he said.

"Really? Won't it be hard to have her along?" I asked.

"She'll sleep in her stroller and the car seat," Mark said confidently. "The girls want to spend the day with her."

Ana and Autumn were crouched by Lottie's feet, leaning into her lap to watch Mia. "Can she come?" Ana asked Lottie.

"She needs to be changed," Lottie said, avoiding the question as she placed the bottle back on the table. I lifted her from Lottie's arm.

"I can do it," Mark said. Lottie and I both looked at him, me in surprise, Lottie with skepticism. "What? I know how to change a diaper. It may have been a few years, but I changed quite a few diapers in my day."

It was true. When the girls were babies, Mark took over every night when he got home from work. I'd often watch him in awe, tired after a long day's work, but still so at ease with the care that the girls needed. He'd prop the two of them in the crook of his arm and then hold their bottles side by side in his hand. When they needed changing, if Mark was home, he was the one to carry them ceremoniously up the stairs.

Mark bent down and lifted Mia into his arms. "Come on, little girl, let's get you cleaned up," he murmured into her ear as he carried her out of the room, Autumn trailing him.

"Can she come?" Ana asked again, sitting beside Lottie on the couch.

Lottie reached out a hand and smoothed back a strand of hair that had fallen into Ana's face. "I guess so, if your mom wants to take her. It's not really up to me." I felt a pang of guilt, though I wasn't really sure for what. For inviting Lottie and her daughter into our home while she recuperated? For flying out here to take care of them both? No, it was for the tug-of-war that Lottie thought we were playing with Mia.

But weren't we? It wasn't only in her head, and we both knew it, try as we might to pretend otherwise.

"I can bring her to daycare, if you'd prefer," I said to Lottie. Her face looked flat, empty, the peaceful calm lost in the chaos of the last few minutes. "Or . . ." I paused, leaning forward, trying to get her to look at me. She was still focusing on Ana, her hand still in Ana's hair. Uncharacteristically, Ana remained still, letting Lottie fuss over her for a moment. "Or I could just stay here with you and Mia, and Mark can take the girls to the park."

Lottie didn't answer me. "You have a scar," she said to Ana instead. Lottie's hand cupped Ana's cheek and hair, but she was staring at the white puckered line just below Ana's eyebrow atop the bone of her eye socket. "She has a scar," Lottie repeated, but this time to me, finally turning to meet my eyes before looking back at Ana's face. It was thin but nearly two inches long. I was surprised that Lottie hadn't noticed it before. But maybe she hadn't been looking.

I nodded, unable to say more. Part of me wanted to brush it off as inconsequential, but part of me wanted to root her to this spot, to force her to see what she had done. The feeling was quickly replaced again with the desire to absolve her, but I knew that would have been impossible.

Ana hadn't said a word, but she watched us both with wide and anxious eyes.

"It's not too bad," I finally said.

Lottie shook her head, her eyes suddenly filled with tears. "Beautiful girl," she whispered as tears began to slide down her face. Ana remained rigid, afraid to move out of Lottie's hold, but her eyes found mine.

"Mommy?" she said, her voice full of confusion and fear.

I reached for my daughter, pulling her toward me and away from my sister, again away from my sister, but this time more gently. "It's okay, honey," I assured Ana as I wrapped a protective arm around her thin frame.

"Why is Aunt Lottie crying?" she whispered, though Lottie was sitting so close that their knees were touching.

"She's just a little sad, but she'll be okay," I told Ana, gathering her hair. "Should we do French braids today?" I asked, to change the subject, to give her some small gift for putting up with the strange moment she'd just had with her aunt. Ana pulled closer to me and nodded, but I watched as she reached out a tentative hand.

"Will you have a scar too?" Ana asked, her fingers resting on the track of stitches above Lottie's ear.

Lottie ran her forefinger over the thick black line of thread. She managed a half smile. "I guess I probably will."

"It's not so bad," Ana said authoritatively. "It's how everyone will tell you and Mommy apart." She pulled her hand back and turned to face me. "So can Mia come with us?" she asked again, this time the impatience creeping into her voice.

I looked from Ana to Lottie, my eyes resting on the scars, new and old, that I'd managed to grow accustomed to in the days, weeks, and months. "She can come."

Ana let out a whoop and took off to find her sister.

"Is that okay?" I asked Lottie, though we had both long grown tired of my solicitousness.

"It's fine," Lottie said, sounding irritated. "Just bring some bottles with you. And don't forget the diaper bag."

I forced myself not to roll my eyes, not to make a snappy comment. "I'll bring everything she needs" was all I said.

I knew the trip was a bad idea as soon as we took the wrong exit. Mark accidentally got off at the exit for Fisherman's Wharf, which meant we had to navigate the traffic of the touristy area as well as downtown. I'd been second-guessing myself from the moment we pulled away from Lottie's house. Mia had been fussing in the backseat off and on since we'd gotten on the road. She'd drift off to sleep, and then someone in the car would make a loud noise—Mark cursing as we missed the exit, me yelling as he nearly ran over a jaywalking pedestrian, the girls squeal ing over the roller-coaster-like hills of Pacific Heights—and she'd be awake again, whimpering or squalling in her seat. I focused on the road and clenched and unclenched my fists, trying not to let my frustration and panic spill over into the car.

The traffic downtown was stop-and-go; we'd have a minute at a red light followed by the rush of several lanes of traffic for a few blocks, only to sit at a red light again. Suddenly the afternoon seemed a foolish idea. What had Mark been thinking, taking Mia and the rest of the family for an afternoon in the city the day before we'd all be boarding a plane to go back to Boston? I'd gotten caught up in his enthusiasm when I should have been back at Lottie's house, taking care of my sister and doing last-minute packing.

As we inched down Market Street, I was overwhelmed by the numbers of homeless people slumped on curbs or slowly meandering down the sidewalks amidst the office workers who obliviously rushed past, clutching cups of coffee. I knew that many, if not most, of these men and woman were mentally ill; some of them likely had the same chemical imbalance as my sister and were unable or unwilling to accept help. I turned around to see if Ana and Autumn had noticed the multitudes of weary and downtrodden just outside their window, but they were focusing intently on the sticker books that Mark had bought them for the airplane.

"I'm going to call Lottie to make sure everything is okay," I told Mark as I dug around in my purse for my phone.

"What the hell is that?" he asked, waving his hand as a bicyclist darted out in front of him, ignoring the narrow bike lane that ran alongside the traffic. "No wonder your sister was hit by a car, if she was riding anything like that moron."

I didn't answer and dialed Lottie's home number.

"Hi," I said when she answered.

"Hi. Are you guys okay? Is Mia okay?" she asked.

"Yeah, everyone's fine. I was just worried about you. Are you all right?" In the backseat Mia whined again, and I fumbled in the diaper bag for a bottle. "Honey, can you give this to her?" I handed the bottle to Ana. "Sorry," I said, turning back to the phone. "Are you all right? I feel bad that we left you all alone."

"I'm fine, Franci. Bored and stir-crazy, but fine."

"Okay. I just . . ." I trailed off, unsure how to finish. "I had a weird moment of panic. I wanted to make sure you were okay."

"I'm fine." Her voice was small and far away. "Franci?"

"Yeah?"

"I'm so sorry about Ana. The scar. What happened last year when you were here. I'm really sorry about everything."

"I know you are, sweetie. So am I. It's over now, though. It's in the past." I turned around to see that Ana was only holding the bottle halfway up so that Mia was sucking down air bubbles. "Ana, you have to lift the bottle all the way up. She can't get the milk that way." When I turned around, Mark was running through a yellow light just as it turned red. About fifteen pedestrians on either side of the street had already begun to cross. "Mark, be careful," I hissed. He was hunched forward over the steering wheel as if he were a racecar driver. "Sorry, it's a little chaotic here," I said to Lottie. "Mark took the wrong exit."

"You didn't tell me which exit I was supposed to take," Mark argued. "You could have given me a little warning."

I waved him away and pressed the phone closer to my ear. "We'll be home soon," I told Lottie. "We'll have dinner together tonight. We can talk more then, okay?"

"Sure," Lottie said, and then she was gone.

Lottie

How had I not seen the scar?

It was so clear against Ana's skin, such a bright white, so close to her eye, so *there*. How had I kept myself from noticing it until today?

The house was quiet now that everyone had left. The Black was coiled around my spine, waiting, my midnight strength suddenly gone in the yellow light of day, in the white of Ana's scar. I forced myself to breathe deeply, to rise above the pain that radiated from my arm, from my hollowed-out heart, from the sleeping darkness.

I tried to watch TV. I tried to read. Franci called to check on me, and I tried to apologize, for everything, but she was distracted and distant, her heart too full of others.

I made my way to the hallway and threw open the front door. Outside the air was sweet and unseasonably warm for February. There was something so hopeful in this, something so very necessary to my spirit that I wanted nothing more than to spend the day outside.

But doing what? I couldn't walk, couldn't bike; I couldn't even sit on a park bench very comfortably.

Could I drive?

The doctor had said it wasn't safe to drive, not till both casts were off. But in my car, I could roll down the windows, feel the fresh air against my skin washing away the pallor of sadness and foreboding that seemed to coat everything.

I wasn't even certain if I'd be able to maneuver the wheel and pedals, but I went back inside to get ready, my heart lifting slightly at the possibility of doing something, anything other than sitting around the house all day long, waiting for Franci and Mark to take me back to Boston with them like a cheap souvenir they'd picked up on their trip.

In my bedroom I managed to take off the pajama pants and replace them with a pair of shapeless black linen pants. I found my purse, wallet, and keys and went out to the car.

I unlocked the driver's-side door and backed my body in, first letting my butt land on the seat and then slowly swiveling to face forward, using my good arm to help lift my leg inside the car. I was fumbling with the keys when I saw Sally making her way down her front steps, holding hands with a man I'd never seen before. They were smiling at each other and talking, their bodies in contact at all times in the way of new lovers. When Sally saw me in the car, I watched her features cloud with concern.

"Shit," I muttered under my breath as Sally made her way toward the car. I managed to get my other leg in and shut the door behind me, pretending I hadn't noticed them. Sally was knocking on the window only a minute later. I unrolled it and gave her what I hoped was a big smile.

"Hi, Charlotte." Sally peered into the backseat to see if Mia was with me. "What are you doing?"

"Oh, just going for a little drive," I said.

"Are you sure that's such a good idea?" Sally asked. Behind her I noticed the tall new boyfriend watching me with curiosity. "I mean, I don't think you're really in any condition to drive." She gave me an anxious smile.

"I'll be fine. I usually only drive with one hand anyway," I joked. "Good thing I'm a leftie, huh?" I started the engine.

"Charlotte, really, if you need to go somewhere, I'd be happy to drive you. Or we could pick something up for you. If you need . . . medicine or whatever." She shifted uncomfortably beside the window.

So Franci had told her. It made sense, of course. But why did I find myself angry at Franci? And why did I find myself more than a little ashamed to have Sally know my secret?

"Who's your friend?" I asked, looking past Sally, ignoring her offer to help.

Sally looked behind her, as if she'd briefly forgotten about her new love. The man stepped forward and put a hand on Sally's back, leaning over her.

"I'm Liam," he said, reaching his hand through the open window. I gave him the fingers of my left hand, and we shook uncomfortably. "I think Sally's probably right. It's not safe for you to drive like that."

I gently tested my right foot against the brake. I didn't have a lot of feeling through the plastic of the boot, but it didn't hurt and I could use the amount of pressure I would need for both the gas and the brake.

"You're sweet to be concerned. But I'm just fine," I told them, leaning forward to roll the window back up. "You kids have fun now," I said as my window closed. Sally tried to talk to me through the closed glass, but I'd already turned the radio on and was shifting the car into drive. They both stepped back, out of the way of the car, and I pulled out into the street. I wondered how long it would be before Sally called Franci.

It took me a few minutes to get the hang of driving. I held the wheel with my left hand and was able to press on the pedals with my right foot. I'd already been on the road for several minutes before I realized that I was on the Bay Bridge heading into San Francisco.

The traffic was surprisingly light. It was late morning, and rush hour had ended several hours earlier, but I gripped the wheel tightly, my heart beating too fast. I had pulled over to unroll the window once I was out of Sally's range, and the noise of the wind cutting through the car was loud, a jackhammer in my brain. But with only one hand, I couldn't manipulate the manual windows to roll it back up, so I forced myself to breathe deeply as the exits for San Francisco started to appear. I took the exit for Market Street and carefully made my way down the off-ramp and onto Folsom.

I didn't go into San Francisco that often. I tended to only go when I had visitors in town or on a rare afternoon when Whit and I decided to go to the museum or to the park for a picnic. It was the East Bay's pretty sister, and though I preferred the funky hominess of Berkeley, San Francisco gleamed and sparkled in a way that my own city did not.

But the area below Market Street was San Francisco's dirty little secret, the homeless and drug-addicted pushed just out of sight of the tourists. I stopped at a red light and tried to force myself to breathe deeply, to allow my heart rate to return to normal.

On my left, a man pushed a grocery cart piled high with what would have been garbage to most people—old clothes, newspapers, and tattered books. On the sidewalk to my right, a gaunt woman in a filthy tee shirt and jeans held a sign asking for change. Her blond hair was matted with knots.

I thought of the stories that Mother used to tell us about Louisa and Mirabella Strout, the ones where they would try to save the homeless with chocolate cakes and stacks of blankets. Looking back now, I realized the stories all possessed a desire to overcome the powerlessness that Mother must have felt in the face of her own sadness, which burrowed its way into her heart like a worm in an apple. It found its way in, but then couldn't find a way out.

I watched the skinny blond woman, and when she moved her cardboard sign, I realized with a start that though her arms were like sticks and her shoulders sharp, her belly was round and low, her hand resting protectively in the way I knew so well. A car beeped behind me, but I was paralyzed.

The woman was sitting on a dirty blanket, and she looked up to see why the horns were blaring, her eyes meeting mine. I flicked on my hazard lights and put the car in park, reaching for my purse, barely noticing the sounds of other drivers honking at me, cursing as they swerved around me. I eased myself out of the car and walked unsteadily over to where the woman sat. As I got closer, I realized she was younger than she appeared, probably not yet thirty. Her skin was deeply tanned, and dirt was visible in the cracks and lines of her face, but she would have been pretty if she were living another life. A book was open on her lap.

"What are you reading?" I asked. She didn't question my presence here, my injuries, my double-parked car, likely recognizing someone else whose life was falling down around her.

Instead, she held the book up. It was a history textbook, and she was turned to a section on the Mayans.

"Is it interesting?"

The woman shrugged. "It's okay," she said, and her voice was soft and young.

I wanted to ask her so many things. How she had gotten here in the first place, what she'd once wanted in this life, if she was sad all the time, or if she hoped for something better. What she was going to do once her baby was born. If she still believed in the future. If she had family or anyone who loved her. Somehow I felt certain she held some special knowledge, some secret understanding that she might be able to impart.

"You want it? I've got others." The woman gestured to the shopping cart behind her. I felt my eyes fill at the generosity of the gesture, but I shook my head.

"When are you due?" I asked instead.

"The end of May." She leaned forward conspiratorially. "I hope it's a girl. I know I'm not supposed to care. I mean, all I really care about is having a healthy baby. But . . ." She gave me a shy smile. "I'd really love to have a little girl."

I nodded, my vision blurry with tears. The Black was in my eyes, my ears, tugging at my hair. I forced myself to smile. "You're carrying low. It looks like a girl," I told her. Her face lit up.

"You think?"

"Definitely." I unsnapped my purse and dug out my wallet. I had forty-three dollars and some change, and I slipped the bills out and emptied the change into my palm, handing it all over to the woman.

"Here. For you." She thanked me, though she didn't seem surprised by the gesture, perhaps by now used to both the kindness and indifferent cruelty of strangers.

"What's your name?" she asked as I turned away.

"Louisa. Louisa Strout," I told her.

"Thanks, Louisa," she called after me as I hobbled back to the car. I got back inside faster this time, the pain of my body seeming to leave me, to hover around me in the halo of Black. As I pulled into traffic, I looked back at the woman. Her hand was resting on her belly, and she'd gone back to her book. *I am Louisa Strout,* I thought, *and I am invisible.* I climbed back in my car and kept driving.

As my car flew down Fell Street, as I fought to steady my breathing while cars inched in on either side of me, as I nearly ran through several red lights and realized that I couldn't really feel my foot on the gas pedal—it was during all this that I grasped the magnitude of the mistakes I had made over the past few days.

I clutched the wheel tightly as my car hurtled forward, all of it beyond my control now, the bottle of pills sitting at the bottom of a diaper pail or already on the way to a landfill. The Black had arrived, unbidden as usual, and he had snaked his way into my heart and soul, leaving his filthy fingerprints on all that I held dear.

As I soared down the four-lane road, I realized I had only one hope left.

Franci.

I spoke her name aloud as if I could summon her up, and likely somewhere in this sparkling city I had. I forced myself to focus, to remain calm, to recall where they had gone today. I remembered them talking of tea, of flowers, of Japan, and then I remembered they were going to Golden Gate Park.

Breathe, Charlotte, breathe, I ordered myself, but it was Mother's voice that I heard. I felt her cool hand on my brow, wiping away the sorrow and grief and sadness that seemed to live there always.

I flew farther down the street, and the cement of downtown was slowly replaced by green, the towering trees of the Panhandle growing thicker as I got closer to the park. The flat brick apartment buildings were gradually replaced by pastel-colored Victorians. I made a shaky one-handed left turn and then a right onto Fell, the street that led toward Golden Gate Park.

I was beside the park, its eucalyptus trees on my right, and somewhere inside were Franci and Mia. Tears had started to slide down my cheeks, but I blinked them away because they obscured my vision. My head ached, my arm throbbed, and I heard the voice of the Black as he pulled back my hair to whisper in my ear.

"I told you so," he hissed, his voice scratchy and raw.

"You're wrong," I pleaded as I turned onto Ninth Avenue. Franci was near; I felt her waiting for me, guarding Mia. "Please," I whispered.

Suddenly I saw the signs for the Japanese Tea Garden, and for a moment my chest filled with hope—hope, the most vital and sacred of all emotions. My eyes scanned the road for Franci; I was sure she was looking for me as I was for her. Pedestrians, bikers, and in-line skaters whirled past on both sides, and music drifted in the window, a chorus of bongo drums and guitars. Before I realized what had happened, I'd driven past the exit for the gardens and had turned onto the road leading to Park Presidio Boulevard.

"No!" I cried, craning to look in my rearview mirror, but it was too late; I was in the green belly of the park, surrounded by the oppressive canopy of trees. Again, cars rushed by on both sides, and I hurtled forward on a narrow road that was nearly as busy as a highway, though it was swathed by the trees. My heart opened with longing and regret, so certain was I that I'd left behind Mia and Franci, my life, my last chance.

As the park receded behind me, I mustered up my strength and courage and tried to find my way back even as the road spit me out on the other side of the park. The cars were flying at fifty miles an hour, and I couldn't find an exit on either side.

"Pull over," I ordered myself, but there was no place to go. I was in the middle of several lanes, and all of the cars were boxed in tightly. My body vibrated with pain, each beat of my heart a blood-surging pang. Thump, my arm. Thump, my foot. Thump, my head. Thump, my heart and soul and very being.

"You've missed your exit, Charlotte," the Black cackled. "There's nowhere left to go." The car barreled ahead, and I realized that I was driving up the ramp toward the Golden Gate Bridge.

The green was replaced with the blue of the sky and ocean. Something inside of me gave in, let go—a sweet release, like I'd been holding my breath underwater for a long time and could finally breathe. The beauty was astonishing, and I couldn't help it. I took my eyes from the road.

The wide wires of the bridge were suspended in air, and as I sped north, the burnished red supports appeared to rise up like arms welcoming me home. Below me churned the cold, dark ocean, but above the sun was bright, its yellow holding magic, the bridge promising good things to come. My heart raced, and I knew that Franci's did too, pounding in time with my own somewhere nearby in this lush city of green and gold, her beautiful and expanding family holding her safe in their orbit. I let my hand rise off the wheel, my eyes on sky instead of road. My heart burned for my daughter, knowing the unhealable pain that she would carry with her forever, just as I had.

"Mother," I cried. "Mother, can you hear me?"

"I'm here" came her answer, and her fingers reached for mine, carrying me up into the blue-and-gold sky. Below me, the crash of metal was deafening.

Franci

It was nearly eleven by the time we arrived at the Japanese Tea Garden in Golden Gate Park. I strapped Mia's car seat into the stroller and ushered the girls from the car. I tried to let the disquiet fade away. As we began to walk, Mark let his hand linger at the small of my back, and we made our way to the entrance of the gardens.

Once inside, I felt some of my anxiety dissipate. The gardens were beautiful, green and lush with brightly colored flowers. Orange koi circled lazily in green, lily-laden pools, and the girls squatted by the ponds to watch the oversized goldfish. They climbed the small foot-bridge, and I took pictures of them holding hands at the top, the sun glinting off their long blond braids. After we finished walking, we made our way into the open hut where tea was served. Mia had been sleeping soundly since I put her in the stroller, and the din of the tearoom seemed to keep her asleep.

We all ordered tea and Japanese pastries, and then Ana and Autumn went to wander around the gardens some more while we waited for the food to arrive.

"Stay on this side so I can see you," I told them as they made their way down the steps. I leaned forward and pulled the hood up on Mia's car seat and then turned back to Mark.

He smiled at me, the blue of his fleece making his eyes bluer than usual. "Are you okay?"

"Yeah. I just feel weird leaving Lottie at home all day." A waitress came bearing a tray of tiny ceramic teacups and a steaming turquoise teapot. Ana and Autumn crouched at the edge of one of the ponds, their fingers dipping through the surface of the water. I poured a cup of tea and took small sips. "Shit," I said suddenly, putting the cup down.

"What's wrong? Did you burn yourself?" Mark asked.

I leaned down and rummaged through the diaper bag and then checked my purse. "No. I think I left my cell phone in the car." I pictured it in the small hutch between the seats where I'd left it after hanging up with Lottie.

"So? You don't need it," Mark said, picking up his tea. The cup looked tiny in his large hands.

"What if Lottie tries to call? I should go back to the car," I said, standing up.

"Franci, we just got here. Will you relax? You talked to her less than an hour ago. She's fine." Mark reached for my hand and tugged at me. I remained standing. I scanned the gardens until I found my children's blond heads by a flowering purple plant. "I have my phone," Mark said. "She can call me if she needs to get in touch with us."

"Does she know your number?" I asked.

Mark sighed, loosening his grip on me. "I'm not sure." He handed me the phone. "Call her. Give her my number."

I sat down and punched in the digits of Lottie's number. The phone rang and rang before going to voicemail. "She's not answering," I told Mark.

"She probably just doesn't recognize the number," he said. He appraised me for a moment, then reached into his pocket for the keys to the car. "Go on, go get your phone. I'll stay here with the girls."

I jogged the several blocks back to where we'd parked the car, and by the time I unlocked the door, I was out of breath. When I looked at the phone, there were two missed calls from a Berkeley number. I listened to the message that had been left. It was from Sally, explaining that she'd seen Lottie getting in her car and driving away. I hung up before Sally finished speaking and dialed Lottie's cell phone number. Again it went straight to voicemail. "Goddamnit, Lottie," I cursed. I called Sally back, only to get the same information as I'd heard on the message. I told her to call me if Lottie came home.

I looked around the park wildly, not knowing where to go or what to do. Around me people skated and biked and walked leisurely, holding hands or tending to children. The park was abuzz with a calm and festive spirit that countered every muscle in my body. I tried to breathe deeply, but instead found myself crouching beside the car, my face in my hands.

It was as I cowered on the ground that I felt it. Lottie rushed through my body with the force of a wave, powerful and dangerous. She was inside me, and then she wasn't. Though I hadn't been aware of her presence, her absence was cold and pervasive. It filled my mouth and cheeks, all the way down to my toes, and I wondered how I was still breathing. I don't know how long I was there, inhaling the smell of grass and dirt, trying to quell the overwhelming sense of doom that had overtaken me, but when I opened my eyes, Mark was saying my name. He was there with Ana and Autumn, who watched me uneasily, and Mia was nestled against his chest.

"She's gone," I told him before I forced myself to rise.

My legs were weak as I blinked into the luminous green and gold of the park and understood that nothing would ever be the same.

Franci

January

It was the second day of the new year, and the snowstorm was just reaching its conclusion. Today was supposed to have been the first day back at school after the Christmas vacation, but it had been snowing since the early morning and school was cancelled, an unexpected gift. An hour ago the power went out, and though it was only midafternoon, we'd lit candles and spread blankets on the floor to play Candy Land.

I stood at the living room window, my fingers pressed against the cold glass as I watched the last flakes of snow pile up in the backyard. Nearly a foot had fallen.

Lottie never liked the cold, had never understood my desire to move to the Northeast, but I looked forward to the giant blizzards that occurred every couple of years. Lottie didn't like the extremes of New England, the sweltering days of summer and then the sudden plunge into winter. Perhaps her desire for the easy middle ground came from her own uncontrollable extremes.

Several years earlier my sister had visited over Christmas. It snowed on the afternoon of Christmas Eve, a giant blustery storm much like this one, and Lottie and I took the girls to hike down the path behind our house. Ana and Autumn showed Lottie how to make snow angels, and Lottie lay on her back with the girls on either side of her, flapping her arms and legs like a bird ready to take flight. It was the only time I'd seen my sister in the snow, and we were both surprised by the sheer pleasure it brought her.

It was always like this. Lottie would creep into my thoughts on a daily basis, often where I least expected to find her. Sometimes the memories would be ordinary—a shirt in a shop window would remind me of something she would wear, or I'd hear a song she loved. I'd see her face everywhere, in the supermarket, at the post office. In the mirror. In Mia's smile. But more and more often, the reminders would be like today: a sweet moment I'd nearly forgotten, a glimpse at the half of me that was no longer here but still ached like a phantom limb.

That afternoon in Golden Gate Park, I was certain that I knew her absence in the moment that it occurred. She was with me, and then she was not. Her leaving me was a whistle through my chest, a whoosh of air and then a barrenness. As I crouched by the car that afternoon, I was suddenly aware of an echo in my heart, a second heartbeat that repeated after my own, an emptiness that hadn't been there only moments earlier. And I knew she was gone.

Mark spent much of that afternoon trying to calm me down and convince me otherwise. But I already knew. When Sally called to say that the police were at the house about a car accident, I was only learning the details—the car drifting across Golden Gate Bridge, veering into oncoming traffic, and striking a bread delivery truck. *Dead upon impact,* the officer said, though miraculously no one else was seriously injured.

She was driving to me and Mia, of this I was certain. Though others might consider her death a suicide, I knew that she had tried to choose us. And though she was not successful, her attempt to clutch at those fragments of her life, to try to reach her hand out of the Black instead of closing her eyes and sinking into it, that meant more to me than she could have realized.

Her death was ruled an accident, and for this I was grateful. She hadn't jumped from the bridge, hadn't sat in a garage while the car filled with toxic fumes, hadn't taken a handful of pills, or slit her wrists in the bathtub, or hung herself from a beam in the bedroom. The various ways that she could have chosen to die often flickered through my brain like the images of a gruesome film. I preferred to imagine her last moments filled with the scent of fresh bread, baguettes and sourdough loaves lining the road and tumbling into the Pacific.

"Who wants to go for a walk?" I asked, turning away from the window, away from my memories. The girls looked up from their game, their heads bent together in concentration. Mia toddled back and forth between her sisters, snatching the game pieces from the board. In her thick dark curls I'd clipped a butterfly barrette of Lottie's, and Mia reached up every few minutes to finger it. Though she called me Mama, I tried to surround her with scraps and snippets of Lottie whenever possible.

Before we could leave, there was the business of clothing. Snow pants and hats and big rubber boots were pulled on, mittens clipped to the sleeves of coats so that they wouldn't disappear. I'd always loved the solid roundness that snow pants gave to children, and I had the sudden urge to clasp each of my girls around the waist and feel their pillowy softness.

Outside, flakes continued to fall, but it wasn't too cold. The snow gave the neighborhood a dampened silence, and the only sounds were twigs cracking and the occasional thump of snow sliding off a gutter and onto the ground.

The trail led from the corner of the backyard through a small wooded area of public land. In the summer it was often crowded with people, joggers and dog walkers, but today it was empty. The trees reached together, their thick skins of snow blocking out the natural light, surrounding us in white. There was something magical about the woods today that we all seemed to sense, and we walked without speaking, each of us taking in the blinding brightness with a certain reverence.

There were times when Lottie's death was crippling. There were moments when I'd forget, when I would suddenly be reminded that she was gone forever, that I'd never again see her face or hear her voice. Sometimes the grief rocked through me like a spasm and I'd have to stop what I was doing to steady myself. Sometimes it was an effort just to breathe.

Loving Mia helped. I could see the goodness of Lottie in her so clearly every day. I was patient in my care of her, calmer and more centered than I'd been when my own daughters were infants, intent on mothering Mia the way I knew Lottie had wanted to.

The weeks after her death passed in a blur—the funeral, the packing up of her things, moving our father to Boston, the matter of Lottie's will in which she'd already named me Mia's guardian in case something should happen to her. I arrived back in Boston several weeks after I'd left, without a sister, but with my father and a baby that Mark and I would raise as our own.

Miraculously, life went on. I still woke up each morning and brushed my teeth. There were still lunches to pack, dinners to make, and the nightly ritual of reading homework. My body still functioned, though at times it felt as if my heart did not.

A few weeks after Mia and I arrived home, Mark asked me if I wanted to talk to someone. I was surprised by how grateful I was that he'd brought it up, and for the past nine months I'd been seeing Dr. Litwack regularly, though it often struck me as ironic that I was the first in my family willing to accept this help. He was the one who asked me to read Caitlin's poems aloud to him, and when I was finished, wrung out and damp with tears, he said he'd throw them out for me.

This past fall I'd started to draw portraits professionally. When I began to decorate our spare bedroom for Mia, I'd hung the series of paintings that Lottie had in Mia's room. One morning when Beth was over, she'd stood by the paintings for a long time, examining each tiny print. When I told her I'd made them, her eyebrows went up.

"Hell, Franci, these are great. Will you do one of Elijah?"

After I did the portrait of her son, she hung it up in her living room, where she had friends ask about it. I was surprised to soon have several commissioned jobs and more surprised by how much I enjoyed painting again. I hadn't realized how much I'd missed the comforting scent of oils, the colored smears on my fingers, and the peace I felt during those quiet hours of concentration. I had business cards made up, and recently I'd even thought about renting a small storefront in Brookline.

Through the white world we walked. I carried Mia on my back, and Ana and Autumn wandered in front of us, turning around every few minutes to point something out to Mia. I was amazed at the ease with which they took in their new little sister. Never had they complained about my attention being divided. The grace and generosity they had immediately shown Mia had left me awed and made me love them all the more.

We trudged along, clumsy and slow in our heavy winter gear, but we were in no rush. The woods grew thicker and whiter, as if we'd stumbled into the center of a snowflake with its intricate carved-out corners. I felt a vast sense of gratitude rise up inside of me mixed with the absence of Lottie. I wondered if the absence would ever leave, if I would ever feel whole without her.

"Mama," Mia called in my ear, her weight warm against my back.

"Look," Ana said, pointing up. A cardinal had come to rest on a branch. Its coat was a brilliant scarlet and stood out against the world of whiteness into which we'd entered. It was unlikely, I knew, but as I often did when something special happened, I imagined it was a sign from Lottie, an absolution, a blessing. What other way was there to survive losing her?

The four of us watched the bird, struck silent by its bright beauty. It bounced on the branch several times, pecking at the thick layer of snow with its beak. The bird hopped twice more on the branch, spilling snow in a light dust around us, and then it flapped its wings and took flight. We all watched, heads tilted back, a dazzling splash of color in the midst of all that white. The bird made its graceful flight up, through the thick silence of the trees, and into whatever lay beyond.

ACKNOWLEDGMENTS

This manuscript went through many incarnations over the years. Big thanks to Jodi Warshaw and the folks at Lake Union Publishing for spotting the synopsis on my website and bringing these characters out into the world. To Marlene Stringer, for your fierce dedication to your clients and for pushing us every day. To Ann Collette, who set me on the publishing path. To Charlotte Herscher, whose keen eye made this a much stronger, leaner novel.

Several books were helpful in understanding what it's like to live with bipolar disorder and the impact it can have on others, most notably *An Unquiet Mind* by Kay Redfield Jamison and *Manic* by Terri Cheney. Reading these moving and brave memoirs helped me to write from Lottie's perspective. Any inaccuracies are mine alone.

To Marya Cohen, for over thirty years of friendship and for medical expertise on an early draft so long ago that you've probably forgotten about it. To my father, for reading like an editor but cheering for me like a dad. To my mother, for endless book recommendations, a shared passion for reading, and for always caring about the details of a story. To my aunt, Lynda Bernard, for a thousand acts of support and generosity over the years—really, a thousand is a modest estimate.

To Cynthia Riggs and the Wednesday night writing crew, including Lisa Belcastro, Catherine Finch, and Amy Reece, who were the first ones to set eyes on this novel nearly ten years ago. To Sarah Smith and

Mathea Morais, the best writing team a girl could ask for. To the writers at 17 Scribes and Lake Union, for expertise and companionship in a potentially lonely business.

To Amelia Angella, Holly Thomas, Skye Sonneborn, Moira Convey Silva, Anna Cotton, Andy Cavanagh, Stefani Mucci Cavanagh, Pete Cavanagh, and Mary Cavanagh, for boundless enthusiasm for my writing.

To Nevah and Olivia, for reminding me every day what's really important. And to Reuben, for always making writing possible and for being my safe harbor when this whole publishing gig gets overwhelming. Thank you.

ABOUT THE AUTHOR

Photo © 2016 Eli Dagostino

A teacher as well as a writer, Emily Cavanagh lives with her husband and two daughters on Martha's Vineyard, an island off the coast of Massachusetts. She is also the author of *The Bloom Girls*. Read more about Emily's work and life at www.emilycavanaghauthor.com.